THE BLADESMITH'S DAUGHTER

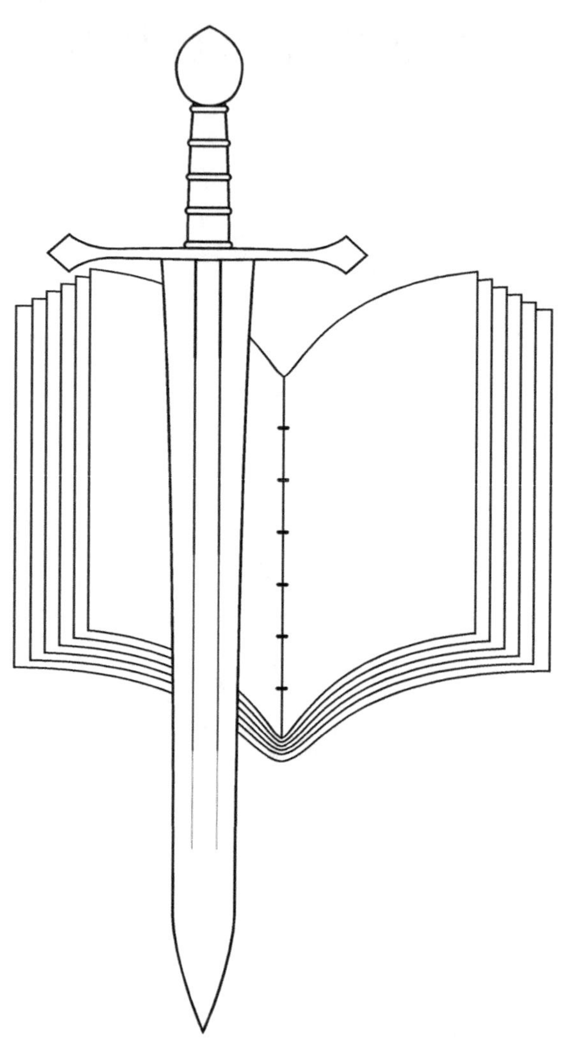

THE LAST STRANGE KINGS

BOOK ONE

THE BLADESMITH'S DAUGHTER

CARLA FRAGA

Quills & Pixels

The Last Strange Kings, Book One

The Bladesmith's Daughter

Learn more about The Last Strange Kings series and download a full-color map: laststrangekings.com

Published by Quills and Pixels

Seattle, WA

quillsandpixels.com

ISBN   978-0-9860686-0-7

Copyeditor: Kyra Freestar, Bridge Creek Editing

Design, map, and layout: Steve Laskevitch, Quills and Pixels

To Beloved Mister S

*Eternal thanks to my beta readers Jennifer Laba, SML3,
and KLH, and to copyeditor Kyra Freestar,
unearther of meaning from thickets of verbage.*

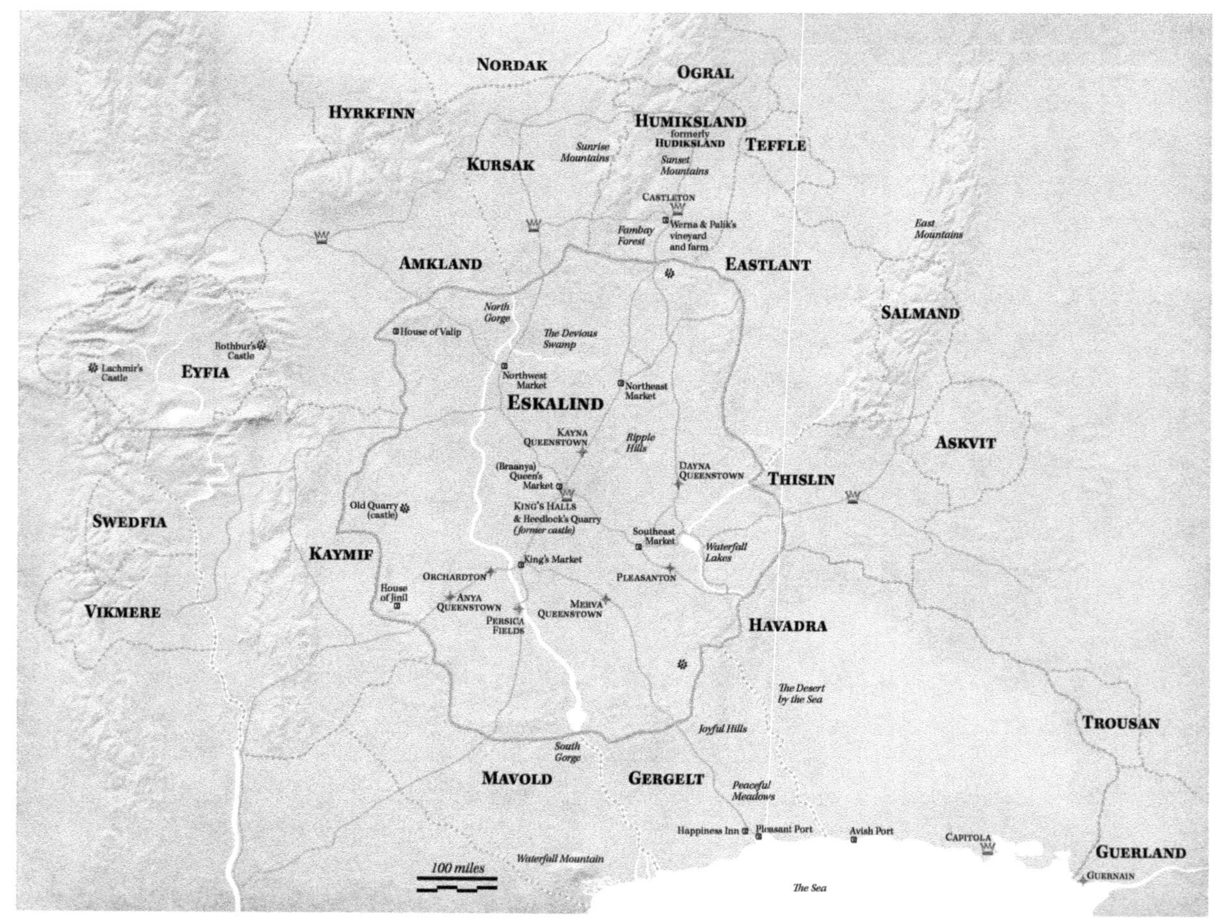
NORDAK
OGRAL
HYRKFINN
HUMIKSLAND
formerly HUDIKSLAND
TEFFLE
Sunrise Mountains
KURSAK
Sunset Mountains
CASTLETON
Werna & Palik's vineyard and farm
Fambay Forest
EASTLANT
East Mountains
AMKLAND
SALMAND
North Gorge
House of Valip
The Devious Swamp
Rothbur's Castle
Lachmir's Castle
EYFIA
Northwest Market
Northeast Market
ESKALIND
KAYNA QUEENSTOWN
Ripple Hills
ASKVIT
(Braanya) Queen's Market
DAYNA QUEENSTOWN
THISLIN
Old Quarry (castle)
KING'S HALLS & Heedlock's Quarry (former castle)
SWEDFIA
Southeast Market
Waterfall Lakes
KAYMIF
King's Market
ORCHARDTON
PLEASANTON
House of Jinil
ANYA QUEENSTOWN
MERVA QUEENSTOWN
VIKMERE
PERSICA FIELDS
HAVADRA
The Desert by the Sea
TROUSAN
Joyful Hills
South Gorge
MAVOLD
GERGELT
Peaceful Meadows
Happiness Inn
Pleasant Port
Avish Port
CAPITOLA
GUERLAND
100 miles
Waterfall Mountain
The Sea
GUERNAIN

NORDAK
OGRAL
HYRKFINN
HUMIKSLAND
formerly
HUDIKSLAND
TEFFLE
KURSAK
Sunrise
Mountains
Sunset
Mountains
CASTLETON
Werna & Palik's
vineyard
and farm
AMKLAND
Fambay
Forest
EASTLANT
North
Gorge
The Devious
Swamp
House of Valip
Northwest
Market
Northeast
Market
ESKALIND
KAYNA
QUEENSTOWN
Ripple
Hills
DAYNA
QUEENSTOWN
THISLIN
(Braanya)
Queen's
Market
Old Quarry
(castle)
KING'S HALLS
& Heedlock's Quarry
(former castle)
Southeast
Market
Waterfall
Lakes
KAYMIF
King's Market
ORCHARDTON
PLEASANTON
House
of Jinil
ANYA
QUEENSTOWN
MERVA
QUEENSTOWN
HAVADRA
PERSICA
FIELDS
The Desert
by the Sea
Joyful Hills
South
Gorge
MAVOLD
GERGELT
Peaceful
Meadows
LEGEND
Happiness Inn
Pleasant Port
Quarry (in Eskalind)
Castle (elsewhere)
Capital city
100 miles
Town or city
Waterfall Mountain
The Sea

Another delicious meal was now a memory. Marna sighed as she walked the length of the hand-hewn oak table, sweeping the last of the dinner crumbs into a rag. With her wide hips she pushed the assortment of chairs and stools under the table, where they would await their next use at breakfast. Stout candles at the table's center gave a warm, flickering glow to the farmhouse's largest room. Reaching the end of the thick slab, Marna flicked her tatter-edged cloth at the dead hearth, then flung the limp fabric to her waiting nephew in the kitchen. Narnik dipped to catch it with practiced ease, dropping the rag into the deep dish tub on the washing counter.

A strand of long reddish-blond hair swept into Marna's vision; she trained it back behind her ear, gray eyes to the hearth. Rain softly struck the thatched roof, interrupted by Narnik rubbing dry a ceramic bowl till it squeaked. He giggled, watching his aunt, mischievous delight in his blue eyes.

Marna shook her head, walking toward him whilst untying the begrimed apron from her trim waist. "You are eleven years old going on eight, Narnik." She gave her nephew a playful slap on the back and stowed the worn apron on a hook under the tall cupboards in the kitchen. "Time for bed." A weary satisfaction laced her voice as she undid the tie crowning her faded green bodice.

On the opposite side of the hearth, the door to the sleeping room swung open. Her eldest niece, a tall, oval-faced girl of fourteen with long blond hair to match her brother's, peered around the hearth's rounded stones.

Marna walked to her, hearing the quieting chatter of the numerous little ones coming from the room beyond. She raised an eyebrow. "Are your brothers and sisters ready to sleep, Palika?"

Her niece nodded. Despite the girl's tender years, a vertical worry crease was etched into her forehead.

"Tell them to settle down and ask The Powers to send their brothers and father home safely."

"And Uncle Malik." Narnik's singsong voice came from behind Marna. He clanked a stack of bowls into a cupboard.

"Yes, of course, and your Uncle Malik." Marna pictured his thick, rough fingers. *By The Powers, I hope he will not be my fate, despite the hopes of my sister and her husband. Yet stuck in the countryside at my age, I have no other prospects.*

"See Palika, I told you she wouldn't forget Uncle Malik. Would you, Auntie? When you join with him, you'll be Mother's sister and Father's brother's wife. Our aunt twice!" The boy giggled, perhaps pleased at his alacrity with family relationships.

Palika answered in a steeled whisper. "It's not funny, brother. We may never see any of our menfolk again." Her cheeks pinked and her blue eyes swelled with a layer of tears.

Marna placed calming hands on her niece's lean shoulders. "They will all come home, dear. You'll see." She hugged the girl, who sniffled against her hair. *Little does she realize I speak from knowledge and not just hope. King Hudik does not sacrifice his sons, even those of low and hidden birth, on the battlefield. Unless Hudiksland loses the day.*

"Thank you, Auntie." Palika murmured. "I hope they come home soon."

Marna gave her slender back a final squeeze and released her. "I do too." Well, three out of four.

The girl returned to the sleeping room and shut its door. Marna leaned her back against the thin lumber, listening as Palika shushed her younger siblings. Their six small voices rose into a soft rhythm as they asked The Powers to watch over their menfolk away at battle. After the rustling of covers, she waited a minute more, at last hearing the calm, even breathing of sleep.

Pleased that they once again fell to slumber quickly after drinking her dinner broth, Marna brought her hands to her mouth so Narnik would not see her proud smile. The deep scent of bay leaves and marjoram still lingered on her skin from preparing their meal. *I told my sister, it makes them sleepy when I make it, even though I follow her recipe to the measure. Except for the mint.*

A solid thud sounded on the thick front door. "Could your mother have delivered the neighbor's child already?" Marna walked the ten paces across the room and called through the barred door, "Werna?"

"Is Mother back?" Her nephew followed her, and she waved a hand to silence him.

A plaintive voice croaked, "Please." A man's voice, but weak. She did not recognize it.

Marna growled her reply, keeping her tone low to not wake the children. "What do you want?"

"… lost … hurt." That was all she could understand.

"We should help him!" Narnik tugged on her elbow. "What if he is one of our soldiers?" Despite his young age, the boy stood nearly to her broad shoulders, and he was quick and strong. *If it is only one man, and he is injured, the two of us could handle him. Unless he is armed.*

Reaching for the thick stick leaning against the wall, Marna stood to her full height. She grasped the would-be weapon with both hands, wishing to The Powers her menfolk had left behind at least one of the swords her father made, rather than this club. How she hated to rely on knives as weapons. For chicken butchering, and herb cutting, fine. But a knife could easily be turned against one. *If only I had a sword.*

Not that she would know how to use it, but she wanted to look as intimidating as possible. A woman of her size wielding a blade—that would shock any intruder. But the stick must do.

Marna nodded to Narnik, who unbolted the door and threw it open. A helmeted man in mud-covered clothing of leather and metal plate slumped to the floor at her feet. She jumped back, but he lay on his side unmoving, the rain and dirt silently pooling around him onto the freshly scrubbed floor.

Narnik knelt to touch him. "He's a knight!" Her nephew looked at her with wide eyes. "Look at his armor!" Even coated with mud, the quality of the materials and craftsmanship was richer than any she'd seen at her father's workshop in Castleton, the dark leather embossed with odd patterning, and bronzy sheets of similar design plating the upper and lower extremities.

Marna peered into the dark drizzle outside. "He's alone, I think." She said it more to reassure herself, as her nephew plainly had no concern for their safety. She bent toward the man and laid the club on the floor. "Who are you? Is the battle close by?" He did not respond. She listened a moment, but only the soft pat of rain on earth could be heard. She turned to the boy. "Double bar the kitchen door." For once she was glad the house had no windows. Cool air flowed through the open door.

Narnik fingered the man's limp hand. "His gloves are stitched with a red sword over a brown shield. Does that mean something?"

"That he's from the Strange Kingdom, Eskalind. Our allies, thank The Powers. Now bar the side door!"

Narnik rose and dashed to do her bidding, gushing, "The Powers sent us a Knight to protect us! A real rich Knight from Eskalind."

She rolled the man over as gently as she could to unblock the doorway. He weighed a good deal, but this bladesmith's daughter had inherited much of her father's strength. A slight repositioning of the stranger's legs, and she was able to shut and bolt the front door.

Marna examined him. No blood that she could see, but a horrible black mark cut across his bronze helmet at the crown of his head, unlike anything she had ever seen in her twenty-eight years. A whiff of a strange, metallic scent wafted as she neared his face. His eyes remained closed.

"Can you hear me?"

The man's eyelids fluttered to reveal light brown eyes with a soft, unfocused expression. A flutter of pity at his condition stirred in her chest. The bladesmith's daughter spoke in a reassuring and confident voice, hoping she did not sound pert or offensive to this man of obvious high station. "You are lucky I am have some skill at healing. I am going to remove your armor and your sword and check you for wounds. All right?"

He said something that sounded like "Sss."

"Can you tell me what happened?"

The Eskalinder sputtered a reply. "It … hurts."

"Where does it hurt?"

He blinked. "My head."

"Anywhere else?"

"No." It was more a wheeze than a word.

"I will see to it. Now rest. You are safe here."

The injured Strange Kingdomer gazed at her, and she felt he understood. He closed his eyes and his head lolled, the metal of his helmet scraping the wood floor.

Narnik reappeared at her side, whispering, "Is he dead? Who is he?"

She shrugged. "He must be a Lord of some kind, but right now it does not matter. Help me get his armor off."

Marna cupped the man's neck with one hand and with the other slipped away his helmet as carefully as she could. Long brown locks stuck to his sweaty forehead, and water matted a trim beard against a crooked jaw. She ran her fingers along his jawline, feeling for a break and watching his expression for tension or pain. But he remained peaceful, and she felt nothing unusual. Accounting it an old injury, Marna deftly moved his hair aside and examined the dark mark across his head.

Something had cut through his helm and burned him. A firebrand? No, the force would have crushed his skull. *It is a bad burn. With the storm, it might have been lightning. Poor man. I hope I can heal him.*

She gently rested his head back onto the floor, wishing for a pillow.

However, she needed to examine him thoroughly before considering such niceties. Marna undid the metal clasps of his breastplate with expert fingers. Tedious childhood hours spent inspecting hooks and latches, of clasping and unclasping the armor coverings her father and his apprentices made, ensured that this was a chore she knew too well. *Would that he had taught me how to better defend myself with his sharper wares, rather than to serve as a mute examiner.*

The healer handed the breastplate to Narnik.

"What armor!" The boy studied it with delight, clutching the leather edges. "And it's light! Did Grandfather ever make pieces this rich?"

"Put it aside and remove his gauntlets and gloves." She undid the greaves protecting his shins, inspecting for cuts and prodding for broken bones.

Her nephew muttered and fumbled with the leather straps anchoring the gauntlets. "You never answer my questions."

"Now is not the time, Narnik. Once we remove his armor, I will check thoroughly to see if he has more injuries." She unbelted his scabbard.

"Oh, let me touch his sword!" Heedless as a chicken, the eager lad leaned across the man to grab for it.

"I will keep that for him. And don't kneel in the mud." She placed the sword and its sheath out of her nephew's reach and shot him a warning glance.

"Hmm, only a few lacings on his inner tunic. We will have to pull it off very gently. I don't want to worsen his head injury. Can you do that?" Narnik nodded, and the pair peeled the shirt over the man's head as tenderly as a midwife unswaddling a newbabe. "Now put his tunic aside."

He obeyed, commenting, "It smells like he's been working in the fields."

Marna surveyed the man's bare chest. The smooth perfection of his skin and modeled tone of his broad torso startled her.

Oh. The muscles of a warrior but no scars. Well, I am certain a man with armor this light and fine, and no cuts, does not lead from the front. Perhaps he is also related to our king. The thought made her smirk. She touched his ribs lightly, dispassionately feeling for breaks, again watching his face for any tic of pain. "He does not seem to have any other wounds."

"I don't see blood anywhere on him."

"Ah-ha, you are paying attention. Good." Marna looked at the prone man's drawstring breeches. Touching him there made her nervous. Yet as a healer, she should check everywhere. Still, she ignored the area between his hips, instead patting his legs. "No, no blood, no tears in the cloth." She removed her hands as the man shivered.

Narnik looked at her. "Should I fetch a blanket?"

She grinned at his initiative. "In a moment. He has no broken bones, so let's move him near the hearth first. I will treat him there." Grasping the man under his arms, the pair dragged him the several paces with great effort. He moaned once as they laid him flat. Marna knelt by his side.

The eleven-year-old scrambled to the woodbox. "I'll get more tinder." He returned, tossing twigs into the dead hearth and working fast to rekindle a fresh fire. She'd always known the boy had pluck, but he hid it behind sass. With the older menfolk away at battle, her nephew had a chance to establish himself as more than the family jester. And finally he was demonstrating it. The concentration on his face as he coaxed the fire brought to mind a proverb of their land: "Crisis proves the man."

She would enjoy relating this incident to his mother someday. Hopefully soon.

"Did he come from the battle, do you think? How far away is Eskalind? Do you know?"

Marna puckered her lips. "Peace, Narnik! I need to treat his head wound. Bring the bag of healing herbs, the mortar, and the pestle." When he did as she bid, she retrieved the dried plants she sought and ground them in the bowl. She spoke in quiet tones, "Lower your voice." She glanced toward the sleeping room, hoping he would get her point.

Narnik sighed but watched her efforts, turning his blue eyes to the man. He spoke softly. "What do you think happened to him?"

"I think he was struck by lightning."

Narnik gazed at the man's face with newfound wonder. "Can he survive that?"

Marna raised an eyebrow, displeased with her nephew's lack of bedside manner. "He will be fine." She scraped the pestle around the sides of the bowl, forcing the herbs to the bottom. "Now get a pillow and a warm blanket from the sleeping room." She hated that the man still rested his head on the floor. Though, with Palika's help, she had scrubbed the wooden planks after dinner. Marna imagined what the Eskalinder Lord would think, waking to find himself on the bare floor of what he would surely consider a hovel. "Thank The Powers the floor is made of wood, not dirt."

Her nephew scurried from the sleeping room carrying a blanket and a lavender and chicken-feather stuffed pillow. She accepted the items and stretched the coarse cloth over the prone man's chest, tucking it around his shoulders. "Narnik, clean the mud off the floor with the floor brush." He mumbled but did so whilst Marna cradled the stranger's head and gently placed it upon the pillow, studying his injury. The tips of his large ears protruded through his dark hair. The unjoined woman shook her head. *A shame he has a face only his mother could love. Though a man this rich must have a mistress in every town.*

His task completed, Narnik rummaged through the pile of armor and leathers, retrieving the man's scabbard. "Did you see this?" He bounded to the hearth to show her, the bronze gleaming through the dirt. The lad dug his fingers along the engraving, scraping away the mud to reveal a clear design of carved swords running the length of the shaft. The polished metal of the cut patterns contrasted in a pleasing manner with the puckered background of hammered brass. Indeed a work of the finest craftsmanship. Marna bit back a smile. "Your grandfather would envy this piece, but put it down, Narnik. A man such as this will not care for you touching his weapon. I think it's time you went to bed." She tapped the pestle against the ceramic bowl, listening for the ringing sound that indicated to her, when she ground medicine, the right consistency of the herbs.

The boy hung his head, his blond locks brushing his shoulders to hang over his eyes. He sulked to the sleeping room.

"Before you go, bring broth from the kitchen, and a clean cloth in water."

He did as she wished, but then stood to watch.

Marna poured a bit of broth into the herb-filled bowl. A fresh, clean scent filled the air.

Narnik shifted his stance, creaking the floorboards. "What are you making?"

"A paste for his burn." She stirred the liquid. "Now go. And don't wake or tell the others." He went to the sleeping room door but lingered. She did not look at him, and without further acknowledgment, he went inside and closed the door—no doubt to rest his head against the wood and eavesdrop.

Marna dipped her finger into the paste and spoke quietly to the stranger. "Can you hear me? This may sting at first, then it will soothe." At least, she hoped it would. She traced the blackened skin with the salve, studying the man's face for any sign of emotion. His forehead pinched briefly, then slackened.

"Does that feel better?"

"Yes." He moaned softly.

"My sword?"

"It's here. Once I treat you, I will clean your sword." A glint of pride crept into her voice. "I know the importance of cleaning a battle blade before blood pits the metal." Another bit of knowledge her father had entrusted to her.

Grasping the damp cloth, she dabbed the man's face. The mud washed easily away; the blood stuck and required more pressure to remove. Trying to maintain a healer's detached manner, she wiped his neck and collarbones, yet her gaze wandered to the smooth skin and musculature of his well-formed chest. When Marna touched his warm hands, her gaze stopped on his long fingers. "Oh." His hands were beautiful. Graceful but strong. She carefully ran the cloth over each of his fingers, forgetting for a moment to breathe. *For hands like this, I may find room in my heart for large ears and a crooked jaw.*

The healer chided herself for foolish thoughts. "I will clean your sword now." She thought it best to tell him what she did, even he if did not acknowledge what she said. One never knew how much a nobleman expected from a woman servant. Marna hoped to The Powers her patient would accept her ministrations and a place to sleep without making any further demands.

As the Hudikslander reached for the scabbard and unsheathed the blade, revealing a watery pattern across the bloodstained metal, her patient's eyes flickered open.

"I'm a bladesmith's daughter. I know how to care for a sword." She lowered her eyes to his brown gaze, which seemed to find her this time. "My father is chief armorer to King Hudik. He and his workshop make all manner of blades and armor for the royal court." Marna placed the empty scabbard by the man's side and rose to approach the tall cupboard in the washroom. From it she withdrew a bottle filled with oil, returning to wipe the sharp metal clean in long, careful strokes.

The injured man watched her with an expression she could not read. He rasped, "I thank you." Studying his face, she judged him to be nearly thirty.

The stranger sat up, and Marna drew away. "You must be feeling better." She wanted to help him rise, but decided against it, and instead backed toward the table. Retrieving a stool, she sat, laying his sword at her side. She worked a second coating of oil into the metal. Keeping the blade between them gave her a sense of safety.

"I do feel better." He looked about the room with a hazy gaze. "Where am I?"

"You are in a farmhouse, about half a day's walk south from King Hudik's seat in Castleton, and you are safe." She smiled to reassure him while considering her situation, hoping she and the children were safe with him in their home. Then she looked at his cloudy expression and her compassion stirred. She figured if she were to tell him to leave, he might drown in a puddle. *May The Powers protect me, this time.* "Are you hungry, my Lord?"

He waited a moment, as though interpreting the words. "Yes."

"Then I will bring you some broth."

Marna stood with a slight "Umpf." A long day directing the children in preparing for the grape harvest, together with her unexpected strange guest, weighed upon her weary limbs and mind. But everything stood in readiness for her menfolk to return and handle the heavier labor. Tomorrow would be easier, unless this man caused trouble. Or the battle had come to her doorstep.

She carried his clean sword to his scabbard, which rested against the hearth. Sheathing the blade, Marna went to the kitchen and ladled broth from a thick ceramic pot into a bowl and brought it to the Eskalinder.

The man drained the bowl, and his eyes lit with wonder and a flicker of intelligence. "That was the best broth I have ever tasted."

"Thank you." She had heard that before. "I will dry your tunic by the fireplace, but first, I will find you a clean one." She quietly stepped into the sleeping room. All the children breathed peacefully, except Narnik, who snored propped against the wall. Marna grinned, guessing he had thought to stay awake till she returned.

The candle in the overhead lantern glowed evenly as she went to the old, stout chest on the far end of the room. She rummaged for one of her sister's husband's tunics. The injured man was not as broad as her braither, but some of Palik's older clothing might fit the man.

She returned with a plain linen tunic for her patient and handed it to him. He passed her the bowl without looking at her, in the manner of a man used to others tidying his table. The Strange Kingdomer pulled the tunic over his head and shoulders, moving without any indication that the act pained him. Marna's guest also did not seem to note the strangeness of finding linen clothing in a plain farmhouse, as though he were used to such fine fabrics. She stifled a smug grin.

The Hudikslander refilled her guest's bowl; the Eskalinder gulped it empty without effort. Then he lay back onto the floor by the hearth, tugging the blanket around him. As he looked much improved, she decided to venture a few questions.

"What happened to you?"

"I . . . I . . . don't know." The disoriented expression returned.

"Do you remember where you are from?"

He blinked, his eyes reflecting the hearth's light. Distress, dismay strained his speech. "No, nothing."

"You must be a High Lord of the Strange Kingdom, given the make of your armor and sword. You bear their King's emblems."

The prone man shook his head as though this were all new information. He stared at the ceiling. "I remember walking here. Stumbling. It was dark. Only The Powers could have led me in such darkness."

"There was much blood on your sword. Was the battle nearby?"

"I . . . I don't remember." He sounded like a lost child, frustrated with his predicament. "I walked and walked. A long way. Oh." The man closed his eyes tightly, as though in pain.

"Perhaps in the morning you will recall. Now you should rest. You will be comfortable here?" She hoped it did not sound like an invitation, as she had nothing else to offer.

He tugged the blanket tight over his chest. "I can sleep anywhere."

"Ah! You remember something."

His eyes opened, glancing about as though searching for something he knew was nearby. "I cannot recall even my name. I try, but nothing comes. By The Powers, what have they done to me?"

"You are lucky they led you to a healer's door."

He faced her. "What is your name, Lady Healer?"

Marna wondered if he mocked her. Clearly she was no lady. And a question like that might contain a flirtation, yet she heard no hint of that in his voice, especially given the lost face he was giving her.

"I am called Marna."

"I thank you for your care, Marna." He rolled the *R* sound in her name, and it sent a tingle down her back.

With difficulty, she inhaled evenly. "You're welcome. And till you recover your name, I will call you Guest."

Her patient leaned onto his back and stared at the ceiling. His lips silently formed the name she gave him, his concentration as intent as though tasked with memorizing an epic tale.

"Don't roll into the fire, Guest." Marna patted his hand as a nursemaid might. She stepped into the sleeping room, and bolted the door with silent fingers.

———

The lost man awoke without opening his eyes. Cool air wafted over his face, and he could sense daylight through weighted lids. But his head felt as though it floated upon water, with an airy, rhythmic sound coming from far away. He quieted his breath a moment, trying to center on the sound—repetitive, and oddly familiar. His forehead itched with the effort to discern what was happening, where he was.

He felt his sword hilt in his right hand. Now he recognized the noise; it was breathing, but not his own. Many people stood around him. Close by. A terrible panic seized him. He was in battle, knocked down, surrounded by enemies.

A childish giggle shattered that thought. He opened his eyes to see a flock of fair-haired children, plainly but neatly dressed in beige homespun fabric and as curious about him as he was about them.

The tallest, a boy with wide blue eyes, spoke. "Look! He's awake! The guest is awake!" The lad crouched by his side. "I'm Narnik. I was here when you came last night. Do you remember that? Where are you from? What's your name?"

He shook his head against the onslaught of questions. He could recall nothing except waking, and the stinging of residual panic in his veins, and he muttered, "Thank The Powers I did not draw my sword." He clumsily brushed the blanket away and groaned as he sat, just as a tall, generously proportioned woman with a tapered waist rushed into the room from the door beside the hearth. A round-eyed toddler with long legs dangled from her arm.

"Children, leave him be. Give the man room." She bent to him, her gray eyes kind and vaguely familiar. "How are you feeling?"

"Tired. Very tired."

The woman nodded. "Then you shall have more rest." She turned to the children scattered about the room. "Off to your chores."

Narnik rose from the floor, standing nearly to the adult woman's shoulders. "But we were just watching him sleep." He looked at the man with what seemed a mixture of awe and inquisitiveness.

The woman lowered the little girl in her arms to the floor. The child waddle-walked to the long table that filled the middle of the room and babbled baby nonsense. "Leave our guest in peace, Narnik. I need to tend to him." The guest turned, watching her brush past the children to the kitchen. She called out from its open door, "Palika!"

The guest leaned back against the hearth and rubbed his hands over his face. He wished he remembered something. Anything.

He glanced up as a tall, slender girl with a thin forehead came to the kitchen door. The woman spoke to her. "Palika, carry Lena outside, and see that the others get to their chores."

Palika did as she was bid, entering the main room and scooping the little girl into her arms, clutching her protectively. She regarded him with open hostility as she left.

The other children fled the room out the main door, leaving it to bang against the wall with a squeak of its hinges. The swinging door sent pulsing, painfully bright shafts of sunshine into the room. The guest shielded his eyes from the light source, straining to watch the smaller children scamper about the muddy yard. As his eyes adjusted to the glare, he saw Narnik, followed by two shorter boys, make for a low building that looked like a stable. Several plump chickens wandered about, clucking at the heels of another little girl until a taller girl he did not recognize scattered grain at their feet.

He fought to collect his thoughts. "So many children. Where did they all come from?"

The woman laughed. "I don't think that needs explaining."

He was not certain what she meant, but her tone suggested he had just said something remarkably stupid. He cleared his throat. "How many children are there?"

"Eight here." She opened a wooden cabinet and retrieved a bowl. Herbs and baskets hung from the ceiling of the small kitchen. She ladled broth from a large iron pot. "And two more at battle with their father, and another in the womb." She brought him the bowl. "Drink this."

He nodded, the thought that she had told him her name slowly surfacing as he accepted the broth from her and drank. The taste was familiar and strange all at once, filling and light, with a hint of peppery spice. It warmed his throat as he swallowed, spreading a healing comfort across his chest.

"That was the best broth I've ever tasted."

The corner of her mouth raised in a hint of a grin. "Thank you."

Again he felt he had said something dim-witted. He strove to sound conversational, instead. "You must have joined at a very young age to mother that many children."

"They are my sister's." She retrieved the empty bowl from him and refilled it.

He tried to recall if he had seen another woman. "Oh. Is she here?"

"No, she's attending a neighbor who is with child."

"And your husband?" A sudden rush of keen interest elevated his heartbeat. It felt as if minutes passed as he waited for her reply.

"I have no husband."

The woman handed him the bowl. His fingers brushed hers as he grasped the pocked ceramic curve. He regarded her, noting her height, pretty face, and pleasingly pear-shaped figure. "Marna." He said it before he realized he spoke. The syllables sounded familiar in his throat, as though he had said her name many times.

"Your memory is returning?" Her gaze met his as she backed into the kitchen.

"I remember your name, and…" His head throbbed from the effort of thought. "That you cared well for me last night." The guest tried to grin, pleased to remember something, yet his satisfaction was diminished by the sense of wariness he felt from her. He wanted to look at her more closely, as though some mystery might be explained in her face, in her form. Perhaps her reticence stemmed from sensing his growing desire to study her.

The guest drank and met her gaze. Without thinking, he blurted, "And I would recall a wife, if I had one."

She startled him with laughter. "Ha! You should rest more. The sleeping room is there." She pointed to the door beside the fireplace. "Finish your broth, and I will call you when breakfast is ready."

The guest felt his face flush with mortification for his witless comments. "Yes, rest will be good." He rose and placed his bowl on the table, reluctant to let it go and to leave her.

The eldest girl entered the room through the side doorway. Her blue gaze darted between them for a moment as if assessing something. "Auntie Marna, where do you want the mint?"

"Add it to the pot in the kitchen, Palika. And don't forget a few sprigs of thyme."

"Mint?" That sounded strange to the guest, and he turned to the woman. He ran his fingers along the edge of his bowl. "Mint in broth?"

She watched his hand for a moment. "When *I* make it." Her gray eyes sparkled, and she smiled.

He watched her as long as he could as he shuffled to the sleeping room. While his head still ached, he found it easier to rest with the fresh memory of her smile in his heart and the thought that perhaps The Powers had led him to this place for a reason.

A female voice called to him. "Come to supper."

"Supper?" He wiped his eyes, a soft, unfocused feeling floating in his head. A distinctly female silhouette filled the doorframe. "Have I slept that long?"

"You needed it." The woman turned away, her hair a brief golden-red flash to his mind. *Marna.* A sense of relief cleared his head as he recalled her name.

He sat up on the straw mattress and surveyed the room. Above him, near the door, a metal-grilled lantern hung from a thatched roof. The thick candle inside illuminated the room with warm light and odd shadows. A hearth of river-smoothed rocks lay not far from his toes. At the far end of the room squatted a dark wood chest. On either side of him, two wide, rough pallets sprawled from bare wooden wall to bare wooden wall. It occurred to him that many people usually slept in this room. He pondered this as he leaned against a surprisingly soft pillow, until something poked his head. Reaching, he yanked the offending material—a chicken feather. Someone giggled.

The guest looked up to see several blond children crowding the doorway, their curious blue eyes on the strange man in their bed. He gave them a tentative smile, straining to recall if he had seen them before.

The tallest, a boy with the height of a youth but the eager, inquisitive eyes of a child, stepped forward. "I'm Narnik. Remember me? Auntie Marna said you might not remember us and that we'd have to remind you who we were."

"I…"

Marna's voice interrupted. "Come to supper!" Most of the children scampered away.

"Come on." Narnik offered a hand and helped him stand. The lad led him into the main room, where the rest of the children scrambled and clambered onto bare wood stools and chairs of different makes and sizes.

Narnik plopped onto a stool and swooped a hand to commandeer another next to him. "Sit by me."

The guest complied as Marna introduced him to the brood. Each of the older children nodded as she called out their names, while the younger ones quietly gnawed fistfuls of bread with unself-conscious appetite. He smiled weakly, perplexed. He would never remember any of their unusual names. Not that he knew what a usual name was. He would be glad if his own name came back to him. By The Powers, he wondered what strange plan of Theirs unfolded.

The lost man watched Marna as she managed the distribution of the meal, standing at the far end of the table ladling broth into bowls, then passing the full bowls into small, eager hands.

Narnik chewed a mouthful of bread and said, "Guest, were you in the battle? Do you remember? Last night I saw your sword had blood on it!"

The lost man gazed at the cup of broth before him. Green and reddish herbs swirled atop the liquid in a mesmerizing spiral. He tried to recall, but felt groggy. Then a flash of ranks of armed men, stretched across a plain, appeared in his vision, as though conjured by The Powers and real for a moment. He inhaled. "I do remember something…" He stared at the broth and rubbed his eyebrows, pressing firmly. "I was with Soldiers and Horsemen. Two groups, side by side. One had pennants of blue, white, and silver—"

Narnik interrupted. "Blue and silver? Those are our king's colors!"

The eldest girl held her shoulders high and tense. "Who won?"

"Palika, Narnik, shh! Let him tell," Marna scolded.

The boy ignored her. "So you fought for our king?"

"I . . ." He squinted, trying to find a sure memory. Pain pulsed along the crown of his skull. He looked at Marna, half expecting guidance and relief from her. Suddenly, the guest wondered how she must feel, harboring a man who might be an enemy. He looked at the children. All watched him, save the littlest, who mashed crumbs with her thumb. A name came to his thought. "Hudik King. I fought for Hudik King."

Narnik whooped. "King Hudik is our lord!"

Palika's shoulders lowered. Marna gave a slight nod. The guest gazed at her as she sipped her broth. In a flash, he saw a battlefield with invaders fleeing. He spoke in a soft voice. "They ran away. I remember them running away."

Her gray eyes met his; her gaze laid his heart bare. "Who ran away, Guest?"

"The attacking army. The invaders."

Narnik banged his palms on the table. "Then we won! We won!" He hugged the boy next to him. The others chattered and cheered.

"And they will be home soon." Palika's voice was serious but glad. "If they are all right."

"Who will be all right?"

Marna's niece's gaze dropped to the table. "My father and brothers." She glared at her aunt. "And my uncle."

He watched his healer, whilst his stomach fell to his feet at this mention that Marna had a husband. She had lied to him.

He bit his teeth as she pulled an empty stool away from the wall and sat across from him. "But you are not from this country," she said.

"What makes you say that?" Narnik interjected. "Oh, right, you said his emblems were of Eskalind."

"Think a moment before you speak," Marna scolded as she reached for the littlest girl, who pounded her hands on her aunt's side. "Recall how he said our king's name."

Narnik scratched his ear. "We say 'King Hudik'. He said 'Hudik King'?"

Marna looked at the guest, a challenge in her gaze. His reply was tense. "It is natural for me to say Hudik King."

"That proves you're from the Strange Kingdom."

"Auntie Marna, how do you know that?" Narnik was ever curious. The lost man had other questions for her, but stayed his tongue.

"Their old King toured your grandfather's forge once when I was a child, and that is how he and his men spoke." She turned to spoon broth into the smallest girl's mouth. "Children, you must learn that Eskalind is Ever Allied with Hudiksland. Our guest wore their new King's emblem and colors."

Before the guest could grasp her meaning, the words slipped away, like sand through his fingers. His head pounded with pain as he tried to form his question, to think. Perhaps The Powers did not want him to think. He watched her wipe the small girl's face with her apron. "You said you are a bladesmith's daughter," he said.

"Yes, I told you that last night."

Narnik launched a barrage of questions. "But isn't the Strange Kingdom where The Powers live? Have you seen them? And everyone is rich, right?"

The guest nearly choked on his broth. "That does not sound right to me."

"But your armor is very fine, and your sword too. I saw it! Maybe you aren't really a Lord, and are just like everyone else there."

"I wish I remembered." The guest sipped the broth. Its taste warmed his chest. His heart eased and his mind drifted. Until Marna spoke again.

"Let the man eat, Narnik." Marna passed him a loaf of dark bread. "Otherwise he may never recover his memory." Her gray eyes glinted at him, and he realized that while Narnik and the other children seemed content with his tale, perhaps she was not. Then again, if she had lied to him, he cared not what she thought.

————

The next morning, the lost man gladly accepted Narnik's invitation to see the family's vineyard. Two of the younger boys tagged after them as they ambled along a path tracing the southern edge of a steep hill. The air smelled fresh; a warm breeze ruffled the grass. It felt good to walk outdoors and breathe the countryside scents. To The Powers, he hoped the change of scenery and motion might help penetrate the continuing fog obliterating his past, and the nagging feeling that his healer had deceived him. He planned to ask Narnik a few questions. If he could get a word in.

Narnik stopped at the crest of the wide, flat hilltop. "Look, Guest!" He pointed to dusty, colorless stones outlining a large rectangle subsumed in the earth. Two piles of stones anchored the center of the short ends of the shape: the remains of chimneys. Dense weeds and grass sprouted amongst the mortared stones, filling the interior like a poorly laid carpet. "That's where my family lived, a long time ago. There was a big fire, and my grandmother died." The two younger boys, Tarvik and Tanvik, tromped around the stones, leaping over every other one. "That's why we live in the little house," Narnik said. "This used to be the main house. But Father and Uncle couldn't rebuild on their own." For once, a woesome expression crossed Narnik's face. "Then Father joined Mother, and we all came along, and there hasn't been a chance to build it up again. Watch this." The boy bent, scooped up a pebble, and skipped it at his brothers' feet.

Tarvik yelped and looked about. "Something bit me!" He spied Narnik watching him. "What did you do?"

Narnik maintained an expression of innocent nonchalance until his young brother lost interest.

The guest shook his head as the lad giggled. "Narnik, I am a little confused about your family. Your mother and your Aunt Marna are sisters?"

The boy nodded, his blond ponytail flopping with the motion. "Uh-huh."

"Then your uncle is Marna's husband."

"No, Uncle Malik is Father's brother." The guest felt an exhilarating sense of relief. But Narnik's next utterance brought fresh worries. "They aren't joined yet."

A sudden catch filled the man's throat, and he stifled a swallow. "Oh, they are betrothed."

Narnik laughed. "Well, Mother wants them to be. Then Auntie Marna would stay with us forever. But I don't think she wants to." He dashed across the wide plain of the hill, turning his head to call out, "Come this way!"

The lost man followed, pondering this new information and feeling weary. He gazed over the neat rows of black-vined grapes below, the ruffle-edged, gray-green leaves fluttering along low trellises.

Narnik gave a brief tour of the land below. "There is the wine house and the mashing tubs, and do you see the wells? Our grapes are a thirsty crop!" The guest observed the structures; their tidy thatched roofs glistened in the sunshine. The boy turned to the guest and straightened. "All our wine goes to King Hudik. That's why we have crowns as our barrel mark!" His brothers raced past him and down the hill, scampering like young colts freed from their pen. "See, Guest, we have royal connections on both sides of the family. My mother's father is an armorer for the king. The chief armorer." Narnik puffed his chest and smote the air with an invisible hammer. "But Aunt Marna almost cost him his position. She told the prince that he wasn't a good enough swordsman for a blade grandfather made him." He laughed.

"Why did she do that?" The more he learned about this woman, the more fascinated and confused he became.

"I don't know. She speaks her mind. So she had to leave Castleton. That's why she's with us. And to help Mother."

The memory of the care she gave his blade surfaced. "I could see her saying that to one who would not treasure a fine sword." His legs felt weak, and he sank to a rock, the burn on his head throbbing. "She is bold, but thoughtful. I mean, I think she speaks her mind, but with good intentions." The pain waned. He felt like a fumbling fool and wondered why he blabbered at the lad thus. A tuft of daisyweed seed floated by.

Narnik sat at the lost Eskalinder's feet, picking at a blade of grass. "I like her too. Even though she's always telling me what to do."

The guest laughed. "You do not mind as well as the others."

Marna's nephew gave a mischievous smirk. "But you like that she speaks her mind—you must not have that happen very often, being from the Strange Kingdom where everyone is a Lord."

"You speak your mind to me."

"But you are going to show me how to spar and be a great warrior!"

The Eskalinder smiled, but his thoughts circled back to Marna and Malik and what happened in Castleton and—

"Guest?"

"Hmm?"

"I asked if you think your men are trying to find you." Narnik chewed on a yellow-flowered plant.

"My men?"

"Auntie Marna thinks you have servants or vassals or someone who must be trying to find you." The boy spat out the plant. "Yuk."

"I … I do not know. Whenever I try to think much, my head hurts." The Strange Kingdomer gestured to the wound on his head.

"That's strange," Narnik said.

"We should go back to the house now, Narnik. I could use more of your aunt's broth."

"Mmm, that would be good. Oh!" The blond lad turned to the man, his eyes suddenly eager, as though ready to impart a long-held secret. "You haven't had her roast chicken yet. That is the best."

———

Narnik and the guest hunched before the live hearth, polishing the bronze-plated side of the lost man's leather armor: the vambraces that protected the arms, the greaves for his shins, and the large breastplate. Behind them, Marna wiped the table of the last crumbs from the evening meal. A burbling murmur came from the sleeping room as the younger children readied for bed.

The boy's enthusiasm was tangible. "I wish I had armor like this. And a sword."

The guest grinned and stole a glance over his shoulder at Marna. "First you must learn how to care for armor, and a blade."

Narnik puckered his mouth. "Are you just saying that so I'll do more work?"

The Eskalinder chuckled. The fire flickered orange light across their faces.

"Watch this!" the lad whispered. He tilted the gleaming vambrace in his hands to reflect the firelight into Palika's eyes as she cleaned the supper dishes. She wiped her eyes, a puzzled expression tightening her features. Then she spotted the source of her troubles.

"Narnik, stop it!"

He giggled.

A stool scrapped the floor behind them as Marna spoke. "Palika, let Narnik finish those dishes whilst you go to bed."

With a satisfied smile, the girl tossed the washrag to her brother.

The youngster whined, "But I was helping Guest with his armor!"

"Then I will help him." Marna brushed the boy aside with a swish of her skirt and settled next to the guest. The youngster grumbled, stomping to the kitchen.

In a low voice, the lost man's host confided, "I always need to keep an eye on that one." Marna shook her head and reached for a greave. "Narnik, you will need fresh water. Just bring it outside."

The boy hoisted the dish tub away with a grunt, slamming the side door as he left.

She oiled a cloth and set to work. "Would you believe my sister already has plans to join him with a neighbor's daughter. When they are of age, of course."

"Would that be the neighbor your sister is attending?" The Eskalinder felt pleased to have remembered this bit of information. At least he could recall something. The more time he spent with his host, the less cloudy his thoughts felt.

"No, another neighbor. Being a midwife, Werna is familiar with all the families in the area."

"Hmm. I do not understand this desire to make matches."

She studied his expression. "Isn't that how things are done everywhere?"

"Not in my land."

"You are remembering more; that is good." The bronze squeaked under her polishing. "Anything else?"

He brought a hand to his mouth as a vague image of a woman formed in his mind. She was seated at a dressing table, holding a dark, onyx-framed mirror threaded with veins of gold. Her whitish-blond hair hung in a long braid, entwined with a silken sable cord that matched her elegant gown.

"My mother." The words escaped as a whisper, a mixture of bewilderment and wonder as he tried to grasp more of the scene. "She loved fashioning new gowns…" As he spoke, he recalled women unfurling bolts of jet-black cloth, interwoven with gilt threads. "She had attendants to help her, and there was one she thought I should like." He tried to envision that woman's face, but could see only the stone hearth before him.

Marna chuckled softly by his side. He was very aware of the small amount of space between them. "Well, that is unusual, to have your mother want to match you with a servant."

"You misunderstand. One's station is of no consequence in matters of the heart. What bothered me was that she would try to encourage me toward one woman or another." He looked at her. Part of him felt glad to know something about his past; another part puzzled at why he felt so adamant about the topic.

Marna's expression was incredulous. She put down one greave and reached for another.

"Marna, The Powers bring people together, and no one should interfere with that." His voice sounded sharper than he meant.

The Hudikslander raised an eyebrow. "That is not the belief in this land."

"Yet it is so."

A mischievous look sparked her gray eyes; he sensed she enjoyed his resolve. He stared at the fire till she spoke again.

"So, you did not care for the woman your mother encouraged you toward?"

He shook his head, frustrated with the teasing bits of his past that came and went, like flitting butterflies in a blooming garden. "I do not even remember what she looked like, I think … No, I do remember. All her attendants seemed the same to me; they all wore their hair like my mother, copied her style of dress."

Marna laughed. "That sounds like King Hudik's … court." She watched his fingers work the cloth over the metal. "It seems some things are the same the world over." She was quiet a moment, as though her thoughts led her far away. Then she spoke in a soft, wistful tone. "My sister would join me with her braither, her husband's brother."

"Surely you have say in the matter. Would you have him?" The guest silently chided himself for the immediacy of his response, and his harsh tone.

"Everyone says it is a good match." The bladesmith's daughter looked at the flames. "Yet I do not feel drawn to him."

The guest ground his polishing cloth into the breastplate. He realized he had been rubbing the same portion over and over. Moving the cloth aside, he saw her face reflected before him, in profile, as she watched the fire. He reached to touch her reflection. *Marna.*

Narnik banged through the side door. "I'm done!" The dishes clanked in the tub in his arms. "Now can I help?" He plopped the wooden tub onto the counter.

Marna rose as one resigned to a familiar task. "Yes. I must be off to bed."

"Can I sleep out here with our guest tonight? I won't ask for stories or anything!"

His aunt turned to their guest. He nodded slightly, not wanting her to go, but uncertain how to manage in front of the boy. He smiled weakly. Her gray eyes glimmered in the firelight, but her demeanor, as she spoke to her nephew, was weary.

"Only if he agrees, and you promise to let our guest sleep when he wants to."

"Yes, Narnik, that is fine," the lost man said.

She left, and he felt her departure as a dull ache, as though he were witnessing her Joining to another man.

The next morning at breakfast, the lost man devoured his third bowl of broth with a hearty slurp, contesting with Narnik to see who could be loudest. Across the table, Marna shook her head, but a smile graced her rosy lips.

Her guest grinned. The more broth he drank, the *clearer* his head felt—and the more he simply wanted to be with her. He imagined this was their home, their children, and that there was a small room, perhaps detached from the rest of the house, for just the two of them. She refilled his bowl, and he swirled the broth while pondering these happy thoughts. Then little Lena screamed, without provocation, shattering his vision of domestic tranquility.

The guest glanced up to see Marna gently stuffing a piece of bread in the girl's mouth, and the child quieted, chewing contentedly.

Narnik fidgeted by his side. "Palika, did you make this bread?"

"Yes, why?"

"I could tell. It isn't as good as Auntie Marna's."

Palika's face turned beet red, and she snapped, "Then learn to make it yourself."

Narnik smirked. "I'm only good for dishwashing."

Marna interjected, "And chicken slaughtering." Instantly, all the children turned to look at her. She rose to collect empty bowls. "We will have roast chicken tonight, if Narnik agrees to this task."

The table erupted in shouts of joy that brought a memory of boisterous men clamoring for ale. The guest pondered this as the oldest boy beamed at him.

Only Palika's expression was sour. "Shouldn't we save the chickens until everyone returns home?"

"No, dear niece. There will be enough for a second feast later."

The lost man caught Marna's eye and gave her his best mischievous expression. "If your chicken is half as good as your broth …"

"It is even better." She smiled, and he felt the warmth in it as though her entire being radiated a tenderness meant just for him.

The intoxicating scent of roasted chicken filled his lungs, and the Eskalinder paid no mind to the blisters forming on his hand from turning the spit. Narnik threw more wood on the fire whilst two of his brothers rotated the opposite handle. Sparks flew against the darkening blue of the sky.

Narnik grinned. "Not much longer, Strange Kingdomer!" He stood alongside the smaller children, who watched, chattering. Little Lena gummed her hand, perhaps in anticipation of the meal to come. Palika leaned against a large wine barrel, a huge plate of finished birds on her lap. She snipped away the strings binding each together.

Marna appeared at the side door of the house. "Narnik, give the man a rest." She walked toward the fire pit. Narnik grabbed the handle from the guest and turned the spit. "And do not pick at the birds that are done! Guest, come into the house and let me see how your wound is coming along."

Palika glanced at her. "Auntie Marna, don't you need help?"

"No, dear. I need you to test the chickens for doneness, and keep your siblings at bay."

Palika nodded but glared distrustfully as the stranger followed Marna.

"Go sit at the table," Marna said, "and I will bring the herbs to you." The house was quiet, as all the children were outside, no doubt facing the certain temptation of their favorite dish.

A sweet scent filled the kitchen, and he noticed chopped herbs on the cutting board. He sat at the long table, watching the broad candles flicker as Marna came toward him carrying a bowl coated with minced plants.

She stood next to him. "Now let me see." He bowed his head and closed his eyes, feeling her fingers part his hair. His breathing quickened.

"Where? I cannot find it!" The buxom woman bent deliciously closer to him. "It's healed. Completely healed!" He looked at her as she whispered, "It could not have healed that quickly." She pulled her hands away as though startled by his expression.

The Eskalinder rose slowly. He spoke in a gentle voice. "Are you certain? Here, look again." He bowed his head.

Marna reached to his forehead. "Yes, it is gone." Her voice wavered; her fingers still intermingled with his hair.

He raised his head, and her warm hands traced the sides of his face, stopping at his beard. Her lips parted as though she might speak.

He reached to touch her face. Her hands fell away from his chin and rested lightly on his collarbones. He wondered if she might push him away; uncertainty clouded her expression, as though something pulled her in two directions at once.

The lost man whispered, too choked with emotion to speak clearly, "I am drawn to you, Marna." Her gray eyes softened, and he traced her smooth, freckled cheek to her jaw.

"And I to you."

His fingers trailed to her lips. She smiled under his touch. The delicious smile from that morning that warmed his being as though he had never known affection before.

Suddenly he tottered backward, uncertain what had happened. Marna grasped him with strong hands, steadying him.

"Guest?" She looked anxious.

"I, I think I was not breathing." He smiled weakly. She gave him a saucy expression and tapped his nose with her finger.

"You use this."

He gulped air and leaned to meet her lips, surprised, and pleased, to find her meeting him halfway.

———

Narnik chewed a delicious chicken leg, staring at his plate, disappointed only a few small morsels remained. He watched his siblings playfully fight over the wishbones. A tempting half-eaten chicken thigh rested on Tarvik's plate. Narnik was considering how he might distract his brother to grab it when he noticed his aunt explaining the wishbone game to their guest. The adults drew sides, and the contest began. In a moment, his aunt held the larger piece.

She grinned, a smile that seemed to come from her entire body. It made him think of a bright lantern, too bright to stare at.

Auntie Marna whispered, but the lad heard her: "I wasted my wish on the impossible."

Their guest's reply piqued the boy's curiosity: "It is already done."

He'd seen that look before, when he spied his parents alone in the wine house just before they kissed. That was the first time he noticed them sneaking away together. Without fail, those little meetings were followed by the announcement that a new sibling was on its way.

Narnik smirked, pleased with himself for figuring out where babies come from.

Palika rose to collect the dishes, casting a disdainful glare at the guest. He wondered why his sister disliked the man. Then again, unlike him, she didn't want to go to Eskalind and have rich armor like their guest's. He sat up straight, whispering into his hands, "The Powers help me keep Palika away from them until they get joined."

———

Marna stood in the open doorway of the sleeping room, gazing at her dozing nieces and nephews. The soft breath of sleep lulled the air. She shook her head, pleased but again surprised how quickly and soundly they fell asleep after drinking her broth. *All I do is add mint to my sister's recipe.*

Her empty bed-place, between little Lena and Palika, did not beckon. She looked over her shoulder to see if the guest was in the main room. Not seeing him, she considered that he might be outside, and smiled.

Palika flung her arm across the empty sheet where her aunt usually slept and mumbled.

The woman wondered if the girl was dreaming of a man who would bring her away from this place. A wry expression crossed Marna's face as she, not for the first time, considered how wretched her life would be if she joined with Malik.

Her youngest niece rolled, sprawling her legs diagonally across the bare spot on the pallet, leaving no more room on the bed for another person.

Marna pulled the metal grate to dim the lantern slowly, trying to stifle the annoying scratching noise it made. She turned to the door and caressed the cut lavender draped from a wooden peg, inhaling the rich scent. Then she slipped into the main room, shutting the door behind her. The candles still glowed on the long table, but she saw no sign of their guest. She craned her head to peek into the side room, just as the front door opened.

He entered, and his expression brightened when he saw her.

She grinned back, her hands self-consciously folding before her in a maidenly gesture. He came toward her and took her hands in his deliciously long fingers. They gazed at one another, and Marna felt she could study his face for hours and still discover new features, new mysteries. She sighed. He paused her breath with a kiss, gentle and heady. His touch felt natural and sympathetic, as though his being would repair old hurts. She lingered in that comfort, till she realized she wanted him closer.

Marna pulled away with a happy hum. Stroking his once well-kept beard, which she might offer to trim tomorrow, she murmured a question. "Care for a walk?"

Her fingers traced along his lips, and he whispered, "Aye."

She could feel the heat in his brown eyes. Turning on her heel, she dashed to the side room to retrieve her knit wool shawl. Realizing how eager she must seem, she lifted her hair slowly, deliberately draping the ash-colored fabric across the back of her neck. It scratched her skin. She wondered how his fingers would feel there.

Taking his hand, she led him out the door. The guest pulled it shut carefully, turning to her. "Which way?"

Marna considered her options. She must decide, and soon, whether this walk was an opportunity to spend time together, to talk and exchange kisses, or if she wanted more. The chance to be with a man she truly cared for was strong, but she didn't want to seem too eager.

"This way." She led him away from the house, toward the main path, at a leisurely pace. The moon lit the surrounding fields and the empty stable with bluish light. The remaining chickens clucked nervously as they passed the henhouse. As they approached the well, Marna found an excuse to linger. "Dinner was a bit salty."

He paused. "Your roast chicken tasted wonderful to me, but let me fetch you some water." His voice was kind, inviting. The Eskalinder reached for the bucket and dropped it into the well. It splashed the bottom, and he turned the creaky crank to hoist it back up. Lifting the water bucket toward them, he offered her the full ladle. She bent to sip the cool, fresh liquid. A bit sloshed over the sides and fell back into the dark bucket, splashing up like silver sparks. She could not help but comment. "Everything looks pretty in moonlight."

"You are beautiful in any light, Marna."

She wiped her mouth, smiling against her hand. If anyone else spoke thus to her, she would raise a skeptical eyebrow. Yet Marna read his expression as sincere, with a softness about the eyes that spoke of contentment.

She passed the ladle to him and he drank. "I wish this was your broth."

Marna grinned as a plan formed. "The hill that overlooks the vineyards—have you been to its north side?"

Her former patient shook his head. "Narnik showed me the south side. With the view of the vineyard."

"Ah. The north side is where I go … to think." She stopped herself from saying, "To be alone," which was true also. She still did not know what she wanted. "Would you like to see it?"

"Only if you would show me."

The bladesmith's daughter offered the nobleman her hand. He smiled at her, and under clear moonglow she led him up the gradual rise of a path along the hill's side. They passed the stable. Patches of freshly thatched roof glimmered in the soft light, evidence of the last work the menfolk had completed before the call to arms swept them away to battle.

Her sister's endless suggestions rang in her mind. "Oh Marna, bring Malik more bread. Marna, help Malik with the hay." She found herself suddenly angry that her family wanted her to stay in this place.

Her eyes trailed to the man at her side. Maybe he would bring her to The Strange Kingdom and everything would be all right. Until she got with child and he had to join her off to the nearest bachelor. She frowned as their shoes crunched small bits of rock. *Father never taught me anything, only told me what to do. And poor Andrik. Father wanted me to join with him, and I would have, gladly, yet The Powers saw fit for him to fall in a battle he should never have been in. And Father sending me to live here…*

Tears threatened to spill from her eyes as all these thoughts tumbled like boulders cascading down a cliff. She must make her decision.

"There." She gestured ahead with her free hand to a wide, flat stone, set just below the thin trees on the hillside's crest. "This is where I come and sit and think." She led him to the spot and sat in her usual place, patting the still sun-warmed rock next to her. He sat by her side. "On clear days one can see quite far. Even at night. See?" She pointed to a dim orange light in the distance. "That's the house where my sister is attending our neighbor. I wonder how she fares." Marna turned to hide her face from the lost nobleman and hastily wiped her eyes with her free hand. Then she laid her head on his shoulder, and he stroked her hair, trailing his fingers down her arm to rest on her hip. The combination of his soft touch and the thoughts raging in her head hitched her breathing.

"How fares my healer?"

"I'm sorry. I'm not much company." She raised her head.

"It is good just to be near you, Marna."

"I'm more tired than I realized." Perhaps the lie affected the truth. Her limbs felt heavy, her shoulders sagged. But she drew closer to him, wondering why she felt so strange.

Her guest spoke. "I was hoping . . . I was hoping now that we are away from the children, that . . . that you might tell me about your life."

Marna studied his face a moment. "Twenty-eight years will make a long tale." She sat up.

He leaned onto his elbow as jauntily as one would expect a man to lean onto a well-upholstered couch, gazing at her with sparkling eyes. "I would hear all of it."

"I shall try to make it interesting, even the boring bits."

With that, she began her tale with growing up in Castleton, of her father's first forge and watching the sparks leap from the pounded metal, the incessant clanging. Her earliest memories. "I thought it exciting. At one point, as a very young girl, I wanted to be a bladesmith. That did not meet with approval." She laughed, then quieted as her thoughts returned to how her birth had disappointed her family. "Father wanted a son to follow him, as he had followed his father. Yet none of my brothers lived long enough for him to name them."

"How horrible."

"Yes, it was. I think my mother blamed herself." Marna knew what that felt like. "She died when I was eight. Before that, she was frequently ill. I think that's why Werna, my sister, and I have had such an interest in healing." She stared at the moon as it climbed higher over the neighbor's distant roof, knotted her shawl across her bodice. "My sister has attended at over forty births and has never lost a mother or a babe. I just wish she had been old enough to help Mother."

Her guest watched her, and she feared he might think her about to slip into a morose mood. The Hudikslander searched her memories for a lighter tale. "Once, when Werna first learned herbcraft, she believed she could make a love potion for a youth she admired." Laughter crept into her voice. "She poured it into his ale when he turned away, but instead of having the desired effect, the poor lad spent the night in the outhouse!"

The Eskalinder shook his head and chuckled. "Then I am doubly glad it was you who answered the door the night I stumbled here." The man lowered his voice at the end of the sentence and looked at the ground, his lopsided chin giving him a shy look.

Marna wondered if he thought it bold of her to bring him here. Given how little she knew about him, part of her could not help wondering if he recalled more than he was telling. Yet when he gazed at her with his kind brown eyes, he looked as smitten as her future braither Palik chatting with Werna at the Castleton market when they first met. And her guest's undemanding touch—despite the obvious strength in his well-muscled arms—ah yes. She watched him teach Narnik and Tarvik sparring yesterday, and the man clearly knew how to swing a blade, even when a whittled tree branch served for practice. But with the boys he showed great patience, good humor, and encouragement for their fledgling efforts.

"Marna, are you cold?"

She raised a questioning eyebrow. He chuckled. "You are pulling your shawl very tight. Shall we go back?"

Again she noted the softness in his brown eyes. "No, my guest." She reclined on her side, facing him, the hard rock beneath her. Reaching a tentative hand to his hair, she followed it to where his large ear protruded from his locks. She smiled, recalling how when he first came to her door, she had thought his face one that only a mother could love.

The Strange Kingdomer reached out his near arm. "Here, do not trouble your head on the rock." His speech was threaded with tender concern. She raised her head, placing it on his arm, and said, "I could grow used to a pillow such as this."

His voice startled her. "Marna, wake up. It is morning."

She opened her eyes. The light had changed from silvery to a grayish blue. A bird tweeted in the trees behind them.

The Eskalinder lay next to her, a lopsided grin curving his lips. "You sleep soundly."

Marna sat quickly, her side sore. The slender gray clouds above were edged in shades of dusky rose. "I … fell asleep?"

"Aye." The brown-haired man rolled onto his back, stretching and bellowing a yawn.

"Did you sleep?"

"Hmm?" Rubbing his eyes, he groaned, sitting up. "No, I …." His expression was sheepish. "I watched you sleep."

"Oh." Not certain what to make of this, Marna stood, shaking her shawl and shivering, more from jangled nerves than chill. "But, I wasn't that weary." Creaky stiffness from dozing on bare rock plagued her bones and she felt a fool, wondering if for some reason her chicken and broth had a hand in making her, as well as the children, more tired. Puzzled, she gazed into the distance where a plume of sputtering smoke rose from the neighbor's chimney.

The guest pulled himself to his feet while she wrapped the rough-yarned shawl about her arms. The thin clouds stretching overhead brightened to a pure pink. "You must think me a dreadful bore for falling asleep on you."

The nobleman stepped closer. "I was well occupied." A hint of mirth tinged his voice, and she tilted her head questioningly. He stroked her cheek. "Though I did miss your eyes."

Marna grinned, glad to feel at ease. "We must return before the children wake."

He nodded, and she thought she caught a hint of disappointment in his gaze.

"We will have more time alone together later," she promised, hoping to The Powers it would be true. Though only They could explain how she had managed to sleep through this opportunity.

Chapter Four—These Few Moments

The long blue shadows of morning shortened under cheery sunshine. The guest leaned his wrist against the side door's frame. Outside, Marna readied the children for a berry-picking excursion, distributing woven-reed baskets to clamoring hands. The memory of the moonlit walk and rest on the hilltop last night brought a sigh to his lips.

Fourteen-year-old Palika glared at him. "Isn't the stranger coming with us?" The youngest girl wiggled in her arms.

"We will follow soon." His healer gave the toddler a kiss. "Bring back lots of berries, little Lena. Then Auntie Marna will make you a pie!" The small girl grinned, reaching for the basket dangling from Palika's hand.

Palika whispered, but the Strange Kingdomer heard her: "Auntie Marna! Think on Uncle Malik!"

Marna turned her back to the guest and spoke to the reed-thin girl in a low voice. Then she called, "Run along!"

The children trundled away with their berry baskets. Narnik led the way, quickening their pace by challenging Palika to a race, even while his eldest sister directed a serious, pleading gaze at her aunt.

Marna waved goodbye to the berry-pickers as her eldest niece brought up the rear of group. Narnik circled the others and rushed to Palika. He grabbed Lena, who giggled at the transfer to her brother's arms, and called to his siblings, "The more berries we pick, the more pies we will eat." With a glance at their guest, he shouted once more, "We'll be gone a long time! And don't forget our sparring practice later!" Then he dashed along the path, causing Lena to scream with delight whilst Palika gave chase after him, admonishing him to slow down.

Marna chuckled at the spectacle, then turned to her guest, radiant and happy. He asked his beloved softly, "Come inside?"

His healer nodded, and they walked to the main room, closing the door behind them. Lit candles gave the windowless room a cozy glow. The Eskalinder sat upon one of the stools by the table, folding his hands over the smooth wood. Despite his desire to touch her, he promised himself to let her make the first move. Last night she had seemed skittish, at times, and he sought to reassure her how the ways of Eskalinders were different.

Marna sat next to him, immediately reaching for his hand, stroking his fingers. After a moment she spoke. "I've been wanting to tell you that I'm sorry I fell asleep last night. I don't know what happened to me. I thought I wasn't that tired." She sighed. "It was as though something *made* me fall asleep." He listened, but could not resist bringing her warm hands to his lips. "I'm sorry, dear Guest. I mustn't be making any sense."

He shook his head, his lips slightly grazing her knuckles. "It gladdens my heart to be near you, Marna. I thank The Powers for leading me to your door."

She smiled, and they gazed at one another a long while. He breathed in the heady scent of herbs on her fingers, feeling both heavy and light with her closeness. His beloved's gray eyes sparkled in the candlelight. He murmured her name and kissed her hands.

"Dear Guest." She closed those beautiful eyes. "This is all the time we have. A few stolen moments." She squeezed his hand. "Let us not waste it!"

Hearing Marna's willingness excited him, but her insistence that this was their only time together—he would not stand for that. "This need not be our only time together."

"Of course it is." His healer looked away, her voice strained as though he tired her patience. "My sister will return, or my menfolk, or your men will find you."

He spoke resolutely, measuring the words. "We can be together."

"Perhaps your wound is not completely healed." She smiled weakly, running her fingers along his hairline.

The Eskalinder shifted closer to her, her arm against his chest. "I *am* healed, Marna, thanks to your care." Closing his eyes, he pressed his lips softly against his love's cheek, but her words sprouted unease in his thoughts. After a moment he pulled away to study her face. He needed her to understand.

"The Powers mean for us to be together, Marna. I am certain of it. Why else did they lead me to your door, to your healing, to my own heart?"

Her lips parted into a smile that hurt him with its tenderness. "Dearest Guest." They kissed again till she broke away, slight glints of red gleaming in her locks and a grin gracing her pretty face.

He made a falsely stern expression. "Are my kisses amusing?"

"No, oh no." She laughed, a light sound that sent a tingle along his spine. "You will think me ridiculous. But I just … sometimes I think your memory will return suddenly, and you will think me an insolent wench for not calling you 'my Lord.'"

"I would never think that. And what does it matter if I am a Lord or not?"

She raised a defiant eyebrow, a gesture worthy of a noble lady. "You are a Lord from the Strange Kingdom. You, you must be."

"I do not see how that matters to our being together, Marna." He embraced her, resting his ear against the side of her head, and whispered tenderly, "What can I do? Would it help if I remembered who I am? We could journey to Castleton when your family returns, see if I recognize anyone or anyone recognizes me. Would that reassure you of my intentions?"

She pulled away, and her eyes looked glassier, as though she might be about to cry. "This is all the time we have. These few moments…"

Muffled, but increasing, shouting reached his ears. He recognized Narnik's voice.

"Guest! Riders are coming! They have armor like yours and a banner! Guest!"

Marna gulped, and they clearly heard Palika shout, "Narnik, no. *No!*"

The clamor grew louder. With both hands, Marna pushed against his chest, breaking their embrace. She stumbled from her stool and went to the hearth. "They have found you. Our time is over. Go and greet them."

He stood. His chest ached where she had pushed him as though branded with a hot iron. He reached to touch her long hair; his voice caught in his throat. "Marna, what are you saying?"

"It is not to be. Just go!"

"Guest, come out!" The sound of Narnik hammering on the side door startled his wits. "Hurry!" The door jangled against its metal latch. He had not realized Marna locked the door.

The Strange Kingdomer gazed at her back. He brushed his fingers against his chest. The pain there was real and intense. Anger and disbelief flooded his veins. The pounding on the door mimicked the pounding in his head and his heart. He must say something. "You wish us to end like this?"

Her shoulders rose and her head hunched forward. "Please go!"

He turned, facing the front door he had stumbled through just a few nights before. "The Powers led me here. Why can you not see it?" Shock and disbelief mingled with a rising anger in his breast. With a curt, last glance at her back, he trod to the side doorway.

"Guest, they're coming! We saw them from the hill!" Narnik stepped aside as the door swung open. "See!" The boy pointed toward the road leading to the house. A cloud of dust obscured all but the silhouettes of riders and their pennants. The pummel of hooves grew closer. A rid-erless horse charged ahead of the entourage. For a moment he feared it might lead a stampede of the house.

But the chestnut mare broke her mad run, trotting to him as casually as if she expected a treat. As she approached, his vision sharpened. In that instant, he recognized his horse. "Breena?"

Breena whickered, batting her long black eyelashes and lowering her head in a gesture both apologetic and joyful. He stroked her fuzzy forelock tentatively, the gesture feeling at once innately familiar yet odd, as though it had been many years since he last touched her.

The mare nudged her great head into his shoulder with unabashed affection. "You know me, I see. Ah, Breena." He brushed his hand through her mane, the clarity of recognition returning. He had done this before. Many glad times before. Her clear love for him caused a lump in his throat, intensified by his healer's rejection.

Narnik was at his side, his mouth wide open with awe. "She's beautiful!" Several of his siblings rushed around him, reaching to pet the mare with berry-stained hands.

Breena withstood the onslaught contentedly, her dark eyes never leaving his.

The mounted men continued toward them, their brass breastplates, coated with dust, giving a dim gleam in the sunshine. The Pennant Bearer held aloft a red flag, embroidered with a brown shield stitched in metallic thread and a crimson sword across it.

The riders halted, and the man beside the flagman spoke. "My Lord, at long last Breena leads us to you!" That man's stallion walked forward, and he dismounted with graceful haste, bowing his light brown locks. He raised his green eyes, and the lost Eskalinder recognized him.

"Jinil!" They embraced as old companions, with a chuckle and hearty pats on the back. The erstwhile guest felt as though a rock had been placed under his feet.

"Thank The Powers you are safe, my Lord. Breena here has led us on a merry chase." A thin scar ran through Jinil's beard, and a quirk of a smile nudged his lips. He lowered his voice. "Are you well, my Lord?"

"I am well, I thank you." The words came easily, as though he had said them before, but he wondered what his face betrayed. "A long tale, best told later."

Jinil nodded with the ease of long-established companionship. Turning toward the mounted men, he called, "Praise The Powers, Dalock King is safely found!"

The lost man froze. "King?" He drew the word through his mouth.

Dalock looked at these men and for a moment saw them gathered in a great stone hall, *his* hall, dark beamed and bannered with billowing crimson and earth-colored pennants. A gathered entourage of Ladies dressed in long red silk gowns and men clad in chestnut tunics and bronze-plated leathers stomped their feet, calling his name.

The memory faded as Marna and Palika came through the front doorway, his armor stacked in their arms. The girl glared at him accusingly, while Marna's mouth was firm. But before he could speak and declare his feelings for her before his men, she looked away, and the pressure in his chest reminded him of the force of her rejection. Words stuck in his throat. His face flushed, and he wished himself anywhere else.

The surrounding men cheered. "Hail, Dalock King!"

Narnik stood dumbfounded by Dalock's side. "King? Truly?"

He turned to the boy. "To you, I am Dalock." He clasped the lad by the arm.

Narnik's grin could not have been wider had the Strange King bestowed the finest blade into his young hands. "I will fetch your sword, Dalock!" He ran into the house, darting past his aunt and sister.

Two of the King's Guards dismounted and received the armor from the women. Marna turned to Palika. "Bring his clothing." The girl hurried after her brother.

Small Lena clung to her aunt's skirts. The healer bent and scooped the child into her arms, straightening her little skirt whilst evading the King's eyes.

Narnik swooped out of the house, carrying Dalock's belt, his scabbard and sword attached. The Hudikslander lad dropped onto one knee and offered them to the King with the ceremonial aplomb of an aged steward. The gathered children watched in gap-mouthed awe as the Strange King accepted the items with a solemn voice. "I thank you, Narnik, Palik's son." He nodded to the blond boy and threaded the belt and weapon to his saddle. With a last squeeze of Narnik's shoulder, he climbed into the saddle, his fingers easily slipping into the impressions worn into the leather from many times before. Breena gave a satisfied whinny as he settled onto her back.

Palika returned with his clothing, which she passed to one of his men as though it were a hot loaf of bread that might scald her. The heavily embroidered sleeve of his undertunic momentarily flopped from the pile as the King's Guard tucked the bundle into a leather pouch.

Dalock gazed at the plain sleeve at his wrist. "I thank you all for your care." He found he could not look at any of them. The Strange King glanced at Jinil, half expecting guidance. His man fished in a small pouch for coins.

Marna spoke curt and quick. "We ask no reward." Her tone cut him to his heart, and he thought to spur Breena and be rid of the place. Jinil's soothing tones interrupted his plans.

"Good woman, we are pleased to find our Lord safe and in good health. No doubt this is your, and your family's, doing."

"No doubt, my Lord." She inclined her head, which gave the appearance of deference, but did not compensate for her brusque voice.

"Then as King's Second, I give you our thanks again. We will make our leave." Jinil's sympathetic voice belied the tension in the air.

Dalock eyed the dusty path, commanding low, "Give the order, Jinil."

His lead officer motioned to the other men, and the King led them away.

Narnik and his siblings called behind them, "Goodbye, King, Dalock King! Goodbye, Guest!" The young Pennant Bearer clomped to the front of the line, and the dust stung Dalock's eyes as much as Marna's words had marred his heart. He managed a faint wave of farewell. With mounting bitterness, he realized that for the last few days, he had lived in an imaginary world, for a while thinking himself a humble winemaker, the children his own and Marna his beloved. A false dream from which he must now awaken to his true life.

Despite his recognizing Jinil, Breena, and his Guards, an odd feeling gripped the newly recovered King. The familiar felt at a distance, akin to going on a long journey and then returning home to find everything as he had left it, unchanged, yet strangely unfamiliar. The King's riders skirted the hill that overlooked the vineyards, then wound past the burgeoning grapes, nearly ripe for crushing. The bucket resting under the peaked roof of the well, the tall wine house, the stomping tubs, all awaiting the forthcoming harvest. The path turned to the main road; they passed a shed painted red. Then the trees and hills lapsed into anonymity.

His Second interrupted his thoughts. "My Lord?"

"Hmm?" The King jerked his head toward Jinil.

His man shouted over the trotting of hooves. "Have you any requests for your return? And shall I give news of what passed during your absence?"

He looked to his Second, noting his steady green gaze, despite the jostling of the horses. Dalock ran his fingers over the smooth leather reins and spoke tersely. "When we return to camp, a bath will be in order. For now, give me your reports."

He listened to the news, glad for the distraction of attending to speech over the clomping and shifting rhythms of the horses. It seemed there had been a battle, though he could find no recollection of it in his thoughts.

Jinil reported in a cautious tone, "Nine of our men slain."

Nine. Inwardly, he knew that was a remarkably slight loss for a battle, yet he felt a pang, for each was an individual, with loved ones and companions who would ache from the absence.

His Second hesitated, as though expecting Dalock to comment. When he did not, the man continued. "Twice that number wounded. All the injured expected to recover fully."

"Thank The Powers for that, Jinil."

"Aye, my Lord. Hudik King wishes to honor you at his halls once you are found."

A sudden feeling overcame him that being under Marna's withering gaze would be preferable to an obligatory visit with the incompetent lord of Hudiksland.

Turning to his man, he asked, half in jest, "How long do you wager

I can delay?"

"Perhaps your bathwater will be slow to boil." Jinil's grin echoed his own. Dalock felt at ease bantering with his Second, despite the odd removed feeling that continued to plague him. His man watched him with a keen eye. "My Lord, may I inquire what happened these past few days?"

Breena snorted. Dalock patted her neck and aimed to sound carefree. "I was struck by lightning, forgot who I was, crawled to a healer's door, and was healed." He cocked his head at his man, gauging his reaction.

"Well." Jinil scratched the scar in his beard. His face remained impassive but his eyes showed a slight flicker of surprise.

"Come now, man, is that all you can say?" It pleased him that his voice sounded mirthful.

"It is the stuff of our Legends, my Lord."

He agreed, but Marna's disbelief sowed anger in his tone. "Tell the men to make a faster pace. North, yes?"

"Aye, my Lord."

Dalock spurred his mare, loosening the reins, and roared for his Guardsmen to follow. The Strange King led the charge, though nothing more tempting than his bath awaited at the end of the ride.

A couple hours later, the King and his Guards reached his camp, on the edge of a field near Castleton, Hudik King's seat. The horses tromped wearily whilst Dalock's men waved at him, bellowing fond greetings as the entourage passed. The returned King raised a fist, growling in reply. His Soldiers cheered. Their open joy thawed his heart. A bit.

He recognized his sprawling crimson pavilion, edged with brown trim and topped with his flag. As he approached it, a tan lad of about thirteen ran alongside to grasp Breena's reins. *Trevil, the elder of my Pages.* The name came to him unbidden, as though an inner voice prompted him, a kind guide leading him back to his life.

"Welcome, welcome, my Lord!" The boy nodded in practiced deference to the King, then smiled hugely. "Breena, at last you found him, after all these days!" Trevil reached in an oiled leather pouch belted to his tunic, retrieving a glossy red apple. "I saved it as a reward. Shall I, my Lord?"

"Aye, give her two if you have them." Breena whickered, lowering her head in greedy acceptance of the treat.

The young ruler dismounted and walked about his camp, clasping arms and bantering with his Soldiers, making a great exhibit of showing his face to all his people.

"My Lord, you're dressed for First King's Day?" asked one of his Soldiers, a sable-locked, thick-shouldered man of about twenty years.

Dalock laughed, gesturing to his whitish garments, borrowed from Marna's family. "Aye, but I neglected to wear red. You are my size—lend me your tunic." The man doffed his upper uniform while his companions and his Lord laughed, teasing the Soldier on how he would account for the loss of his clothing to the Uniform Master. The King playfully slapped his man's back, thanking him for fulfilling his service. Two lean and lank youths stood watching nearby, too old to be Pages, too young to have earned their swords and be accounted men. Dalock queried their status. "Standers?"

"Aye, my Lord." The taller, tanner-complected one spoke. "But my sixteenth Naming Day is next month. Then I hope to come to my sword and be a Stander no more, but a true Soldier."

"And perhaps court a certain young woman back home," interjected the second. The first Stander gaped, speechless.

The King knew he should grin or make jest, but found he could not, merely muttering, "May The Powers protect you all."

At long last the Lord of Eskalind entered his pavilion, glad to find himself alone, his only immediate obligation a hot bath. The proud face of King slipped away and his thoughts numbed. Despite recognizing his surroundings—his men, his Pages, his horse, even the ivory comb carved with his initials lying on a hammered brass tray by the steaming tub—the same odd feeling of benumbed removedness cocooned his senses. Shedding his Soldier's tunic and the plain breeches from Marna's home, he regarded the scalloped, embroidered trim on the scarlet undertunic draped over a large upholstered chair. He recalled how few clothes Marna's family had. "I must see the loaned garments returned to them."

Dalock lowered himself into the soothing water and reached for the honey-colored soap. It slipped from his grasp, and he fished for it, catching the bar in his long fingers and working a lather. "Yes, a good plan. I could see her again, and convince her we are meant to be together." Again the soap escaped his wet fingers. Groaning, he retrieved it once more. "If she would have me."

One more time the slick bar slid from his hand. That did it. The spurned King pounded the water in anger, splashing the crimson-edged tapestry screening his tub from the entryway. The drops rolled down the fabric; dripping liquid prickled his cheeks and beard.

Dalock shut his eyes tightly, breathing hard, and a rush of images swept his thoughts, as though The Powers had unlatched the coffer of his memories.

He saw troops arrayed against the invaders of Hudiksland, and himself and Jinil, alongside Crown Prince Humik, conferring along the front lines. To one side of the top commanders, the farmers of Hudiksland, an army weaponed with mere pitchforks, scythes, and rusty, notched swords. On the other side, Eskalind's Second and Ninth Companies, their Captains at the forefront, their Soldiers and Sergeants with short spears in hand, swords or long knives scabbarded to their belts, shields at the ready. Far behind, at the rear, white-haired King Hudik with his younger son, Prince Huprik, sat their steeds, heads bent in conference as though debating the fastest path to the safety of Eskalind.

Ahead of the allied armies, the enemy loomed under a smokeclad sky, fire and destruction the dark fruit of their labors as they scourged the northern range of Hudiksland. Then Dalock, the heirless Strange King, challenged their leader to single combat, hoping to spare the lives of his own men and the impromptu army of King Hudik. Yet despite his victory, a final mob of marauders surged forth, intent on avenging their leader's death. Nearly a dozen Strange Kingdomers and far more of Hudik's men gave their lives to dispatch them.

Violence, death, trauma; all weighed hard upon him as he compared those moments with the leisurely activities of the past days at Marna's home. He muttered, "By The Powers' Will, Eskalind fights to preserve the peace in the borderlands. Yet I have known little peace in my days as ruler, until I met Marna." Dalock King opened his eyes, gazing about his pavilion. "Surely They had a hand in leading me to her."

Marna put the last berry pie in the oven with a sigh and traipsed to the woodbox. "What, I thought there was more?" She stuffed a small log into the fire.

"Narnik, I need more wood!" She stopped. "I have not seen him since Guest left." The Hudikslander inhaled a deep breath. "I suppose I should use his true name now." Fighting back tears, she suddenly realized how unusually quiet it was. She opened the side door, seeing no one in the yard. "Narnik! Palika! … Tanvik?" No one answered. "Lena?"

"Tarvik? Malka?" She walked into the dusty yard, brushing past a chicken. She heard the children, in the distance, chattering and laughing. A familiar voice peppered the mix—Werna was back! Marna hurried toward the sound.

Seven youngsters swirled around their mother, who carried her youngest daughter on one arm whilst holding the next youngest's wrist with her free hand. Narnik faced Werna, walking backward, recounting their adventures since her departure. Palika hung by her mother's side, interjecting corrections of her brother's stories. She regarded Marna with guilty eyes as her aunt approached.

"Werna!" Marna threaded her way through the brood, leaning over to hug her sister's shoulders. "What news?"

Werna broke the embrace. "Much to tell." She shifted Lena over her swollen belly and narrowed her blue eyes. "Though I hear you have news of your own."

Marna did not pause but was instantly on guard, wondering what Palika had told her mother. "How fares our neighbor?"

"Well, and a healthy boy for her. Perhaps a nice husband for my youngest, hmm, Lena?" Werna kissed the girl dangling on her arm. "Or perhaps for my next." She laughed, glancing at her belly. "Our neighbor's husband returned safe from battle."

"Did he have word of Palik?"

"Yes, he spoke with our menfolk. It seems there was very little battle—anyway, they are all safe and unharmed but Tuvik, who cut his arm carrying something. Tuvik, my clumsy, dear son! How I wished the midwife had not dropped him." The expectant mother adjusted Lena on her arm. "But the bottled salve you gave them for the journey healed him, Marna; he says he is as good as new and ready for the grape harvest."

"Welcome news! When will they be home?"

"By nightfall. And, sister, you and I must talk first." Werna glanced at Palika.

Her eldest daughter reached for the tot. "Here, Mother, let me carry her."

Lena fussed as her older sister pulled her away from their mother.

"What a good girl you are, Palika. Hard to believe you will be of age in only a couple years." Werna shook her head, the twin blond braids tied at the nape of her neck making a swooshing sound. "But first we must find a husband for Auntie Marna. We have neglected her for too long."

Marna gave her elder sister a wry look, not in the least looking forward to their later conversation.

————

"No pies till our brave warriors return tonight!" Werna shooed her children away from the kitchen and the sweet, steaming temptations. "Palika, let them outside for a while. Now there's a dear girl. And Narnik, you and Tarvik ready the fattest chickens for roasting."

Narnik grinned. "We had them when King Dalock was here."

Werna looked at her sister, blond eyebrows arched in surprise.

Marna eyed her nephew. "Then ready the fattest that are there now, Narnik." She turned from her sister and threw a pile of herbs on the chopping board.

"Should I kill the brown feathered one with the red wattle?" She could tell from his tone he was grinning, and wondered what he found funny. Then she pictured their guest's armor, and his men's clothing, all in shades of red and brown. She slapped more mint onto the cutting board as her sister responded, "No, Narnik, that hen gives the biggest eggs. Now run along." Werna waved her son away.

The boy grabbed the axe and followed his siblings out the door.

Werna waddled to her side. "Marna, you served that man *your* roast chicken? You were wooing him!"

"He was already wooed." Marna chopped the herbs with vigor, her imagination bent on inventing the vilest chore ever for her nephew.

"Narnik said he is a king!"

Marna turned from her work, the blade embedded in the wood. "How was I to know he was a king until his men came and called him such?"

Werna spoke in a raised whisper. "Did you lie with him?"

"No." Marna did not restrain her bitterness at her sister's question. "Though I wish I had had opportunity." The once-firm green herbs turned to minced ooze under her knife.

"Do not say that! What would Malik think?"

"I care not what Malik thinks."

"Marna, be reasonable. You cannot fancy a noble, let alone a king; there's no hope of ever having a true family."

She could not resist. "Would you say your husband did not come from a true family, as his mother was one of the king's mistresses?"

Werna's blue eyes opened wide. "Shh! What if the children hear you!"

"Then they'd know why their menfolk are called to battle but never fight."

"Would you want them to fight? To be hurt or—" Werna's voice caught and her face paled. Marna instantly regretted her remarks.

"No, dear sister. I'm sorry." She placed her knife over the herbs and embraced Werna's round shoulders. "Forgive me. I did not mean it. You know I wish them no harm." Werna nodded stiffly. "They are my family too, and I love them."

The two women broke their embrace and resumed their kitchen preparations. Marna brushed a tear from her eyes. Her one chance to enjoy the affections of a man of her own choosing had slipped away, replaced with the unavoidable prospect of joining to fat-fingered Malik.

Werna spoke, her voice gentle, like when they were children and the elder sister aimed to soothe the younger's dark moods. But her words belied her soft tone. "Did this man feel … encouraged?"

Heat colored her cheeks in mute wrath. But Marna was no longer certain what had happened. Only that Dalock was gone and she would never see him again.

"Ah, so he encouraged you. Sweet promises and such, hmm? Tell me, what did he say?"

The unjoined woman ground out the words. "He said that in his land, one's station was of no matter in affairs of the heart."

"Men!" spat Werna. "They will say anything to get a woman into bed."

Even as her sister spoke, a feeling of clarity grew in Marna's mind. "I think he believed it."

"Did you?" Her sister's voice rose.

"Well." Marna looked at the little piles of minced herbs. A green stain swelled across the damp wood board, bleeding to the far edge and the line of ceramic bottles filled with cooking greases. She stared at the cork stopper on the oil flask. "I think he thought he was telling the truth." Grabbing a handful of orange-skinned onions from the hanging basket, she returned to her chopping.

"Marna, think a moment." Werna placed a hand on her sister's arm. The sharp, stinging scent of onions hung in the air. "There's no future with him. But with Malik, half the wine house would be yours and your children's." Her voice was gentle, persuasive. "Don't you see, if you do not join with him, you will find yourself caring for Malik's children anyway?"

Her sister's reasoning surprised her, but she had her reply ready. "Malik would not join with someone else."

"He is already twenty-six! He has waited long enough. You have waited long enough." Werna lifted the mortar and pestle from the draining board and reached for the salt canister, her voice soft as cooing to a newbabe. "And you know, a man must have a wife. Hmm. Our neighbor has a niece, just of age, he might consider." She scooped salt into the mortar and ground it with a steady hand. "Sister, I know you have been … hurt, in the past, but time heals old wounds. And Malik is a gentle man."

Marna watched her a moment, considering her words. Her deeply annoying choice of words. Once again Werna had strung her along in a conversation only to trump her at the end with words that sounded harmless but cut acutely. She looked her elder sister in the eye. "I can say it no plainer: I have no feelings for Malik."

"Oh, they will come. Malik is a good and gentle man."

She steeled her voice for her reply. "Feelings have come, but not for him."

Werna shook her head while pulverizing the salt. "We shall see."

CHAPTER SIX—IN HUDIK KING'S QUARRY

Dalock Strange King rode the straight road leading through his army's camp to the northwest, toward the thatched-roof houses of Castleton. Hudik King's stone fortress rose loftily above the dense town. Stiff pennants bearing his crest of the silver crown stood erect in their wire frames as though an unseen blast of wind had unfurled them. Thinning orange light glowed mutely on the upper battlements of the dark structure. As his entourage approached the rock walls, Dalock distracted himself with admiring the construction, muttering, "A fine quarry this king has. Would that he were not such a fool to need it."

Jinil called to him, "My Lord?"

"Hmm?" He turned to see his Second regarding him with a quizzical look.

"Shall we announce you, my Lord?" At least, that was what he thought Jinil said.

"Yes, fine." He gazed at the raised portcullis, which yawned overhead like a bored, iron-toothed beast. A Guard shouted his arrival: "Make way for Dalock Strange King!"

———

King Hudik called with open arms from the far end of the cavernous stone hall, "My Lord King Dalock! Or rather, Dalock King, as you say in your land!"

Dalock strode the length of the narrow, cobalt-shaded carpet that ran in a long line to steps crowned with two chairs, King Hudik's silver-gilt throne and another, for himself. Behind him, Eskalind Guards and Jinil trailed. The pale-haired lords and ladies of Hudik's court bowed as their Ever Ally passed, the men dressed in overtunics representing every shade of the dye makers' invention. The ladies' long veils framed their faces and clashed with the various shades of their high-waisted, low-bodiced gowns. How untidy foreign courts felt, with their mishmash of colors.

The Strange King ascended the short series of steps to accept the elder king's hand and to smile before the people as though all were well.

"You will forgive me, King Dalock, Dalock King, I am set in my ways!" King Hudik chortled, his reddened nose and purple-stained lips comical accents to his neat white beard. Midway through his fifth decade, his countenance had aged apace of his years, as if it enjoyed the surprise on people's faces when they discovered he was well shy of sixty. "Please, sit by my side, my Ever Ally. We will drink." The last phrase suffered from an abundance of enthusiasm. The ruler of Hudiksland swept a hand to the vacant chair next to his, whilst his eyes roamed to a tray of twin begemmed chalices borne by a servant. In the midpoint of Dalock's seat, a large blue cushion fringed with silver tassels rested. "You deserve the place of honor in my kingdom, my Ever Ally King Dalock."

"I thank you, King Hudik." Dalock resisted the temptation to call the man Hudik King. He would save that for later, when he and Jinil recounted the evening together in his pavilion.

The Eskalinder motioned to his man to stand nearby. As Dalock settled onto the cushion, he discovered that the tassels decorated not only the edge of the pillow. A rather prominent tassel occupied the center of the cushion. It prodded him in an extremely uncomfortable place.

The tray-bearing servant approached, presenting the two kings with chalices of wine. Dalock edged forward, grateful for an excuse to extract himself from the troublesome bolster. King Hudik raised his silver goblet, a fond look upon his swollen face. "I trust my countryfolk cared for you well."

"They did, King Hudik." Dalock rubbed his fingers on the bejeweled goblet, wishing it were plainer and served by another. He thought to question the older man if the wine came from Palik's vineyard, but decided less conversation suited him better at the moment.

The ruler of Hudiksland swirled his wine whilst his nostrils flared in a noisy inhalation. "I shall be certain to send them a reward for their kindness." He drained his cup in one go, smacked his lips, and announced, "But first I will demonstrate our gratitude, our appreciation for your alliance, for the continuing amity between Eskalind and Hudiksland." A page collected Hudik's chalice, and the lord of Hudiksland clapped his hands together. Blond men clad in the colors of clear sky and white clouds entered the room lugging two curved-lidded chests, one after the other. As they neared, Dalock discerned the chests' decoration to be matching painted scenes of men hunting in a forest. The first trunk clanged slightly, as if it contained stacks of pewter dishes. The young King tentatively rested his elbows on the upholstered arms of his chair, hoping to find nothing bothersome lurking in their padding.

The porters lowered their burdens to the ground. On signal from their ruler, they opened the noisy box's lid, revealing a gleaming stack of finely wrought swords. Dalock tried not to think of the bladesmith's daughter.

King Hudik spoke. "I am certain many of these will fit your hand well. The rest, your men will find to their liking, I do hope."

"You are most generous." A thought wagged him that the blades would have found better use arming the common people of this frequently invaded land. But he stayed mute.

The older lord gestured again. The servants lifted the lid of the other chest, unveiling bolts of rich red silks and velvets.

"Your color, I am told." Hudik motioned for his refilled chalice.

"One of my colors, yes."

Hudik's cherry-nosed face beamed with pride. "Fit for a queen."

Dalock did not like the reference, replying coolly, "I thank you,

Hudik King."

"We will hold a feast in your honor tomorrow night, here in this hall. Please extend our invitation to your officers."

"I thank you again."

The bottom of Hudik's chalice rose in the air once more. "It is we who thank you, Dalock King." His voice changed to a conspiratorial tone, and he leaned closer. "But come, I would show you my chief treasure." Dalock suspected a trip to the wine cellars would follow.

Rising from his throne, Hudik led the Lord of Eskalind and Jinil, King's Second, through a passage hidden by a brocaded, sapphire-hued curtain. They walked up a wide stone stairway to a room with a thick wooden door. A guard opened the door into a close-arched room lit by many slender candles arrayed along the wall. In the middle of the room was an elaborate wooden cradle, hung with King Hudik's colors. A woman veiled in white sat nearby. She rose as they approached, stepping aside.

"Look." King Hudik's voice carried an odd tone, almost childlike, vulnerable. "My son's son." In the candlelight, the lord of Hudiksland's white locks appeared golden blond, perhaps as they had been when he was a younger man, looking at his own newborn son.

Dalock came to gaze at the small babe, sleeping peacefully under lace-edged blankets.

"He was born during the battle. I dare not think what would have happened, if..." The grandfather's voice trailed off, touched by a remoteness and vulnerability at odds with his earlier manner. Then King Hudik cleared his throat, the loose skin on his neck jiggling. "My grandson's future is secured thanks to the victory you brought us."

The sincerity of his tone surprised Dalock, who offered his grace. "May he grow to be strong and wise."

"Yes." The old king's voice returned to his former tone, as though he were a tired traveling player uttering well-worn lines. "If he is gold to me, then surely, here is silver." He beckoned to the veiled woman, who stepped from the shadows. "My daughter, the Princess Huma."

Huma brushed aside her sheer veil to curtsey to Dalock, displaying a ruby gown bodiced with a deep, curved neckline showcasing a pleasant swell of bosom, crowned with a firm gaze in her deep blue eyes. Most men would call her beautiful, and Dalock found himself not immune to the woman's enticing physical attributes. Perhaps it was the wine.

"You are a man steeped in riches, King Hudik." He nodded toward the lady. "Princess Huma."

She smiled with a slow tilt of her head, as though the action demanded a count of three to be performed properly. "We are most grateful to you, my Lord." A strand of pale blond hair brushed her face, a tether of spun gold resting on her cheek. "All of Hudiksland is." She curtseyed with a gentle flourish of her arms, her bosom rising, yet the gesture called attention to the slightness of her shoulders, her thin arms. Dalock doubted they held enough strength to lift a breastplate, or even a vambrace.

The proud father nudged the younger man. "Huma will be at the feast tomorrow night; perhaps you can become better acquainted then."

Dalock acknowledged her in a resonant voice. "It will be an honor, Princess."

As Huma bowed low to Dalock once more, he feared she might overflow her bodice. He recalled his father's words of long ago. "Be wary of the designs of those in the borderlands. Until you are joined, many will want to find you a wife of their choosing, not yours. Your wife must be a woman of Gift, and only you can decide who she will be."

Dalock exchanged glances with his Second. He made his leave of Hudik King and his progeny, his thoughts on the simple table and hearth in a now distant farmhouse.

———

"Marna, have some ale!" Werna shouted, leaning against her sister. The children ran around the long table whilst the men sang, and the chicken bones and empty pie pans on the table were all that remained of the homecoming feast.

"You know I don't care for it."

"It will soothe your mood." Her sister spoke close to her ear, pouring a full cup. The song came to its boisterous conclusion, and the children cheered for more.

"I would have some more. More ale." Malik scraped his tankard across the table toward Werna. His hair hung loose around his face like straw spilling from a hayloft. His cheeks and forehead blushed red from exuberant singing.

"Marna, pour for him." Werna slid the pitcher toward her sister.

Marna grasped the handle and emptied the pitcher into his large mug, avoiding his blue gaze. "Oh, we are out! I will refill it." She turned to stand.

"No no, I will do it." Werna pressed firm on her sister's sturdy shoulder and rose.

"Cheers, Marna." Malik raised his large mug to her. Ever since his return with his brother and nephews earlier that evening, something about him struck her as different. He seemed more certain of himself. Determined. Well, perhaps it was all the ale.

Marna looked across the room, into the kitchen, where Werna stood, replenishing the pitcher from a tottering barrel. "Go on!" Werna mouthed.

The younger woman lifted her cup and met Malik's smile. She rummaged for something to say, settling on, "You have a fine singing voice." His clear blue eyes watched her with a keen expression as he drank. To The Powers, she wished Dalock were here to look at her like that.

"Marna, Braither, you make such a fine pair sitting there." Werna placed the pitcher between them and guided her sister's arm toward it. Marna refilled Malik's tankard whilst he winked at her, his broad lips breaking into a smile.

"You read my mind," he said.

"I'm not certain I'd want that ability," Marna said.

He laughed, and it surprised her that she found the sound pleasant. She laughed as well, amazed at the sudden giddiness she felt. Then he reached for his mug, and Marna caught sight of his thick fingers gripping the grooved ceramic container. She sighed, and drained her cup.

———

Dalock leaned back into his chair, considering the question Jinil had just asked him. The Strange King rapped his fingers on the bronze wall of his full wine goblet, sending ripples across the aromatic liquid. Thick tapestries covering his pavilion's walls muffled the comings and goings of carts, horses, and people outside, whilst the embroidery depicted sleek steeds cantering across an open field. Perhaps when he returned home he would finally have opportunity for a long, peaceful ride, free of any purpose or intent save the exhilaration of movement.

The bronze brazier burned tall in the center of the tent, providing more light than heat on this warm, late night. Yes, he should have answered Jinil's inquiry by now. His Second waited patiently across the table, swirling his wine with a quiet slosh. King Hudik did provide fine wine. Perhaps this vintage came from Marna's family's winery.

That did it. "Well, Jinil, I would say Princess Huma's performance tonight lacked only a mirror, for surely she has practiced it many times before." His man chuckled, a low, comforting sound. It seemed ages since they last sat together sharing a cup whilst discussing their day. Yet he felt an absence he could not describe or name. "And dressing her in my colors! What was Hudik thinking?" He shook his head, knowing full well what the man thought: the Strange King would be an excellent addition to his family.

"Subtlety is a lost art in Hudiksland." Jinil drained his drink.

"Ha! Especially with Hudik's younger son." For some reason, any thought of the Prince Huprik provoked a prickling annoyance. "Still, though, I pity the princess; she is at the mercy of her father's wishes." He drained his goblet, tapping his fingers on the table. "I hope she does not suffer for my lack of interest."

"Your interest lies elsewhere."

"Am I that easily read?" Dalock's voice was tempered with surprise, not anger.

"Usually, no."

"Hmm." Dalock squinted at his Second. "Tell me what you see, Jinil."

His man glanced at the wine goblet and spoke softly and intently, as though espousing a conviction. "I see my King returned after a strange disappearance as a changed man."

"Your meaning?"

Jinil poured a half measure of wine for his King. "I'm not certain how to describe it, my Lord, but I sense a distraction in your thought not seen before."

The King leaned back, tilted his cup to his mouth, and swallowed. He placed the goblet on the table and stroked the pattern carved into the metal. His symbols—the sword, the shield, his initial. They reassured him, reminded him of his place in the world, recalling The Powers' Gifts to his ancestors, to himself. To his lonely, familyless self. "It is a woman."

Jinil nodded. "From the house where we found you." A statement.

"You are ever my observant Second." Dalock folded his hands before him.

"My Lord, I have wondered if The Powers had a hand in Breena's uncharacteristic bolting after the battle."

The young King started, recalling an odd moment, after the battle against the invaders of Hudiksland. "Interesting choice of words, Jinil. I… I saw the impression of a hand on my horse's neck. After the battle." He stretched his hands before him, regarding their size.

"Truly?" Jinil's voice was light with wonder.

"Aye, right before Breena charged away. The memory is coming back. Yes, I was picking up her reins, and I saw a handprint on her neck." Dalock King exhaled slowly.

"Breena's reins were completely cut when we found her, as though sliced by a sharp blade." The men sat in edgy silence a moment, and for once, his Second shuffled slightly in his seat, as though he could not contain a thought. "My Lord, interpreting The Powers can be an awkward business, but perhaps this happened to lead you to the woman at the farmhouse."

"I thought that myself." Dalock placed his hands upon the table. "After all, she healed me completely in a few days' time. Though that may simply have been The Powers' Gift to the heirless Strange King." He could almost smell the wonderful calming scent of her broth.

Then he recalled their fraught parting words, how she had purposefully avoided his gaze when his men rediscovered him, how she pushed him away.

"She will not have me, Jinil. She . . ." His voice caught in his throat. Dalock shook his head as regret replaced simmering resentment. "I do not understand the ways of this country, with their matchmaking and concern with one's station in life." The spurned man lunged for the ewer and poured more wine, bringing the red fluid to his face, and catching a reflection of his eager lips. He thought of ruddy-faced King Hudik. Dalock lowered the full goblet onto the table, sliding it away as Jinil spoke.

"We all know the Strange Kingdom is different in many ways from its borderlands."

"And you know better than most Eskalinders, my well-travelled former Ambassador."

"Indeed. Most borderlanders find it hard to comprehend our ways." He tapped his bronze goblet. "But if The Powers brought you together…" His green eyes darted to the King's.

Dalock snorted. "And perhaps The Powers meant for me to meet this king's daughter." The words came cold and cruel. He reclaimed his abandoned chalice.

"Perhaps, my Lord. Yet The Powers do not always disclose their wishes clearly, and while they show us the path, they still may block it, leaving it to us to find another way." Jinil sipped his wine.

"You still have time for reading Haarshil, Jinil?" He cast a serious eye at his Second, but his voice hinted at his gladness at returning to their customary banter.

"Not these past few days, my Lord. Whilst we searched tirelessly for you, I placed my hope in The Powers, and that your disappearance and eventual recovery was Their plan, though toward what end, I can only guess."

The young ruler traced a finger around the smooth edge of his chalice. It was his turn to quote a Loremaster of long ago: "'To what end is always the question. What lives we men follow, ever led by the Will of The Powers.'" For an instant, he thought he tasted the satisfying savor of Marna's broth. The sensation brought a tinge of longing for the freckle-cheeked healer, and a bloom of confidence to his chest. "I will write the healer at the farmhouse. Bring my quilling desk."

Jinil leaned forward, smiling. "I have never known my King to agree to defeat."

Dalock grinned, pleased with the encouragement. His Second stood and brought his portable writing desk.

"Call a Messenger, Avaril if he is here, to deliver this note at first light—for her eyes only."

"My Lord, as I recall, Hudikslanders seldom educate their womenfolk to read." Jinil shook the ink bottle and unplugged the stopper. It made a hollow, ringing sound, but to Dalock, there was more joy and promise in it than in a long line of trumpeting heralds.

"Then tell the Messenger it is a private note, but that he may read it to her, if need be." The young ruler reached to his quill, stroking the mottled red and russet feather as he composed his thoughts.

Chapter Seven—A Visit from a Messenger

Avaril, Messenger to Dalock King, slowed his gelding as he approached the windowless farmhouse. The sun pierced the high clouds overhead, and the dirt path and simple homestead were bathed in the cool blue light of early morn. Under his Lord's orders, the Messenger had left at the end of the main road his guide, the Standard Bearer, the accompanying pair of Guards, and the extra horse. Now Avaril arrayed his roan-colored riding cloak as though he were posing for a formal portrait. His was a private mission of great import to his Lord the Strange King, and he held himself high and proud in the saddle, glad he had polished it well the day before.

Avaril silently thanked The Powers for his elevated status. For years before, he had served as a Swift Rider in Eskalind, racing letters between one Swift Riders Office to another to another, changing horses at each station, ten to twenty-five miles a trip. All those long-disposed-of missives, relayed north to south, east to west, to King's Halls or the borders, were significant back in their day. Now, as a King's Messenger, soon he would deliver a note to the woman rumor claimed had enchanted his Lord. If the hour of his departure from the Strange King's camp—so late as to be called early—did not announce the import of his mission, then surely the inclusion of the riderless horse in the entourage bespoke his task: to fetch their new Queen. At least, that is what Avaril had jokingly wagered with one of the elder Guardsmen.

Outside the front door of the low house stood two broad-shouldered blond men alike enough in face to be brothers. The larger, older-looking man rested the flat blade of an unsheathed longsword on his shoulder. Laced around his thick neck on a wide blue velvet ribbon was a fist-sized, polished silver medallion at odds with the Hudikslander's plain peasant garb.

The second man had folded his brawny arms across his wide chest, but his eyes looked dull and unfocused. Two tall youths lingered behind them, blocking the open doorway; the handsome one hefted a large stick like he knew its weight and balance, and a territorial gleam shone in his eyes. The other, a homely youth, balled one fist; his other arm was wrapped in a thick bandage. *I wager Medallion and Handsome are most likely to cause trouble.* In Avaril's line of work, gauging reactions, a bit of gambling, and always keeping one eye on the way out served one well, if one desired a long career.

The good-looking youth with the club hissed over his shoulder at a boy jumping in the doorway behind him, trying to catch a view of the outside. *Ah, and the lad's the wild card.*

His assessment of the scene complete for the moment—one never knew when the situation might change—he cleared his throat to make his introduction, but the man with the medallion interrupted his plans by growling, "This family and land are under the fair protection of King Hudik. What do you want?"

This terminology was unfamiliar to Avaril, though he guessed it meant if there was trouble, Hudik King might hear of it. "Good man, I mean no offense. I come from the Ever Ally of King Hudik, Dalock Strange King of Eskalind. I'm sent to deliver a message to Marna, daughter of your King Hudik's chief armorer, Wernik. Is this her dwelling?"

The man glared like a father ordered to yield his daughter to Prince Huprik.

The messenger added, "Marna is also aunt to Narnik, Lena, Palika, and several others. Are these names familiar to you, good man?"

"He's asking about the children?" The smaller man belched, the sickeningly stale scent of last night's ale on his breath. Avaril waved a gloved hand to hurry the stench away from his nose.

The older man with the out-of-place medallion ordered his band, "Go inside, all of you." He grabbed the elbow of the other man, bending to his ear, whispering low. Avaril strained to hear but could not gather the exact remarks. Medallion announced loudly, "Fetch her without a word, Malik, then bar the door." He tapped his sword against his shoulder whilst regarding the mounted man. Avaril watched the hastily choreographed show calmly from his horse as the so-addressed Malik stumbled into the house, pushing the youths before him.

A door slammed nearby, and a boy came running around the corner, stopping in midstride with a gentle whoosh on the loose dirt. "Can I come with you? Please?" he breathed. "I want to live in Eskalind and have armor like Dalock's!"

"Back in the house, Narnik!" bellowed the man with the medallion. "And bolt the side door." The lad lingered, raising pleading eyes to the Messenger.

"Young lad, my Lord Dalock Strange King"—he enunciated his Lord's title carefully so the child might perhaps realize his impropriety—"sent me solely to deliver a written message to Marna." He glanced at the older man. "No orders concerning bringing boys of Hudiksland to Eskalind." He hoped a bit of levity might reassure the belligerent, sword-bearing man.

Medallion ordered, "Narnik, do as I say!"

"Yes, Father." The boy turned his back, departing just as the door creaked open and a young woman crossed the threshold. Clad in a plain skirt, bodice, and blouse that looked of similar weave as the men's clothing, she was tall and bone thin. The door thudded shut solidly behind her, and the unmistakable sound of a stout board drawing across it was heard. She swallowed hard when she looked up to the Eskalinder, her face unblemished and smooth with young, wide eyes, clear and blue. Dalock King's Messenger doubted she was much past her sixteenth

Naming Day, but he supposed she was pretty enough to be Queen. He fondly recalled the King's Mother as a lovely woman who dressed with impeccable elegance.

Avaril had hoped he might sense some Gift from The Powers about this new Queen, yet nothing in her face or bearing struck him as extraordinary—though that was the King's pleasure to determine. "You are the woman called Marna?"

The man answered. "She is." The blond woman looked at him, her small mouth opening, as the man added, "And she wants no part of you people. She told me last night. Didn't you, dearie?"

The young woman stared at Medallion, stammering in a most unregal manner. Had it not been his duty to observe and report, Avaril would have turned away to spare her the embarrassment. "I did … say that," she managed in a timid voice.

Medallion gave the Messenger an I-told-you-so look.

"Good man, by my Lord's request, I'm to give her a note in private. I mean no harm." He did not think this would endear him much to Medallion, but it was his stated mission. As much as was possible, Avaril hoped to not disappoint his King.

"Marna, you know what to say. You two go speak over there so it can be private." The last word had a sneer in it, and the man gestured with a toss of his disheveled blond locks toward the bare dirt track meandering away from the house.

The young woman paced away from the house, and Avaril followed slowly on horse till she turned and stopped. "What do you want?" she queried, keeping her eyes away from Avaril's.

"You *are* Marna?"

She glanced back at the stout man as though seeking permission, then nodded. The Messenger managed to keep his tone steady and formal, though he felt he knew the outcome of the conversation already. "Then I am bid by Dalock King to bring you a message."

She nodded again.

Avaril, King's Messenger, dismounted smoothly and turned from her to reach into a small leather bag. There he retrieved a brown parchment envelope marked with his Lord's glossy red seal. "It is a private message." He held out the note to her, bowing his head, his eyes to the ground and her worn leather slippers. Nothing happened. After a moment, he glanced up, only to see her oval face turned away from his hand.

"This is for you." He wiggled the smooth parchment slightly in his hand, as though offering a treat to a skittish horse. "Would you like me to read it to you?"

The thin woman was silent. She looked terribly young and alone, staring into the distance as though he had not spoken to her. Indeed, as though he were not even there. Her lower lip trembled.

"May I read the note to you?"

"No! Please don't!" She bent her head and hid her face in her hands.

Her reaction confused him. This was not the stuff of Legends. Perhaps this chapter in the King's chronicles would go unwritten. Still, he pressed on with his mission. "Kind woman, the King himself authorized me to read this to you, even though it is a private message. I am a Messenger, trained to read, recall, and relay. It's all right."

"No, I'm … Please don't!"

"I will return it to my Lord then. Unless?" He paused, hoping she would acquiesce. Her slight chest lifted heavily as she unsuccessfully fought a sob. "Marna of Hudiksland, I do not know what is troubling you, but I am sorry for your condition, and I may be able to help by read—" And to his utter surprise, she dashed away, running toward the vineyards tracing the road. Her sudden exit unnerved his horse, and the gelding jerked backward on the reins.

The Strange King's man pulled the reins, speaking soothingly to settle his mount while watching the blond woman dart behind a row of vines trained along a trellis and disappear from view, though he thought he saw a light-colored flicker behind the dark, entangled shadows as she sped away. With a slow exhale, he stuffed the unwanted envelope back into his bag, careful to place it in the long pocket he reserved for finished business. Avaril swung a leg over the saddle, noting a spot near the horn his polish had missed, and trotted back to the house. Sounds of a commotion inside could be heard.

After a brief nod to the man with the sword, who looked well pleased with himself, the King's Messenger made his leave, riding away and wondering what to make of the woman's strange behavior. He had the distinct, unwelcome feeling that his tale, once told to Dalock King, would be met as warmly as at the farmhouse. "May The Powers see to it he does not post me to Havadra for this! Or to Gergelt; those folk think poorly dyed potato sacks are the apex of style." Avaril shuddered in the saddle and mourned his imagined fates.

Marna awoke slowly under dim lantern light in the sleeping room. A muffled clamor of voices burbled in the main room. Her thoughts swam lazily, her head feeling too large for the pillow; her cheeks burned. Worse, she could not recall how much ale she had drunk the night before, apart from Werna emptying a pitcher at least twice into her mug. "Umpf. By The Powers, I'll never drink ale again."

She rolled over on the pallet and stretched wide, forgetting for a moment that she might crush one of the children. The utter stillness in the air slowly dawned on her, and she realized she rested alone in the room, on the pallet farthest from the entrance. Then the door flung open, and Malik stumbled into the room, landing flat with a soft thud on the pallet nearest to the door.

That woke her instantly. Marna bolted out of the bed, creeping hip first for the door, a cautious eye on him for the length of the quick journey. Just as she placed her hand on the doorknob, he snored, thunderous as a waterfall. It made her head ache worse. She exited the room to find her braither Palik rebuking Narnik whilst the entire household gathered round. Werna sat uneasily on a stool, little Lena leaning against her, pawing her side, anxious to be picked up by her mother. Marna closed the door behind her as Palik bellowed, "You are to do as I say, young lad, and no more talk of running off to Eskalind."

"But Fa—"

"That is the end to it; I have spoken. All of you, no more of it and off to your chores. Now!"

The children scampered out the doors, even Lena, eager to flee their father's anger. Narnik was quickest of all, causing Palik to bark, "Marvik! Tuvik! Palika! Keep an eye on him. See to it he doesn't stray far." With a curt nod of his reddened face to Marna, her braither looked to his seated wife. "Have words with your sister, Werna. I must check on the grapes." With that he left, the orange glow of sunrise striking the outbuildings visible for just a moment before the door slammed closed.

"What's happened?" Marna asked her sister as she pulled up a stool. Werna gazed away, sad, forlorn even. Her manner recalled to mind their mother's despondent, distracted look when she was last with child. The younger sister touched her sibling's arm. "Werna, are you all right?"

She shook her head. "I hate to see Palik this angry. But Narnik…my boy wants to run away and leave us." Palik's wife lifted her apron hem to wipe a tear away. "You don't want to leave us too, do you, Marna?"

Marna sighed and embraced her sobbing sister, hoping to comfort her, yet also sad for herself. By The Powers, if Dalock came back and asked her, she would go with him and suffer what might come. She might even bring Narnik, if it would annoy her braither, but she would never do such a thing to harm her sister. She kept her thoughts to herself.

After a moment, they broke their embrace, and Werna managed to speak. "My dear little sister. I don't know what I would do without you. It is all too much sometimes, looking after the children, keeping enough food in the house, mending the clothes, feeding the animals, tending the vineyards, a newbabe coming soon."

Managing a weak smile, Marna glanced about, spying the basket of dirty clothing by the front door. "Ah yes, and today is the day I should attend to the laundry."

"I will help."

"No no, you rest. Palika can help me."

"Oh no, no, I will need her here." Werna said animatedly. "If you see her, just send her to the house."

"All right." She stood slowly, puzzled by her sister's anxious change of mood. Then she spied her braither's sword, sheathed, resting in the corner. Perhaps the sight of the weapon made Werna anxious that her husband and sons might soon be sent again to battle. Marna patted her sister's arm and retrieved the laundry basket.

Inside the Strange King's crimson pavilion, Dalock and Jinil discussed the breakdown of the camp, and how best to arrange Marna's arrival and presentation to her new people. "Perhaps an honor guard of Hudik King's men to accompany her, as well as our own. An entrance fit for a new Queen!" Dalock beamed. "Schedule the Joining Ceremony to occur just inside our border."

His younger Page, Moril, announced the return of Messenger Avaril, who entered the King's quarters with the brisk aplomb of a man wishing to rush through a troublesome task. The King's stomach locked. "What happened?"

The Messenger bowed low. "Marna of Hudiksland . . . refused my Lord's note."

"You did tell her you would read it to her?"

"I did, my Lord. But she would not allow me to do so." Avaril's dark eyes looked straight ahead at the tapestries as he addressed his Lord.

Dalock walked into his line of sight, meeting his gaze. "Truly?"

"Aye, my Lord. I relayed that the note was private, I presented it to her with great care, I offered to read it to her. I asked in the gentlest of terms and she . . . my Lord, she ran away."

Dalock could say no more for a moment. Marna fleeing his Messenger in such a way? Perhaps she felt the man might harm her. But since his father's time, he had known Avaril as a steadfast, duty-bound Messenger, and he felt he heard truth in the Eskalinder's voice. He also felt as though Hudik King's throne had dropped onto his chest.

Jinil asked, "Who was with her?"

"Two burly farmer-type men, one armed with an impressive longsword." He retrieved the King's unwanted love letter from inside his cloak and handed it discreetly to Jinil, who placed it on a nearby table. "Brothers I would guess, given the likeness of their looks. Also two youths, one quite handsome, the other plain and clumsy looking."

"Her menfolk have returned," muttered the King.

"You spoke to her alone?" ventured King's Second.

"Aye, outside the dwelling, beyond earshot but under the watchful eyes of the larger man." Dalock glowered as his shock tingled into anger. His Messenger continued, "My Lord, by your leave, one last, odd report." The King flicked his hand for Avaril to continue. "My Lord, the larger man, he wore a medallion, a silver medallion, and told me his house and family were under Hudik King's fair protection."

Jinil reached for the scar on his chin and looked at his King. Dalock nodded, and his Second dismissed the messenger. Once the man exited the pavilion, Dalock angrily swept the envelope from the table, turning away from his companion. He muttered through his teeth. "We meant her no harm. She would not even have the note read to her! What manner of woman refuses a King?"

Jinil's voice was irritatingly quiet and calm as an Ambassador relaying ill news. "A woman protected by a king, my Lord."

That realization caused Dalock to bristle further. "What?" He wheeled to face his Second, unable to follow his man's logic. His brain felt muddled, like a piece of bread dipped into too many sauces.

"In Hudiksland, fair protection means one is under a lord's guardianship. Usually some token is given as proof of that charge. Perhaps, in this case, the man's medallion in the silver of Hudik King's house." Jinil's green gaze held the King's steadily.

It irked him that his Second recalled this bit of Hudikslander custom faster than he did. "Her father is chief armorer to Hudik, her braither the king's winemaker. It makes sense." He strove to sound even, but the young ruler battled surging emotions, well aware that his Second had seen him lose control in the past. Part of him did not care, a large and growing part of him. "It does not matter."

He caught Jinil glancing at the red-sealed envelope, lying forsaken near the tawny leather toes of his boots. Dalock surrendered to the smoldering rage expanding within his breast. "Burn it. And leave me."

His Second scooped the offending parchment from the carpeted floor, placing it inside the low flames of the brazier by the entryway. He bowed and left the spurned monarch to dark thoughts and fantastic plots.

The Lord of Eskalind contemplated calling for his horse and riding hard and fast across far fields of Hudiksland to rid his chest of the ache that squeezed his ribs. Ah, or charging to Marna's home and challenging that usurper Malik. Perhaps he would demand an immediate audience with Hudik King and threaten to sever the ancient alliance between their nations if the inebriate ruler would not grant her hand. These thoughts glinted in his mind as he turned them over, examining their weight and worth.

At the last, he hung his head at the recollection of his words to Jinil. "'What manner of woman refuses a King….' By The Powers, I speak as the rulers of the outerlands do, full of self-importance, nepotism, prerogative. I am not, I *will* not be that manner of man. I am an Eskalinder."

He leaned his forehead against the sturdy wooden pole that held aloft the crimson fabric roof. The carved patterns of his initial and emblem pressed hard into his skin as he recited, "Heedlock King's Son sought to expand Eskalind, but his father Heedlich First King told him to conquer no more, the boundaries with the borderlands were set, drawn by The Powers. No man should alter them. Ever." Dalock backed away from the timber support, pinched the bridge of his nose, and moaned as though this were his last breath. "And The Powers' answer to Heedlock, to his ambition and schemes, was to lead him to his wife, whose Gift it was to assuage his aspirations, to soothe him."

Dalock stood, raising his shoulders and comporting himself as the noble sovereign he hoped himself to be. "Ha! I need no wife to soothe me." Approaching the entranceway, he raised his voice to call to his elder Page. "Trevil! Send for my Second. We will manage the departure preparations. After Hudik King's feast, we will leave this place."

Yet a part of him pled to make his own journey back to the farmhouse, and whilst he gave orders, and wore the face of a man in charge of his own fate, a gleam of determination that this was not all, not yet, flickered still.

"Oh, my head!" Malik tottered out of the sleeping room, reaching a hand to the hearthstones and sinking to the wooden floor by the cooled embers of the fireplace.

Werna watched him from the tidy kitchen, thankful he was finally awake again, and that the children were out of the house.

"You've nearly slept the morning away, dear braither." She whisked a foul-smelling concoction in a small bowl with her arms stretched out before her as she walked toward her braither. "I've fixed a tonic to heal your pains." Werna handed him the bowl, watching him drink. He grimaced at the taste. "If Marna were here, she would cure you in a moment. Her herbcraft exceeds mine." Malik drained the potion with a groan and panted.

"I do not want to blame my sister for your condition, but she did serve you a lot of ale last night."

"No no. I wanted it." He staggered to his feet, belching.

Werna backed away from the stench, the child in her womb giving a strong kick as though it too wanted to retreat. "You know, Malik, Marna just wants to please you." From a safe distance, she watched him sway slightly on his feet.

"You think so?" He plopped into the seat where his troubles began the night before.

Werna smiled as sweetly as she could. "She's just shy about it."

"Marna, shy? She always struck me as bold."

She smiled, sitting across from her husband's sole sibling. "Malik, I will tell you a womanly secret." He regarded her with a flicker of life in his dull blue eyes. "Often we women want to seem different from how we truly are. It is a form of… protection."

"Protection from?" The poor man looked befuddled.

"Our true feelings."

Malik thought on this a moment. "Saister, I am not certain if I dreamed something or if it really happened."

"What is it?" Her voice rose with expectation.

"Was there a finely dressed man here this morning asking for Marna?"

"Oh. Yes."

"Um, who was it?"

"A messenger from that injured man who stayed here. Nothing to worry about."

"But… she turned him away?"

"He was turned away, yes." She knew the truth would out at some point, but hopefully not till all was settled and Marna and Malik were joined. "My, you are fuzzy-headed today."

Malik, when his thoughts turned in a direction, was like a stone rolling down a hill. Werna knew not much would change his course. "Narnik told me that injured man was a king allied with Fath— uh, with ours." He shook his head. He looked like he was trying to put his thoughts together. "What a strange story. The battle was many miles from here."

"Yes, east of Castleton, I know." She tried not to sound too exasperated, and lowered her tone to get her braither's attention. "Apparently the man took a fancy to Marna."

"Oh. Well that makes sense. She's a good cook, and pretty too, and…" His blond eyebrows rose as he turned to his saister. "Did he try anything?"

"Don't worry, Malik! She refused his advances." Werna looked away, a niggle of guilt at wanting to keep her sister in the household threading her thoughts. "My sister's a strong girl, you know." She gave her braither a knowing look.

"Strong-willed, yes." He smiled, leaning into his chair. "A king fancying my Marna. Ha!" Malik snorted. "He probably has twenty wives already, like those foreign men do."

"Men in this land need only one."

"Mmm." His blue eyes twinkled.

Now was her chance. "You know, Palik tells me the grapes need another day to sweeten on the vine, thus today might be a good time to talk to her ..."

"Ah-ha! I see your point. Because once the grape harvesting starts tomorrow—"

"There will be no time for anything but work for a long while."

Malik nodded. "Then I will go find her."

"Wonderful!" Werna exclaimed, in the tone of a mother leading a dim-witted child to an obvious conclusion. "Marna went to the wine house, getting the laundry done before the harvest." Her braither stared at the table. She glanced at the wooden slab to see if something crawled upon it, but saw nothing amiss. "Malik?"

"Hmm?"

"Weren't you going somewhere?"

"Um, yes." He looked at her, his eyes wet and anxious. "Perhaps another spot of ale might help."

Seated at Hudik King's table, to the king's left, Dalock chewed a roasted duck's leg, the meat lacking any whiff of spices or flavor. Before him, performers dressed in multicolored costumes frenetically juggled or leapt in a blur of acrobatics. Their performance gave the impression of a Summer garden buffeted by a windstorm.

Dalock dropped the bone onto the gold-edged pewter plate with a dissatisfied clank.

"Allow me the pleasure of serving you more wine." Huma, Hudik King's daughter, leaned toward him from her seat by his side. Her attire for the feast mimicked the uplifting bodice of the previous eventide, save only that tonight her gown was a rich walnut hue. A sheer scarlet veil framed the princess's high-cheekboned face, accentuating the colorlessness of her fair skin and the azure of her eyes.

Emboldened by the strong wine, Dalock spoke aloud his next thought. "Do you always wear my colors?"

Huma lowered her gaze. "They do not please you?"

"It is not a question of pleasure." The Strange King suddenly swiveled toward her, and their noses nearly touched.

She seemed startled and backed away, her burgundy-stained lips slightly parted, glimmering from the wine. "I am . . . very fond of red."

Huma's gaze strayed from his to the crimson velvet of his overtunic, from the dark leather cords at the neck of his shirt down his chest, which was crossed with a stitched emblem of a chestnut-colored sword. He got the distinct impression that if they were alone, she would touch him there. A corner of Dalock's lopsided mouth twitched, pondering if he would like that. He feigned absentmindedly loosening his laces, allowing a slight peek of his chest to show. He glanced away, pretending to find great interest in how many blue balls the nearest juggler could manage.

The princess inclined toward him, her delicate shoulders but a hand's breadth from his biceps as she stretched forward, intent on the oblong saltcellar resting on the table before Dalock. Her gaze cut to his torso as she did this, whilst Dalock obliged her pretended need for the salt by reaching for the dish with his far hand. He lifted the silver piece in the air just high enough for his tunic sleeve to drop, revealing his well-honed musculature.

He set the salt before her with a gracious nod.

"Thank you." Never had a voice carried such boundless gratitude and promise. Here was a woman who would not push a King away. He smiled smugly, deciding that, yes, yes indeed, he was glad for the provocative, rapt attention. As though through a thick haze, he became dimly aware of someone shouting his name.

"Dalock King!" Huma's elder brother, Crown Prince Humik, called from across the room. The prince beckoned with one hand whilst using the other to open a white brocaded curtain shrouding a passageway. "Your Majesty, by your leave, come! I wish to introduce you to someone." Uncharacteristically, he grinned like a young lad at long last allowed to race his horse.

Huma spoke in alluring tones. "Ah, the crown prince calls." She cast a smoldering glance at Dalock. "One never denies a king … or his son."

The breath went out of him as he pushed his chair back, mumbling a hasty excuse to Hudik King's buxom daughter. Flushing, Dalock fled the table, gulping air whilst crossing the hall, his cheeks a keen match to his overtunic.

Two of his scarlet and tan clad Guards followed at a discreet distance. The clamor of the feast dissipated as he entered the small, torchlit passageway, which led to a long room brightly illuminated with many tapered candles. Several young court ladies, dressed in bright hues, lined the far end of the stone-walled room, standing beside a cut-stone hearth large enough to lay abed inside. Closer to the entrance of the corridor, Prince Humik waited, his long formal tunic emblazoned with the crests of his parents: the glistening, solid silver crown of Hudiksland and the golden claw of Nordak. At his side a slight woman waited, wearing a cream-colored, bepearled gown and a thin veil of transparent gold cloth.

Humik beamed as Dalock approached, his usually strained features replaced with an eager, buzzing joy. "Your highness, Dalock King, allow me to present the former Princess Zala of Kursak, now crown princess of Hudiksland, and most importantly, my wife."

Zala lifted her glimmering veil. Dalock found her face pale, framed by black hair, with hooded, deep brown eyes that drew attention to dark circles below.

The prince's wife raised her left hand before her face and bowed her head to touch her forehead to her fingers, a graceful execution of the Kursak gesture of respect. Then she made a stiff curtsey, as though the movement pained her. The Kursak lady straightened, reaching for her husband's arm to steady herself, her cheeks blooming crimson.

Humik murmured in discreet tones, "This is the first she has come from childbed." The Hudikslander prince placed an affectionate, steadying hand around his wife's shoulders. She leaned against him; an expression of bewilderment added to her ailing appearance.

Dalock regarded the dark-haired woman with sympathetic eyes. "I am honored, Princess. May The Powers protect the new prince, and his fair mother."

Zala's eyes brightened at his sentiments. She spoke with fervor: "Thank you, Lord of Eskalind, for your grace, and for Eskalind's alliance to Hudiksland and my homeland."

Dalock bestowed his best gentlemanly smile upon the Kursak-born woman and bowed.

"Perhaps you should rest, my princess." The warmth and concern in Humik's voice would melt stone. Dalock envied the obvious tenderness between the prince and his wife, yet it also brought a bittersweet hollowness to his chest. The promise and attentions of Huma fell far short of what he witnessed here.

Princess Zala nodded at her husband, and he replaced her veil with deliberate grace. Her dark eyes glistened behind the spun threads, intent and adoring. Dalock felt this an intimate ritual between them, heartbreaking to watch from what felt like a gulf of loneliness surrounding him.

Prince Humik motioned quickly to his wife's attendants to accompany her, and the ladies rushed close to their princess's side to escort her away. As they passed, their jewel-colored gowns flickered in the candlelight. To Dalock it recalled stained-glass windows dappling light onto the stone-paved corridor that led to his chambers, far away in his own Halls. He searched for something to say that would not betray the sudden longing that seized him. As compliments bridge the gap in any land, he cleared his throat and spoke in a lowered voice. "Prince Humik, count yourself a fortunate man. A fine son and a beautiful wife."

"By The Powers, I know it, Dalock King, and am grateful." He spoke quietly, with none of the reserved anxiety that marked their previous discussions. "Ours was an alliance joining, a peace pledge, but when we first met, we realized it was a love match." He watched his wife's procession turn a torchlit corner and disappear from view. The prince turned to his ally, a spark in his blue gaze. His tone bespoke a return to the matters at hand. "Perhaps I may be alone amongst my countryfolk, but I understand that arranged joinings are not the custom in your land?"

"In my kingdom, all joinings are, as you say, love matches. Arrangements are not allowed in our traditions."

"If I may ask, even amongst the nobility, my Ever Ally?"

"Yes."

Humik canted his neck toward his companion, his baritone attentive as though the topic held immense interest for him. "Fascinating and unusual." The royal men walked toward King Hudik's great hall, shadowed by red and brown clad Guards. The crown prince clasped his hands behind his back, pacing alongside his ally. "Dalock King, it is the belief in your land that The Powers bring couples together?"

"It is." Despite his efforts, the Eskalinder's voice hinted at disappointment.

The thin worry lines on the prince's forehead deepened. "I see."

"Many find our ways curious." The pair approached the white brocade curtain that separated the passageway from the great hall. Lively music, punctuated by loud laughter, echoed from the feast. A waiting page drew aside the fabric. Dalock looked across the hall, past the servants bearing large trays of roasted meats and the ever-present, ever-active jugglers, to the long, raised table occupied by the Hudiksland royals.

Prince Humik's younger brother, Huprik, stood in the narrow space between his father's throne and his absent brother's seat. With a movement reminiscent of a pouting child, he pushed aside his brother's place with his rear end, spreading his stance to make advantage of the roominess his maneuver afforded him.

Meanwhile, his sister leaned across the Strange King's empty seat and nodded as her father animatedly babbled, her scarlet veil bobbing with her movements. The pointy polished red nails of her fingertips gripped the far arm of Dalock's chair. From this distance, safely removed from her provocative presence, and after witnessing the sincere tenderness between the crown prince and princess, Dalock realized he found nothing appealing in Huma's manner or appearance. To wit, she reminded him of a piece of unmarked parchment, a blank surface on which others seek to distinguish themselves. Whereas another woman of his recent acquaintance brought to mind the experience of reading a well-loved Legend scroll, a tale one returned to again and again, finding each time undiscovered depths and aching beauties. By The Powers, how he hoped Marna might reconsider her rejection of him.

Dalock looked to Humik. "It is unfortunate that some … forget … the traditions of my land." A flash of recognition enlivened the prince's countenance.

"Aye, my Lord." The crown prince bent toward Dalock, muttering close to his ear, "And some forget the tradition in my land that the elder son inherits his father's position." Worried blue eyes sharpened as he glanced again at the royals' table, just as Huprik sat on the arm of the crown prince's chair.

Dalock gave a knowing, steady nod. "Perhaps we will speak more on this later, Prince Humik." They waded more deeply into the cacophonous room.

The heir to the throne of Hudiksland shouted above the din enveloping them, "I would be most honored."

"After the feast then, at my pavilion." Not for the first time, he wordlessly thanked The Powers he had not elected to quarter in Hudik King's halls.

"King Dalock! Come, come!" The elder king beckoned across the clamorous main hall. "Do bring my son." Hudik emptied his chalice with a throaty gulp, cackling like a man The Powers had neglected to endow with good sense. "We have a special performer for you!"

The Eskalinder caught sight of Jinil, seated at the head of the table adjacent to the royals. The commanders of the Strange Kingdom exchanged slight, neutral-faced nods. Dalock and Humik crossed the hall, stepping past serving girls bearing silver-chased ewers of their king's favorite beverage and pages balancing laden platters of bland meats and foodstuffs.

Dalock whispered to his Second, as he brushed past, "There is hope in the elder son." He resumed his seat next to King Hudik, who motioned for more wine.

The Lord of Hudiksland cast a purple-lipped grin at Dalock, then turned to the blond princess. "Dance for us, daughter!"

Huma hastened to the center of the hall. Nobles, servants, and even the jugglers yielded the wide stone floor to the next round of entertainment. The princess paused a moment, slowly surveying the room and ascertaining that indeed, everyone was watching her. Then she stretched her scarlet veil across her pale arms, slowly undulating her shoulders as the drummers pulsed a deep beat.

King Hudik leaned toward Dalock. "Isn't she lovely?"

"The women of your land are exceptional." Dalock no longer cared if he sounded grumpy. The thudding sound increased; Huma's slender hips took up the dance.

"She will make some lucky man very, very happy." An absurd twinkle glinted in his eyes, brighter than the hammered silver chalice raised in his bony hand. Behind him, his younger son, Prince Huprik, stood, clutching his father's gilt chair, leering at his sister's performance as though . . . as though she were not his sister.

The princess's blue eyes met Dalock's. Perhaps she thought him a brick of butter she could melt with her gaze. He wished Jinil nearer so he could mutter this thought. Watching his Second's diplomatic restraint at the absurdity of borderlanders' customs always gave the young King a chuckle. A chuckle he did his best to restrain until after, as duty and etiquette prescribed.

The elder king's daughter turned and turned again as her father bent to Dalock's ear. "Do have some more wine, our honored Ever Ally."

The Eskalinder slurped at the jeweled edge of his chalice, watching the performance, wagering with himself whether the woman would overflow her bodice. Menfolk pounded their tables, a clanging call urging her to twirl faster, faster. But the more Huma spun, the less he saw her before him and the more his thoughts turned to the last few days at Marna's house. He could not fathom why she would refuse his note. If he could only explain. The thought brought an ache to the top of his head, and the spurned man touched his hairline, leaning his cup hard upon the azure table covering. "She cannot accept Malik."

He lifted his goblet. The distinct impression of a hand appeared where the cup had rested. Whilst the hall erupted in shouts of approval as Huma finished her dance, Dalock blinked, and the handprint evaporated, leaving only a circular wine stain upon the tablecloth. All about him men cheered, some drawing the ladies at their sides close in a strong, clinging grasp, as if to say, "This one is mine." Dalock glanced at King Huprik, hopeful the borderlander lord had witnessed the hand's impression, but the older man just applauded, eyes intent upon his feminine progeny.

The princess bowed to Dalock, long golden hair flowing around her sculpted bodice down to her slim waist, once again presenting her bland smile. He had seen it too many times. If The Powers were to grant him a way to instantly transport himself and all his men across the border, he would spring at the chance.

After an inattentive nod to the performer, Dalock leaned toward the half-laden platters to address her brother the crown prince. "Humik, to our appointment?" The Hudikslander nodded, making low-toned excuses to his father. The elder waved a groggy hand, then called to the pair as they escaped the celebration. The younger royals pretended not to hear. Dalock's attention was grabbed by the sight of Princess Huma in a shadowed corner with her younger brother, Huprik. The siblings rubbed noses, giggling with a familiarity that struck him as unnatural.

"And they call us the Strange Kingdom," muttered Dalock, quickening his pace.

Arriving at the torchlit Eskalind army camp on horseback, the Ever Allies entered the main thoroughfare with an entourage of Humik's retainers, including a Pennant Bearer, following. Dismounting, they continued on foot, the King describing to his companion the arrangements of the camp. Frequently invaded Hudiksland could certainly benefit from Eskalinder lessons on military training and order.

Dalock's armyfolk greeted the party with mostly hearty cheers, though some lost their enthusiasm when they saw King Hudik's banner. The Strange King attributed this to feelings he shared; namely, that the lord of Hudiksland was an inept ruler, whose poor decisions cost his countryfolk and his much-abused Ever Ally. Yet he hoped his people might discover the worth he perceived in the crown prince, and he smiled and patted Humik on the back to show his favor whilst he introduced the prince to many along the way. Prince Humik, for his part, thanked the Eskalinders for their aid, clasping the hands of Sergeants, Soldiers, Cooks, Healers, and Standers with equal enthusiasm. Perhaps there was hope for Hudiksland's future. Just as, he now considered, if he went to see Marna rather than grousing about it, perhaps there might be hope for himself as well. If The Powers showed her the handprint, might that convince her?

Approaching Dalock's pavilion, the royals saw a hooded, cloaked figure in close conversation with the King's Guards. These door wardens, exchanging ribald grins, allowed the figure to pass between the bright torches and enter the King's quarters. A heady scent, akin to a basket of heavily perfumed blooms, drifted in the air. Prince Humik fell victim to its charms: he unleashed a tremendous sneeze, followed by a rain of apologies. "Your pardon, my Lord Dalock King! Perhaps a later time might be better for our meeting."

"I am not expecting anyone, save you, Prince."

The heir to the throne of Hudiksland croaked a whisper. "By The Powers, I know that perfume!" Another sneeze punctuated the sentence, but he managed to stifle most of it inside a silver-trimmed handkerchief, hastily proffered by an obsequious, long-faced member of his entourage.

The Lord of Eskalind regarded his fellow royal. "Then perhaps you should enter first," he said, gesturing. Humik nodded, his eyes reddened and teary, much like his father's after several chalices at the feast. The Guardsmen stepped aside, and the two lords entered the pavilion, Prince Humik wobbling slightly. The crown prince's attendants waited outside, chattering.

A veiled figure sat on the King's bed, illuminated by the bronze candelabras scattered about the spacious interior. The figure stood as the nobles entered, casting the opaque veil to the floor and revealing a sheer red gown that left no doubt to her sex. Dalock neglected at first to look at her face, with so much more on display.

The woman did not glance up, instead saying, in an alluring voice, "I hope you do not mind this intrusion, my Lord."

Prince Humik gaped. "Sister, what are you doing here, dressed in this, this, bedchamber attire?"

Startled, Huma's gaze rose, and she grabbed at the bed, pulling a crimson coverlet to shield her skin. "Humik? How? Oh, do not tell him you saw me!"

Her brother's forehead bunched into a knot above his brow. "Tell who what?"

"Do not tell Father you know he sent me here!" The princess pawed at the blanket, hastily arranging it to cover her body.

"Sent you to King Dalock? But—" He stopped, and when he spoke again, his voice growled low and sharp. "How could he do this to you?"

"Because he bears no love for me anymore, not since you joined with Zala!" Huma bowed her head, wordlessly sobbing, pale fingers clutching the coverlet.

Dalock turned to leave, wishing to spare the young woman further indignity—and himself his hosts' family intrigues.

The crown prince spoke, his voice keen. "My father has lost his mind. Long have I seen this coming." He raised his voice, in formal tones staying the Strange King. "My Ever Ally, I ask your forgiveness. I realize this is entirely against your custom, and I beg your leave to add, it is also against mine."

"I thank you." Dalock cast a quick glance at the princess, then at her brother. "I sympathize with your situation, Princess. Remain here while I distract from your exit. A discreet Guard will accompany you home." He made a short, cool nod to Huma, as though she stood bedecked in her finest gown in her own halls. "Lady Princess." The King's daughter did not whimper but calmed herself enough to mutter a proper goodbye.

Her brother followed him as they exited the pavilion. The nobles exchanged the prescribed farewells with impassive expressions, and Prince Humik, accompanied by his populous entourage, returned to his father's castle.

Jinil stepped close to his commander to hear a brief version of what had transpired. The two men spoke in lowered tones.

"Send for Avaril to accompany the princess home. If she accuses him of touching her, we will know it is false." Dalock snorted, shaking his head. "First we ride here to save them from invasion, then their king throws his daughter into my bed." He scoffed. "The sooner we leave, the better. None of this is to my liking."

King's Second nodded coolly. "As you say, my Lord. The timing is good, for the wounded are well enough now to travel to the border. I will see the departure preparations fully under way, and word relayed to Hudik King. Your men will be ready upon the morrow for the march home."

Dalock smiled grimly as he plotted. "Good. We leave at first light. Thank The Powers that is not long from now. Ah, Jinil, it will be good to be back in our own land."

He watched his man give the orders, thinking for a moment to relay to his Second the strange vision of the handprint on the tablecloth. With a slight twinge, he realized that early journeying would deny his men a good night's rest. Perhaps he could leave immediately for Marna's home, alone, in secret. But then he would be absent from the departure ceremony, and The Powers only knew what would greet him at her sister's house. Forfeiting the notion of sleep, he enlisted in assisting with the departure preparations. The sooner they departed, the gladder he would be.

CHAPTER TWELVE—DISCOVERIES

Awaking from her impromptu bed in the wine house, Marna heard her stomach growling for breakfast. After Malik came to her yesterday, asking for her to join with him, she had barricaded herself inside to be alone, to think and to weep. Mostly to weep. She sat up, holding her head, a dried handkerchief stuck to her arm. Marna peeled it away, trying to think, angry at herself for giving her heart to a man who turned out to be a king. "There is no hope for you," she muttered, wiping her eyes.

In her right pocket, Marna fingered the wishbone she had broken with her guest. Turning the smoothened bone between her thumb and forefinger, she breathed deeply. "Malik asks to be my husband, and I see two paths set before me: to join with him and have my own family, perhaps to find joy in my children, or to stay as I am and continue as a second mother to my sister's little ones. And to Malik's when he joins with another." Tears rolled down her cheeks again. She wiped her face, her only solace the fact that no one could see her. Just then, tentative knocking sounded on the door.

"Go away, Malik! I have yet hours to answer you."

"Auntie Marna, it's Palika. I'm alone. Please let me talk to you!" Her niece's voice was as plaintive as a girl's half her age.

Not wanting the youngster to discover her distress, Marna tried to sound cheerful. "Have you brought me breakfast?" She walked to the door, straightening her bodice and skirt along the way. With a last pass of the handkerchief over her face, she pulled aside the sturdy bench propped against the door, then undid the thick latch. The door swung open, revealing her niece, red-faced and with tears brimming down trembling cheeks.

"Palika! What's wrong?"

"Oh Auntie! Forgive me! Please forgive me, I didn't know what I was doing."

Marna stood stunned, a tangle of thoughts and fears in her mind. "For what? What happened? Is everyone all right?"

Palika stepped back, as though afraid she would be struck. "Father made me lie."

"That's all?"

"Yes … I mean, no! I had, I told Father, the night the menfolk came back, about…" Her gaze dropped to the threshold. "That you, you really liked the guest, and that I didn't like him—because I was afraid he might hurt you." Her teeth bit into her lip as she seemed to struggle to go on.

Marna found some comfort in that Palika's ongoing dislike of Dalock had had, at its root, concern for her well-being. Marna stepped through the doorway, placing a comforting hand on her niece's thin shoulder. "I don't understand, Palika. Why are you this upset now?"

Her niece inhaled loudly through her nose, her shoulders taut. "Yesterday, early, a man came to the house. In the guest's colors! And he asked for you."

"What? How did I not know this?"

Palika shook her head. "You were still asleep. But Father sent me, outside the house, where the man was. And the man asked if I was Marna, and Father answered that I was."

"No!" Marna covered her mouth with her hands, a tingle speeding along her back.

"I'm sorry! Before I could say I wasn't you, Father said something about how I had said I didn't like Guest, which was true, I couldn't deny it."

"Oh, Palika!" Marna's knees felt weak, yet she wanted to run to Castleton and find Dalock to explain. After she had given her braither a sound tongue-lashing.

Her niece continued her tale, standing tall whilst her thin frame trembled. "And the man wanted to talk to me alone, and Father said it was all right, and I didn't know what to do, but I went with him. The man tried to give me a note, but he said it was a private note from the King to you, that he would read it … but it was private, and I'm not really you, so I didn't want him to read it to me." Palika's voice dropped to an ashamed whisper. "So I ran away." The girl's chin dropped to her chest and she covered her face with her hands.

Marna looked out at the vineyards, her mouth open in disbelief. The view seemed to recede from her; for a moment she felt light-headed. Thoughts tangled one over the other as she muttered, incoherently, "He sent a man for me. He must want to see me. But the man was sent away. Why did my braither lie?" A sharp inhale. "Because they want me to stay with them."

Werna wanted her to stay. Palik wanted her to stay. None of them wanted her to go. She grabbed her niece's elbows and shook her gently. "Palika, listen to me. I must go to Guest, tell him what happened. Will you help me?"

The girl raised her blond head, her eyes red, tear rimmed. "Yes, but… what are you going to do?"

"Walk to Castleton and find his camp, hopefully along the way." For a moment she wished they kept horses, but then she was glad they didn't, as Palik and Malik would be slower to follow if they came after her. She released her niece and gazed north. "I may find a wagon traveling along the way that will bring me there faster. I'll need food for the journey. I haven't eaten and there's no food here." She turned her attention to Palika.

The girl almost smiled. "I'll run back to the house and get you some. Mother's already making meal pails for the harvest."

"Good. And Palika, if anyone asks, tell them I am still in the wine house." She looked back to the dimly lit room. "I'll latch the doors and climb out the window. They will think I'm still inside."

———

For Dalock, the morning dawned radiant clear and hopeful bright, with glad sunshine raking the trampled fields where the Eskalind camp had stood. The crushed grass lifted skyward again, released from its weights of wheels, tents, and feet. Eskalind's Second and Ninth Companies, arrayed upon the road in prescribed positions of men, horses, and wagons, awaited the order to depart Castleton. Not surprisingly, a delay in the arrival of the Hudikslander royals from their quarry postponed Dalock's plans for an early withdrawal.

At the behest of the irked Strange King, his Second and his men began their march homeward whilst he and his Guards tarried for the briefest of formalities with Hudik King and his sons, the younger bleary-eyed from The-Powers-knew-what revelry the night before. Dalock regarded the uncouth royal with scarcely restrained disdain. Only three years senior to the younger prince himself, he considered Huprik more akin in attitude and manner to an unproven, entitled youth clamoring to have his sword without test or trial. The Lord of Eskalind muttered to himself as he rode away. "Typical borderlander royal. For ingrate fools like him, my men gave their lives." He wagered with himself how long the prince would last in single combat—The Powers forgive him for such thoughts.

At last the Strange King trotted his chestnut mare away from Hudik King's seat for what he hoped would be the last time in a long, long while. Breena raised her proud head in a triumphant manner, as though she shared that thought.

Reaching the head of the column, Dalock exchanged grins with his Second. The pair rode wordlessly alongside one another, the King keeping his inner plans to himself, his heart racing with anticipation.

Their shadows shortening with the steady rise of the sun, the Companies and King rode forth along the main road, south to Eskalind. It felt almost as though The Powers had a hand in slowing their journey, but the sedate pace resulted from the need to accommodate the laden wagons of gear creaking behind him. As Lord of Eskalind, he could ride ahead if he desired, but he would not chance missing the red shed that heralded the path toward Marna's home. Still, the soft, monotonous clomp of horse hooves on dirt threatened to become a lullaby. His eyelids felt heavy.

"Fine weather for the march home, my Lord," Jinil offered.

Dalock shifted in his saddle, fighting grogginess. "Ah. I was just thinking about the situation we left behind us."

"Which?"

"Old Hudik King and his … spawn."

Jinil chuckled.

"Still, Humik King's Son has my sympathy. Between his father and scheming younger brother, the man is caught between the sword and the grindstone."

"Indeed."

As the sun rose higher, they rode past farm families gathering cut grain in golden fields, the women singing in melodic voices.

He wondered how Marna fared at this very moment. Perhaps the sun fell upon her face. Dalock removed his right glove, the light warming his fingers. He massaged Breena's mane and looked ahead, spying a familiar tree-crowned hill. "I know this place. We are not far from her home." His eyes shifted to the left and to the right, and he wondered if anyone could sense the anxiousness that seized him. As though it had manifested from the air itself, he spotted the red shed not five horse lengths forward.

The King beckoned his man closer. "Jinil, I am going back to get some of that healer's broth. It was quite good." He stared straight at his man, knowing his excuse sounded ridiculous. But he also knew he could count on his Second to act with discreet aplomb. After all, the man had weathered Ambassadorships in realms as treacherous as Havadra and as annoyingly insipid as Gergelt.

Jinil's smooth voice conveyed no indication he saw through his King's ploy. "Very good, my Lord. I will ready some men to accompany you."

Not long thereafter, Dalock, feeling annoyingly clumsy and befuddled, departed, bringing with him a cadre of four Guardsmen, which he led more by instinct than knowledge till at last he sensed a familiar path nestled amongst the long trellises of burgeoning grapes. Urging his men on, he sought to steady his pulse, muttering to reassure himself. "I am just coming for broth. And the recipe. And hopefully for the cook."

The Strange King's contingent rode to the low farmhouse, from which an unfamiliar woman emerged. The small girl in her arms nestled her blond head against the woman's shoulder, her toddler legs draped around the woman's belly, which bulged with child. The woman regarded the men and horses with fear, but the little girl raised her head, blinked her big blue eyes, and smiled. "Hul-lo, Guesth!"

"Hullo, Lena." He grinned back, heartened that she remembered him. Breena snorted.

A well-known shout came from the side of the house. "Guest!" Narnik charged toward the King, who steadied Breena's backstep. "King Dalock! You came back!" The Lord waved his men off, dismounted, and tossed Breena's reins to a Guard. The lad rushed forward, embracing him in fond greeting.

Narnik laughed with joy, then pulled away. His face was red and glossy with sweat, his light eyes eager and wide. "Did you come for Auntie Marna?"

Dalock eyed his men, intent on keeping up his ruse. "I came for her broth."

Narnik's cheerful expression drooped. "Truly?"

"No." Dalock spoke in a low voice. "I—"

The woman in the doorway interrupted. "You cannot lay hold of Marna by force. She is betrothed!"

Dalock cast a startled glance at Narnik, who shook his head. "Not yet! Uncle Malik asked, but she told him she would not decide until candletime." The boy stole a look at his mother, who glared at him.

"Into the house with you, Narnik. Help Palika with the food pails, and we'll bring them to the harvesting." Her tone brooked no argument. Yet the lad ignored her, leaning close to the Strange King.

"You *must* go to her. Please."

Dalock hesitated. He looked at the woman, who he gathered was Marna's sister. She eyed him as though willing him to burst into flames. He saw a bit of a resemblance in the downward curve of the mouth—akin to Marna's lips when she told him to leave. Lena waved goodbye.

"I know where she is now!" The boy grabbed Dalock's crimson sleeve with grape-stained fingers. "See that hill there?" Narnik inclined his head. "I saw her go, when Palika came back! She's there now. I'm certain of it."

His mother growled. "She's not on the hill, Narnik, and if you do not do as I say, you will be roasted with the chickens!"

The boy whispered, "Please say you'll go?"

Dalock regarded him a moment, hoping The Powers meant this to be, his arrival at the farmhouse just as Narnik happened to be here too. "I will go."

The boy squeezed the King's arm and darted past his mother into the farmhouse.

Dalock nodded at Marna's sister, dipping his chin as though she were a great queen. "My lady." Her expression softened into puzzlement. "By your leave, may my men wait here? They will be no bother." She nodded mutely, and he turned to his Guards. "Wait for me." And the Strange King made for the hill.

———

Marna stood alone on her hill, looking across the fields, lined with green vineyards and golden-grained crops, that stretched into the distance toward Fambay Forest. She had been waiting too long for Palika and thought that she should just leave, in case Palik or Malik, or one of the other children, discovered her.

Before she could act on her last thought, footfalls sounded behind her. Glancing over her shoulder, she saw Malik approaching with a lumbering gait that belied the nervous apprehension on his face. It was as though his body had made a firm decision and charged ahead while his mind continued mulling other options. Bits of grape stem clung to his worn tunic; dark purple stains dotted his sleeve. He stopped a few feet away.

"Marna, forgive me, I know I said I would give you until candletime, but I could not wait." He interleaved his stubby fingers before his waist, a gesture that had always struck her as cloying.

"How did you know I was here?"

"Narnik, he told me he saw you leave the wine house and come here."

She wanted to weep; more, she wanted to run, and she turned away to not have to bear the sight of him. But if she joined with him, she would have to bear the sight of all of him.

Trying to find a way to buy herself more time, she spoke softly, willing herself to find a reserve of calm. "You should be at the harvest. Palik will need your strength." She nearly spat her braither's name, but Malik didn't seem to notice.

"I, I was wondering … do you have an answer for me?"

"I told you I need time to think. Alone." She tried to moderate her bitterness, but it wasn't working.

"Marna, you were all I could think of when I was away at battle."

"You would have done better to think on the moment."

He sighed. "Why delay starting our life together?" He reached for her arm, brushing the bare skin below her rolled-up sleeves.

She stepped aside, but Malik pursued, grasping her arm. "Malik, what do you think you are doing?"

His sticky fingers tightened on her exposed skin, but his voice was gentle, apologetic. "I know you have thought me, uh, spiritless, in the past, but I want to show you I am a changed man. Please, look at me. I must tell you something."

He relaxed his grip, and uncertain what would happen next, she regarded him warily. Sweat beaded his forehead and a crimson flush shone on his cheeks. His clear blue gaze pled with her to stay and listen to his words. Despite the fluttering of fear in her chest, she waited.

Malik swallowed audibly, as though forcing down an unpleasant morsel. "I was … scared, at the battle. I, somehow … I don't know what happened, I …"

Marna's ears rang with annoyance at his blubbering, which spewed like a Spring cloudburst.

"I lost Palik in the crowd, and soldiers found me first and thought I was a common peasant and were going to send me to the front lines, and I thought I would have to fight and that I would die. Marna!"

His exclamation startled her, and she tried to back away. His thick fingers tightened on her arm. "I thought I would be killed! You were all I could think of. How I never told you how I feel about you." Malik's tone dropped to a reverent hush as he bowed his head, staring at the ground. "You are strong and commanding and all the things I am not. Was not. But now I want to be strong and say my mind. Like you. For you, Marna. All for you." Again, his pleading gaze belied his actions, as he jerked her closer to him.

"Let go of me. Please."

He looked confused, that old, familiar Malik expression. He stared at her blankly. Then, as though someone had whispered a reminder that he was a new man, he lurched forward. "Let me kiss you and all will be decided."

———

Dalock crested the hill, and just below him, near the flat rock where they sat together on that moonlit night, stood Marna with her back to him, tall and proud as a Queen out of Legend. Her hair flowed past her strong, straight shoulders to her waist. A patched brown bodice flared over his beloved's skirt around her hips. He knew how well his hand fit the tantalizing curve of her waist, and his senses filled with a vision of encircling her warmth with his arms. A certainty that she would be his filled his heart, the sting of her rejection dissipating like a slender cloud on a hot Summer day.

But she was not alone; a blond man stood in front of her in the posture of one reaching for a kiss. Dalock stopped, swaying where he stood, his heart falling, despair entangled with disbelief. He leaned to the side, dumbly watching Malik pull Marna into his arms.

Just then, she kneed Malik where no man should suffer such an injury. Even Dalock, for the briefest of moments, sympathized with his pain, but his spirits rose as fast as they had fallen a moment before.

Marna fled from Malik, charging up the path straight toward Dalock, teeth gritted, hair flashing amber red behind her. Spotting the King, she stopped short, wobbling for a moment. Her lips parted in wordless wonder, her face flickering with a rapid succession of emotions: surprise, shock, and perhaps relief.

Uncertain how she would react to him, he resisted the urge to embrace her, asking, "How fare ye, Marna?"

"Better." Her voice sounded lower than he had ever heard it before.

"I hope he was not asking for your broth—or to be your husband." She gasped, and he ascertained the latter was correct.

Malik's coughing interrupted his thoughts. "M-marna, why did you… Who is that?"

Marna looked over her shoulder. "What idiot doesn't understand a kick in the crotch?"

Dalock called to the crimson-faced man in a commanding tone, gripping the bronze pommel of his sheathed blade for good measure. "She does not desire your company."

His hoped-for echoed his sentiment with a throaty shout: "Go, Malik!" The defeated man groaned and, bent-backed, stumbled away. Marna sputtered like one saved from drowning, her bosom rising and falling. "How is it … What are you doing here?"

Her beauty was different when she was confused, with a singular intensity in her eyes, as though she were searching the entire realm for wisdom. He smiled, hoping she understood his interest and intent, and purred, "I did not come asking for more broth." She did not return his smile, but stared at him wordlessly.

"Marna, I came to ask why you refused my Messenger and—"

"It was not me who refused him."

While a sense of relief flooded his veins, he did not quite understand. "Not you?"

"My braither tricked Palika into pretending to be me."

"Palika? It was not you?"

She brought her hands before her face, her chest heaving with sobs. The Lord of Eskalind was torn between wanting to skewer her braither, berate his Messenger for thinking a fourteen-year-old girl could be his intended, and comfort his beloved.

"Marna." His voice ached with tenderness, and he reached to touch her shoulder, hoping to The Powers it was the right thing to do. She threw her arms around him and cried against his breastplate.

"But you are here now." She whimpered as he stroked her hair. "You came back. I … had just found out from Palika about your Messenger. I was going to walk to Castleton. I wanted to explain. And see you again."

He held her warmth close as she clung to him. How soft her hair felt under his kiss, a slight whisper of mint. Then he realized she had no idea how he felt, what he had written to her. He spoke in a warm voice. "Shall I tell you what the note said?"

He felt her nod against his shoulder.

"It said that in Eskalind the King may choose his wife from all the women in the world, regardless of their station, and that Dalock King chooses Marna. If that be her will."

Her breathing stopped. Raising her head, she said, "You would join with me?"

"Aye."

"Not just have me be your mistress?"

"What?" Certainly he knew the meaning of the word, a common word in the borderlands, or the odd outerlands with their bizarre ways, where a man would bed a woman while he called another wife. "Marna, beloved, my people and I do not believe in mistresses." Dalock released her, but cupped her face in his hands. "I would have you as my wife." He gazed intently at her, willing her to truly know, to understand the great depth of his feelings for her. "If you are full willing, by The Powers, I would have you as my wife, as my Queen. Believe this." His voice quavered. He was alone without her. "Believe this or break my heart."

The edges of her lips trembled and a fresh tear spilled down her round cheek, glinting in the sunlight as it glided past her freckles. "You would have a bladesmith's daughter, who cannot read, and speaks her mind, as your Queen?"

"And no other."

Her fond smile branded his heart with its tenderness. "Then I would have you as my husband, and thank The Powers for…" Her voice dropped to a whisper, quiet, yet clear. "I will thank Them for the light in your eyes and the warmth of your hands and all the days that are given us."

"Marna!" He brought his lips to hers.

Dalock and his Guards tarried outside the farmhouse, whilst inside the sleeping room, Marna dressed in her nicest clothes and packed her meager bag. Her sister slumped on one of the sleeping pallets, quiet and perhaps finally accepting that Marna would depart. Then Werna spoke, her voice cool. "Marna, heed my advice on this one thing: do not tell him what happened to you."

The newly betrothed woman blanched at the memory. "If he is to be my husband, then I feel that I should." Marna pulled her best bodice over her head and straightened the waist.

Werna frowned, folding her arms over her protruding belly. "Then do not tell him until you are publicly joined and he cannot change his mind." She stood, sighing, and pulled on Marna's sleeves, evening the cuffs, then plucked an errant bit of straw from her sister's skirt.

"It would not be right to tell him afterward." Marna's fingers flew through the bodice laces, and she nearly elbowed her sister in the ear. To The Powers, she wanted to be free from the conversation and quit of the house as fast as possible.

Werna touched her arm. "If he refuses you for it, where will you be left? In a strange country, without friends or family." Sad blue eyes peered up at her. "Think on it, my dear little sister! You will always have a place here, no matter what happens."

Marna barely nodded, unhappy at the intrusion of sad thoughts and uncertainty on this suddenly wonderful day. In all haste, she gathered her bag and marched from the house, her sister trailing her with leaden feet.

Outside, Narnik bounced next to Palika, who held Lena by the hand. Marna bent to hug her littlest niece, kissing the toddler goodbye. "Say farewell to your brothers and sisters for me, little one." The small girl giggled, trying to rub noses. The departing aunt indulged her a moment, with a pang of regret that she would not see her absent nephews and nieces to say goodbye. No remorse touched her for forgoing goodbyes to her braither or Malik.

Embracing Palika, she whispered, "Thank you," quietly into her ear.

Her eldest niece clung to her, whispering back, "Please, bring us with you. Please!" Surprised, Marna pulled away and studied the anxious expression on Palika's face. "Auntie, I don't want to be joined to a man in two years."

Pity flooded her heart at leaving the fourteen-year-old behind. Palika was as trapped at the farmhouse as she had been. "I can't, not now, but you'll come visit someday soon, hmm?" The tall girl closed her eyes. "And maybe you can stay, when you are of age."

Narnik jumped up and down. "Dalock, bring us too! Auntie Marna, he wants us to come with you. Don't you, Dalock?"

Werna slumped against the doorframe, her hand to her forehead. "Please, do not carry off my children! What will I do without them?"

Marna, half wanting to gather the pair into her arms and carry them off, was irked that her sister would accuse her betrothed of abducting the children. But she also pitied her sister, who would be without her greatest helpers if Palika and Narnik left. Narnik could be troublesome, but when he obeyed, he did his tasks faster and better than even his older brothers.

Dalock smiled pleasantly, as though Werna's outburst had been but a fond goodbye. He spoke firmly to the lad, who leapt in place expectantly. "Narnik, your mother needs you here now."

"Aw!" complained the boy. "But—"

"But perhaps some day soon you can come visit. All of you." Marna's betrothed nodded to Palika, then locked eyes with Werna. "I will send a Scribe once a month so that you may have letters brought to Marna. Each of you," he glanced at Palika, "will have time alone with the Scribe to craft a personal message to your aunt." Returning his brown-eyed gaze to Werna, he continued. "If there is anything your household requires, ask. I will provide what you need to make your loss easier to bear." The King stepped forward, holding a hand to his betrothed's sister. "By your leave, saister."

"Oh." Werna's expression wavered between confused and expectant; it was the exact look she was known to exhibit right before announcing that the newbabe was coming soon, very soon, and all must be readied. Marna's heart nearly stopped in anticipation, but her sister reached to accept Dalock's hand. "Yes, my Lord Braither," she replied. And all felt right with the world.

———

Jinil gave the order for the army to halt on the road, as the King's somewhat unexpected side journey was lasting longer than anticipated. To The Powers, he hoped this portended happy news. Meanwhile, the kitchen wagons pulled alongside the dusty dirt track and men erected awnings with practiced haste for the distribution of the midday meal. A woman brought a slick water sack to the Soldiers reclining on the dried grass along the road. Jinil calculated how swiftly they might break camp if his Lord's broth-retrieval excursion was unsuccessful. "Hmm, broth or Betrothed?"

The rumble of riders approaching called his attention. King's Second turned his head toward the sound—the direction Dalock King and his Guards had ridden. A patch of trees interrupted his view for a moment, then he caught a flicker of a crimson and brown pennant.

A nearby horsed Sergeant called in a firm voice, "Our Lord returns!"

Jinil nodded stiffly, rising slightly in the saddle and squinting to glimpse Dalock King amidst his Guards.

"Look!" The officer pointed. "Is that a woman with the King?"

Jinil spied a glint of golden-red tresses against his ruler's chest, and recognized the woman as the healer from the farmhouse. He fought a smile.

The Sergeant grinned. "Might the King's Joining feast be in our near future?"

"I would not wager against it." Jinil spurred his stallion to greet his Lord, who grinned more broadly than a youth at his sword-earning ceremony.

"My Lord." Jinil nodded from his seat. The King's horse lowered her grand head to the track with an expression of weariness.

Dalock spoke. "Marna, my dearest, this is Jinil: my Second, my mentor, and as close to me as a brother."

The woman spoke. "My Lord Jinil, I am honored."

While humbled by his master's praise, Jinil realized this was not the ideal time to correct her on the proper way to address him. As a non-noble who held the second-highest rank in the land, it was a fine point that he was only called "my Lord" when the phrase was followed by his title of King's Second, and he hoped his Lord would mention it to her later. It was never best to start a relationship with a superior by pointing out an error.

The healer and his Lord were nearly the same size across the shoulders, and likely in height as well. While it looked like an uncomfortable riding position for both parties, the couple showed no hint of awkwardness or unease. The woman's broad, red-cheeked face was a spot of color above her beige bodice, middling white blouse, and simply hemmed skirt, which fluttered above her leather slippers, revealing a bit of bare leg. He made a point not to glance in that direction, but directly into her colorless but cheerful eyes. Any traces of the resentment or pride that he had gleaned from their brief earlier acquaintance were gone, thank The Powers. Given her ear-to-ear smile, he would be a fool to think anything was amiss.

"The honor is mine, Marna of Hudiksland." He inclined his head in solemn deference, thanking The Powers for his Lord's compliments and for his own small part in the Legend unfolding before him.

Dalock King grinned. "She has agreed to be my Queen. You will perform the ceremony, the day after we reach our own lands."

"My Lord, I am deeply honored and offer gladdest congratulations."

"I thank you." The younger man's smile could not have been broader, even were his jaw to be straightened. It heartened Jinil, seeing his master well pleased.

"My soon-to-be Queen will need her own pavilion, a Page, and Ladies to attend her when we reach our border. And yes, a horse, though I would have her ride with me a while longer, if all is in order." King's Betrothed twisted slightly in the saddle to face him, and he bestowed a love-struck expression upon her, his brown eyes hazy but gleaming.

"All is well here, and I will see to the preparations." Jinil's reply, perhaps unheard by the newly reacquainted lovers, was nonetheless sincere and grateful.

Word passed through the ranks quickly that the woman with Dalock was King's Betrothed.

One man joked to his neighbor, "I see our King prefers a woman with meat on her bones."

"Aye, she is a well ripe dumpling! I bet his horse wishes it were otherwise."

"Then she is rewarded for running away with him after the battle." They chuckled a moment, their laughter fading against the squeak of the wagon rumbling in front of them. Then the two men, each to himself, silently admired the joyful expressions of the freshly engaged couple.

Marna stood alone in her tent, which could easily have housed her sister's entire family. The brown linen inside walls glowed warm orange from the setting sun. All her possessions rested on the small bed: her herb bag, a patched bodice, a plain skirt and simple blouse.

Noting the dirt lining her unadorned hem above her shoes, King's Betrothed shook her head at the contrast between her spare, dirty clothing and the rich surroundings and beat her skirt with her hand to dislodge the soil till it was passing clean. People chattered as they walked by the tent. The Hudikslander straightened, muttering quietly, mindful that only thin fabric walls stood between her and the outside. "I should not have worn my better clothes for the ride."

Her thoughts turning to the day's events, she grinned, but it faded quickly as she wondered what was happening at that moment with her family. Were they eating the evening meal in the fields as they worked the harvest? She hoped Palika suffered nothing for her honesty earlier this day, though as she reconsidered all that had happened, it seemed unlikely Palik would ever know what his daughter had told her. Silently, the Queen-to-be thanked The Powers that Dalock had assured her his Scribe's first monthly visit would begin tomorrow, to make certain all was well. While she doubted Palik would raise a hand against his eldest daughter, she wanted to be certain her niece fared well.

Unbidden, her sister's last words, during their final moments alone in the house, returned to her. She pondered what and when to tell her betrothed of her past.

These recollections were interrupted by a boy entering the tent. He was garbed like a Hudikslander peasant, and for a moment she thought it was Narnik, but he was too slim and small, only perhaps eight years of age.

The blond lad bowed to her. "My Lady." He looked to her with gray irises rimmed with blue. "Is there anything you need?" His reserved eagerness reminded her of a combination of Palika and Narnik. Even his hair color resembled theirs, a bright straw, like any child of Hudiksland.

"Who are you?"

"My name is Favik. I was sent to be your Page by my Lord Jinil, King's Second." He relayed the Eskalinder's title in a steady tone.

"I see." She must adjust to the idea of having a servant. Eyeing the boy's simple tunic and breeches, she asked, "Have they dressed you to match me already?"

"No, my Lady, these are my own clothes." Favik lowered his head, as though ashamed of his appearance or thinking he had disappointed her.

"Then you have not served long?"

"Just since the battle." The boy raised his head, speaking softly but deliberately. "My family is gone now, and I would try my fortune in another land, if I am able."

Her mouth parted slightly at the diplomatic way he described his orphaned state. "I am very sorry to hear of your hardships, Favik." Marna gazed at the child, protective concern stirring. She lowered her voice. "We will both be strangers in a strange land then." Her Page nodded, a hint of gratitude in his fair eyes. "I thought you looked like you were from Hudiksland."

"Aye, my Lady, I am. King's Second thought you might like a fellow countryman to serve you."

Marna gave the lad a warm smile. "I am not happy unless I am usefully occupied, Favik. If you remember that, you will serve me well."

The boy grinned. "What would you like to do, my Lady?"

"I would like to be of some use, though I am not certain what I am allowed to do, or what is proper for me to do."

"But can't Queens do what they want?"

She smiled at the child's innocence. "Not always."

Favik looked concerned, then said, "My Lady, they say you're a healer, that you healed the King." Marna nodded. "Would you, would you help the wounded men here? There are not many of them, but they would get better faster with your help."

The lad's earnest expression touched her heart, and she hoped not to disappoint him. "I could try."

"Would you like me to show you where they are?"

"Aye, let's go!" Marna grabbed her herb bag and followed the youngster outside.

As Favik led her through the encampment, she admired its organization and the clear pathways between tents. Flags in red and brown identified one section from another with stitched symbols of horses for the stabling area, a bowl denoting a food-serving section, a horseshoe for the smithy; all with numerals distinguishing whether an area was for the Second or Ninth Company. She kept an eye out for Narnik, half expecting to discover her nephew had somehow managed to escape the family vineyard.

In the deepening dark of evening and without the King by her side, no one recognized her as King's Betrothed, or if they did, they said nothing as they went about their business grooming the horses and distributing supplies. "And Father always said I was difficult to miss in a crowd." For once she strode at her full stature rather than cowering to appear smaller.

Under a red pennant marked with a four-petaled white flower, she found the wounded, who gladdened to hear she was a healer from Hudiksland with new medicines to ease their aches. Learning that the Eskalind Healers and their Apprentices were away at the kitchen tents,

Marna talked freely to the few men under care. Instructing one black-haired Soldier to rub a handful of her herbs over a swollen cut on his leg, she said, "I see there are not many injuries."

"'Tis true. Ah, this is quite soothing." His eyelids drooped with pleasure in a manner that Marna found almost comical. Then he jerked his head up, like one catching himself falling asleep. "Well, ahem, it's thanks to our King challenging the invader king to single combat. That saved many lives, it did."

Marna started at the news, trying to picture Dalock, who had stumbled into her life weak and injured, risking his head to prevent a battle. Then she recalled the sticky blood on his sword the night that he came to her house. She shuddered. "My good man, how were you hurt?" A tended fire crackled behind her. Favik broke sticks to add to it.

"After our Lord killed that forked-bearded invader king, one of their companies charged him. That was not their wisest act." The man grinned, firelight reflected in his eyes. "Certainly not their wisest act, but certainly their last. My rank and another, and some Hudikslander men, charged them. They all fell. But not before inflicting a bit of damage." The Soldier gestured to his leg. "The King himself attended me on the battlefield."

Marna smiled. "Then you are a fortunate man."

"Not all were fortunate." Favik's small voice had a sharp edge to it.

The healer turned to him. He looked away, with a whisper, "My father." He faced the fire, splintering another stick.

She turned back to the Eskalinder. "You men are well looked after, yes?"

The injured man nodded. "May I offer my thanks, fair Healer?"

"I will check on you tomorrow." Patting the man's arm, she rose. Leaning toward Favik, she placed a caring hand on his small shoulder. It surprised her how bony it felt. "Let us be off."

The lad nodded, rising to lead her back to her tent. But he kept his face turned from her, and she guessed he shielded tears.

An anxious-faced King's Guard stood by the torches outside her tent. "Oh, my Lady King's Betrothed!" Marna stepped back, eyes searching for the person the man addressed. "The King is looking for you," the

Guard continued, "but we could not find you." He had a long nose and graying, bushy eyebrows that exaggerated his pleading expression. "Are you all right?"

"Why, certainly." She placed both hands upon the youngster's shoulders. "I was very well cared for. I had my Page Favik here with me."

The boy turned to her, a glimmer of pride in his position as he spoke. "My Lady, shall I run to the King's tent and tell him you are returned?"

"Oh yes, thank you." Entering her tent, Marna stopped in midstride. The inside was lit with many candles anchored into two ornate bronze candle stands that rose to her shoulder. A red blanket of smooth, soft-looking fabric graced the bed, and tapestries stitched with glistening threads hung from the walls, their placement reminding her of windows. Each depicted a view of horses grazing, some in verdant valleys and others in hill-dotted fields. On her right beckoned a rectangular table with rounded edges, set with many bronze and copper dishes.

Casting a chagrined eye at her clothing, she noted that her right sleeve was rimmed green from grinding herb paste for the wounded. "Well, I certainly don't look like I belong here." A bronze bowl rested on a nearby three-legged stand, the exterior engraved with an odd repeating mark. A circle cut in half, sealed on its left side. Peering into the bowl, her reflection greeted her, and when she dipped a cautious finger toward it, her image rippled. It was filled with water.

King's Betrothed traced a finger along the carved edge, breathless before such finery. Then she set to soaking and rubbing her sleeve. Cool water cascaded along her arm, dripping to her elbow. "Umpf. I need a cloth."

Marna spied two folded cloths amongst the plates on the small table. "My, what luxury, a linen cloth each for drying and for washing." The Queen-to-be gathered the linens, rinsing her hands, face, and neck. Just as she glanced around for a place to hang the cloths, the Guard outside announced the King. She dropped the linens onto a chair as Dalock entered the tent, arms wide.

"Hullo, Marna." He embraced her. "Your Page tells me you tended the wounded. Are they all cured now?"

King's Betrothed spoke confidently: "They are on their way." His brown eyes beamed at her with pride, giving her a warm feeling in her chest.

"Is it true what they told me, that you fought the invader's king alone?"

His smile faded, his lips forming a hard line. "Aye." He spoke without zest, glancing away.

"I do not wish to trouble you with sad thoughts." Marna cupped the firm muscles of her beloved's arm with both hands.

He shook his head, auburn strands in his handsome long locks glimmering in the candlelight, but the slight drop of his chin bespoke sadness and unpleasant memories. "It is what happened."

"That was very brave of you, my love."

Again he shook his head, but the motion had a changed character, no longer of resigned weariness and sorrow, but rather an element of impending mirth. "I must share with you a state secret. I enjoy the unjoined Strange King's Gift." She raised an eyebrow with curiosity. The Lord of Eskalind took her hand, peering into her eyes. "Marna, I cannot die until my son is conceived."

"Oh?" It came out as a question, though she was not certain how she meant it. The breath went out of her.

Her betrothed kissed her hand, a naughty grin playing on his lips. "There are many reasons my land is called the Strange Kingdom."

Before she could ask if her future husband was serious, the tent flap peeled back. Two boys she did not recognize entered, each bearing a tray laden with covered bowls. They wore identical short crimson tunics and caramel-colored breeches.

"Ah, our dinner is ready." Dalock released her hand, gesturing grandly for her to sit. The cloths she had used for washing cluttered her chair. Feeling a fool for not knowing where to place them properly, the for-eigner from Hudiksland gathered her skirt and plopped onto the chair, surreptitiously batting the linens onto the ground. A clandestine kick sent them under the table. Her beloved's fond gaze never left her eyes. Captivated, she stared at him from across the table.

The boys approached and waited.

The King smiled pleasantly at his future bride. "Ladies first."

Marna studied the arrangement before her. A stack of three nested plates occupied each place setting. Around the plates clustered a host of small bowls, containing substances of various colors and consistencies. Scents of cinnamon, rosemary, and roast meat spiraled into the air. Three cups crowded near each set of plates; a small pitchfork rested on the table. Ever so slightly, she raised an eyebrow at her love with a pleading expression.

A glimmer of response registered in the brown depths of his gaze. He turned toward the Pages. "Why is this table set for a formal dinner? Remove everything but the sauces."

The boys scrambled to fulfill his wish. "No, no, Trevil, leave us each a plate. And the sauce bowls and a cup each." His voice tightened. "Leave the food here, Moril! Now be off. And bring napkins, there are none."

The tent flap closed behind them as they scurried away with the excess plates. When he spoke this time, his voice was serious, eyes bright. "Better?" Dalock reached across the less-crowded table to touch her hand.

Marna nodded, grateful for his shielding her from embarrassment before his Pages. She leaned toward the table slightly, whilst long fingers slid from her palm to her bare wrist. The heat in his fingers was palpable. She stuttered an explanation. "I was uncertain how you eat."

"The food goes in the mouth."

She gave his arm a playful slap as he chuckled.

Long rosy rows of clouds trailing toward the south greeted the morning leg of their journey. Marna rode sideways in a woman's saddle atop a gentle-tempered chestnut-colored gelding. Her Page Favik had earlier related that the saddle came from a farmhouse along the way, hastily purchased yesterday for King's Betrothed. The boy also told her that women in the Strange Kingdom wore breeches when riding, under their skirts. How Marna had laughed at that!

"Did you sleep well?" Dalock asked as they rode alongside one another. His horse regarded her with curiously narrowed lids.

"I'm not used to sleeping alone." Only after she said it did she realize how it might sound. She glanced at the King's two Pages, walking on the other side of him. They chatted amongst themselves.

"You will not be sleeping alone for long." Her betrothed grinned, apparently unconcerned by the boys' presence.

"Ha! Well I hope you snore, because I am used to dozing off to the sounds of many breaths."

"At your sister's?"

"Aye. I used to sleep holding Lena, or whoever was small enough at the time, with my back to the wall so that Malik could not approach me in the night."

"Did he ever?"

"Oh no, he was too timid. Although once, after too much ale, he troubled Werna. Her husband put a stop to that!"

They both enjoyed a fine chuckle, but Marna's was tempered by the knowledge she kept hidden from her betrothed.

Dalock's horse snorted. The King patted her dark mane, braided with a thick crimson thread and hung with twinkling brass decorations in that odd half-circle design, like the washbasin in her tent. "There, Breena, do not be envious."

The mare gazed at King's Betrothed with an unmistakable look of loathing.

"Your horse is quite … expressive."

"Aye, she is forgetting her manners. But you have only yourself to blame, hmm, Breena?" The mare tossed her proud head, whooshing her tail. For a moment Marna feared she might bolt. But she settled into staring ahead indifferently, though she clomped her hooves with excessive vigor. "My dearest, have your Page sleep in your tent, if you think that would help you fall asleep."

"Would that be proper?"

"You are King's Betrothed. You set the rules."

Marna smiled, gazing at her future husband with a slight squint. "I think I will enjoy being joined with you."

Deepening lavender tinged the clouds smudged against the darkening blue sky as the sun made its rest below the western horizon. Dalock's army counted itself twenty miles closer to home than when they arose that morning. Marna had made her way alone to the Healer's area. She stooped to examine the swollen cut on the leg of the injured Soldier she had attended the previous evening, as the man chatted amiably. "I walked a bit on my own today. Before your healing, the pain was too great."

"I'm glad you're feeling better. Your wound is much improved." She smiled, pleased at the diminishment of the angry, swollen scar.

"And I feel a great fool for not recognizing you as King's Betrothed. Please forgive me."

Marna laughed. "All that concerns me is that your wound looks and feels better. Now is someone seeing to your dinner?"

"Aye."

"Then I will be off to my own."

"My Lady?" Favik's voice came from behind her. She turned to face her blond Page. "Your … pa-vil-yon … is ready." His bemused expression and the strange word invited questioning, but instead she thanked The Powers to see his bright expression.

The lad led her to a fancy red tent, much larger than yesterday's. Favik stepped aside, gallantly sweeping a thick tasseled rope away and opening the flap to allow entrance. Thick rugs welcomed her feet. Hanging tapestries covered the walls, their metallic threads glistening in the candlelight.

"Oh my." Marna surveyed the room. On a raised platform, a sizable bed rested, bedecked with pillows of differing shapes and designs—some oval, others round, a few square shaped—but all clad in splendid fabrics, inviting to the eye and to the touch. To the right, a dining table, stouter and longer than the one from the night before, was set for two. A small bedroll and pillow lay next to the door.

Favik approached her elbow. "Do you like it?"

She grinned, placing a light hand on his head. "Yes. Someone has made it very lovely." The lad beamed up at her as she surveyed the elaborate interior. Off to the side, a pair of roomy chairs with a small polished cherrywood table nestled between them. An open scroll lay atop the nearer chair, as though its reader had laid it down in haste. Marna frowned. The soon-to-be Queen picked up the scroll, staring at the incomprehensible gold ink squiggles on the black parchment.

"My Lady?" Favik's voice was timid, and the uncertainty in his tone touched her.

"Yes, child?"

"I have been wondering, how can people look at something quiet like that scroll and then talk, like someone is telling them words? Is the scroll speaking just to them?"

"I think I know what you are asking. It's called reading." She held the open scroll out to her Page. "Do you see these gold lines?" His blond ponytail bobbed as he nodded. "They are spoken words made into a design. If you know the patterns, you can understand what it says."

"Oh." The effort of thought was clearly writ upon his face. He came closer to her, his gray eyes on the scroll. "What does it say?" The lad raised a curious gaze to her.

"I don't know yet." The Hudikslanders studied the parchment. "When I learn how to read, would you like me to teach you?"

Favik brightened. "I would know everything that I can."

King's Betrothed arched an eyebrow. "Then I will teach you as I learn."

"Thank you, my Lady." She replaced the scroll on the chair, the boy's eyes following her actions.

"I think I might know one thing about that scroll," he said.

"Yes?"

"It may be from the reign of the King's father?" Her Page reached to touch the black parchment. "The Guardsmen and other Pages told me that red and white were the First King's colors, but that each Strange King has his own colors too. Everything at their court is made in the colors of the current King, or the First King. And the colors of the last King were black and gold."

"Everything at court? I hope that does not include the food!" They both laughed lightly.

A Guard, cloaked in the current Strange King's red and brown, entered the tent. "My Lady King's Betrothed, Dalock King sends word that he will be delayed at least an hour or two."

"I see. Well, Favik, you must keep me amused." The Guard bowed and left.

The boy looked troubled. "Would you like to play a game, my Lady?" he asked in uncertain tones. Then his demeanor lightened. "Or would you like to be of some use?"

At this, Marna smiled. "Yes, I would like to be of some use. Hmm. I would cook the King's meal for him."

"I know the way to the nearest camp kitchen!"

As they left the tent, the bushy-eyebrowed Guard watched them with an anxious face. "My Lady King's Betrothed?" he called after them. "Might I inquire, to where you are going? If the King asks?"

Favik looked at her hesitantly, then at her subtle nod, he turned to the Guard, speaking on her behalf. "King's Guard Damil, my Lady would tour the camp kitchens. You may send for her there."

"Very well!" The Guard bowed in acknowledgment, a playful spark in his eye.

Favik gave Marna a sheepish grin, but his eyes beamed with pride.

"Well done, lad!" she said in conspiratorial tones, trying not to break into a wide smirk.

The Lord of Eskalind stood, baffled, before his betrothed's pavilion. "She has gone to the kitchens?" he queried her Guard. "Why did she not send her Page for food if she was hungry?" Guard Damil shook his head. Dalock looked at his Second.

"She is used to fending for herself, my Lord. And perhaps she is making some broth."

"Would that she would make her roast chicken." Longing touched the King's voice. "When did she leave?" He cast a mildly baleful gaze at the Guard.

"Not quite two hours ago, my Lord."

Jinil spoke: "Ah, that would be enough time to roast a chicken."

Dalock cut his eyes at his man. "I *may* save some for you."

Jinil chuckled, tracing the scar in his beard with his thumb.

"Come, let us find her." The King eagerly strode toward the nearest cooking section of the camp, inhaling with relish the fond, familiar scent as they approached the kitchen tents.

A long line of chickens turned on a spit, rotated by Marna's Page and another boy. "Ah, thank The Powers!" Under the open-walled tent, his betrothed stood behind two women chopping herbs, monitoring their progress. Two large pots boiled behind them. The enticing scent of broth filled the air. A girl dipped a spoon in the broth and brought it to Marna, who tasted it.

"Put those herbs in now; it is ready. And chop more mint."

Dalock called to his future Queen, "Hullo, Marna!"

The women by her side turned to their Lord with gaping surprise, bowing. The girl hid behind the pots.

"Not now! Hurry, get the herbs in the pot! Quick, quick!" Marna grabbed one of the wooden cutting boards, whisking its contents into the steaming pot. One of the other women repeated her actions.

Marna turned to Dalock with an apprehensive expression. "The timing is important." Her voice betrayed a hint of embarrassment.

"Ah, I know how good your cooking is." He gave her a sly grin and kissed her hand, breathing in the seductive scents of the herbs on her fingers. "Much longer?"

She drew closer to him, murmuring her response. "Not too much longer."

Dalock gazed into the gray depths of her eyes as he took her other hand. Her fingers were invitingly warm, the fresh scent of mint hovering as he brought her hand to his lips. One by one he placed a soft, lingering kiss on each of her knuckles. Her eyes lost their focus as she sighed.

Jinil cleared his throat.

Dalock turned to his man with an overly stern look. "You do want some of that chicken, yes?"

His Second grinned, then echoed his King's laughter.

———

"My Lady King's Betrothed, that was indeed the best roast chicken I have ever tasted." King's Second slurped the clean bones like an eager Page. "Even without sauce."

Dalock beamed an I-told-you-so grin, while Marna could only smile, with a nervous glance at the King. The three of them sat at the dining table in King's Betrothed's pavilion, the candles burning low at the late hour.

Her betrothed interrupted her thoughts. "Tomorrow, Marna, we cross the border. The day after, we will be joined." His brown eyes twinkled at her.

Jinil was speaking to her. "Many Eskalinders, even Ladies from King's Halls, gather at the border to welcome the King's Companies home. I sent a Swift Rider yesterday to ascertain which Ladies are present and can serve as your attendants. These noblewomen will assist you in your preparations and in sewing your gowns."

"Will I keep my Page? I do like him."

"As you desire, my Lady King's Betrothed."

"My dear, I thought you might want some womenfolk to attend you as well." Her future husband reached across the linen tablecloth to gently grasp her hand. "That is why I asked Jinil to inquire about the Ladies who have come from King's Halls."

"How kind." She gently stroked his fingers, giving him a steady, serious gaze. He purred. She considered pinching him to bring him back to the moment at hand, but instead stopped the motion and pressed his skin. He awoke to his surroundings.

"Um, Jinil, my man. Perhaps you have some business elsewhere?"

"Of course, my Lord." King's Second rose. "My Lady King's Betrothed." He bowed to Marna.

"Thank you, Jinil. I look forward to meeting the Ladies."

"You are most welcome." Jinil departed the pavilion.

Dalock edged his chair closer to hers. "How are you adjusting to your new life, my soon-to-be Queen?"

"Well, thank you." The warmth left her hands as she prepared her speech.

She heard someone pulling open the tent's entrance.

"My Lord?" Trevil, one of the King's Pages, entered the pavilion.

"What?" Dalock's tone was gruff, clearly unhappy at the interruption.

The boy stammered. "My Lord, I'm sorry, but an Ambassador's letter has just arrived. From Gergelt."

"Gergelt, truly? Nothing ever happens there."

Marna leaned closer to her beloved. "I suppose it is urgent?"

"Ambassadors' letters always are." Dalock's voice was pinched with annoyance. "Trevil, stop Jinil and have him meet me in my quarters. Deliver the letter there."

The boy left to do his master's bidding.

Dalock kissed her hand. "A few stolen moments." At this recollection of their days together in her sister's home, Marna smiled, hoping her eyes did not reveal her inner struggle.

"Till the morning then." He rose and exited her tent with a sigh. That caused her to giggle. Then she calmed, and pondered when she might speak with him.

"Do you require anything, my Lady?" Favik stood in the tent's doorway.

"No, just sleep. Come in."

The boy entered and gathered the dishes.

"Favik, did you have the chicken I left for you?"

"Yes, my Lady. If I had known how good it was, I would not have offered to share it with the King's Pages." He clacked the plates and bowls into a stack.

She laughed. "Ah, but food makes friends." Favik grinned with a cheerful expression that showed he recognized this ready-phrase from their land. She smiled too, and made to prepare for bed.

"My Lady?"

"Yes, child?" She reached for her hairbrush.

"Something else I have learned that is different from home. The Eskalinders never say 'friend' except as a noble title, or when a noble is talking with another noble."

"How odd." She brushed her hair. "How did you find this out?"

The plates in his arms clanked, and he steadied himself, gazing at them. "I was talking with Moril. He doesn't have parents either." He raised his gray eyes. "I told Moril I hoped we would become friends, and he laughed and said that meant we would both be nobles."

"Oh. Then what do they call friends?"

"Companions."

"I see." She nodded. "Thank you, Favik. Between the two of us, we will learn all that we can about Eskalind, together." He beamed as though she had called him friend.

Around noon the next day, the King's party and his Companies arrived at the Eskalind border. The road sloped gently to a crest crowned with a crumbling, charcoal-colored stone wall no taller than two feet at its highest. Two Guardsmen stood at an opening in the wall, long, tapered spears in their hands, the bronze points glinting in the sunshine. These men wore Dalock's colors, red tunics belted with bronze scabbards, and brown cloaks and boots. Beyond them flew the King's banner atop the solitary visible rooftop of a nearby building. As the road rose south into Eskalind, the dusty beige of the dirt Hudiksland track yielded to a yellow powder that spilled from the path by the Guards' boots.

Marna recalled a merchant in the market at Castleton who wore a clear glass pendant filled with what appeared to be a yellow spice. Inquiring about it, she was told it was part of the Strange Kingdom. "The Strange Kingdom, where The Powers live." She recalled her nephew's words with a slight smile. "And everyone is rich."

The improbably short wall of stacked stones before them stretched into the distant west and east. Sections of it lay under a gnarled, red-vined plant bearing white flowers with crimson centers. She whispered to her husband-to-be, "What is that creeping plant?" Squinting, Marna noted the four ovoid petals that formed each bloom. "I've never seen it before."

"King's Flower. They are the colors of the First King, my ancestor Heedlich. He established the borders, built this wall. The flowers grow only along the border and in the garden at my Halls."

She almost asked if the plant had any healing qualities, but doubted he would know; in their brief acquaintance, Dalock had exhibited little knowledge or interest in herbcraft. "Do the colors have a meaning?"

"Yes, white for the snow that once covered the land and red for his love."

"His love for his kingdom?"

"No, his wife. She was one of The Powers."

"What?"

Dalock grinned.

"Don't tease me," she whispered as their steeds trod the yellowing soil.

"It is truth." His eyes twinkled at her.

"You are descended from The Powers?"

"Aye."

"Dalock, if my people knew that, they would worship you!"

"I would not like that."

Not knowing what to say, Marna looked to the border entrance. The two Guards were only a few horse lengths away now. The clamor of many unseen people burbled.

"You and I will walk across." Dalock pulled on Breena's reins, and Marna halted her mount as well. Over the crest of the hill peeked the tops of many tents and a few elegant, peak-roofed pavilions, all in crimson and a warm brown. Excited shouting ahead and a low murmur behind resounded as Marna and Dalock steadied their horses. They waited till the long line of men behind them came to a halt. No one spoke. Dalock dismounted, helped Marna from her horse, and bid her to wait a moment. The two Guards at the border saluted him as he walked between them. It was an odd gesture, for they each raised their left forearms and open palm in parallel to the ground, than flexed their wrists so that the palm faced the King. Crossing into Eskalind, Dalock bent to the ground, reaching with his left hand to touch the soil with his palm. Straightening, he held his hand aloft, announcing, "I thank The Powers for Their Gifts and Their protection." He turned to her. "And for leading me to my wife."

The gathered people cheered as Dalock beckoned her to come to him. She glanced about, trying to pull her lips into a smile, her heart rising in her chest as though it would escape.

Somehow, she made steady steps to her betrothed. As she passed the Guardsmen, they saluted her as they had the King. For a moment she wondered if she might feel a tingling or awareness as she stepped into the legendary Strange Kingdom. But she neither saw nor felt anything different, and her attention was drawn to Dalock as he offered her his clean right hand.

When she reached him, he called to the crowd. "I invite you all to our Joining Ceremony and feast—here, tomorrow!"

Another wave of glad exclamation swept through the gathered Eskalinders. Marna turned for a last look at her birth land, murmuring, "May The Powers help me be a good wife and Queen to my new people."

All along the Hudiksland side of the wall, the returning Eskalinders drew closer, pressing in deep files against the stacked stones. Jinil raised his voice for silence; the cry echoed amongst the officers on either side of the line. All eyes turned toward the King, as though awaiting a signal.

After the crowds quieted once more, Dalock raised the palm yellowed with soil. "Welcome home!" he shouted. Men charged the wall, some leaping, others scrambling, all roaring with vigor.

Their barbaric zeal startled Marna, and she feared she and Dalock would be trampled. But no one made for the road she stood on: Soldiers, Healers, Pages, everyone clamored directly over the short wall; even horses were being led over the lowest parts of it.

She looked at her betrothed, grinning fondly at his people. "Look, Marna." He pointed to a Soldier rushing toward a woman and two small children, twins perhaps, their little outstretched arms bobbing as they toddled to embrace him. "Thank The Powers this many came home safe."

Marna watched the joyful reunion, then turned to see a trio of men lock their arms together and leap over the short wall in unison.

"Everyone has their own traditions," Dalock commented. "I have not seen that one before."

"But Dalock, why don't they use the road?"

"The road is for me, and King's Son when he comes, and you, as his mother."

King's Betrothed fought a gulp but managed to stutter, "Always?"

The Lord of Eskalind chuckled. "Only for an official homecoming ceremony. They will bring the wagons across the road at the end."

"Does this have something to do with being descended from The Powers?"

"It has everything to do with it."

Not for the first time, Marna felt bewildered, and she wondered what other strange traditions awaited her in her new home. To The Powers, she hoped she would rise to the lofty expectations of her.

A slight breeze pulsed the canvas walls of the spacious traveling tent assigned to Jinil. Charged by Dalock King to select only capable Ladies from the many who had gathered at the border to welcome the King home, King's Second waited to review his future Lady's attendants before they met the Queen-to-be. His Lord expected them to provide companionship to King's Betrothed as she transitioned into her new role as Queen, and to sew dresses for her trousseau. He wondered how much clothing the King truly expected these noblewomen and their servants to fashion before the Joining Ceremony tomorrow. He suspected they would be up all night.

In truth, Jinil was looking forward to seeing familiar feminine faces from the court. Dalock King's eight-year reign had been beset by pleas from the border realms for military aid. Jinil's years as an Ambassador for Eskalind, and earlier as an Ambassador's Apprentice, ensured that he knew not only how to swiftly pack for journeying but also the customs and ways of the outer kingdoms. Yet after twenty years of traveling, he longed for opportunity to settle. Now that the King had found his Queen, perhaps his chance would come. If The Powers willed it.

The quiet chatter of the women and their maidservants filtered through the fabric walls, and he thought he heard an unexpected, and unwelcome, voice in their midst. Jinil strained to listen.

A Page entered, announcing, "The Lady Dara."

He nodded, pleased it was one of the Ladies he expected.

Lady Dara, a tall, slender young woman who served at King's Halls not for any family obligation but for her own amusement, entered his tent. She wore a floor-length ruby-red tunic-style gown with a silky brown cord that crisscrossed in the middle of her slight chest and belted at her trim waist. A thick plait of long dark hair hung over her shoulder, and a vermilion and umber striped cap encircled her head like a cushion. The current fashion at court, it added at least a hand's breadth more height to the Lady's already tall form. Dara's reputation as a skillful and expeditious seamstress had led him to request her presence, as otherwise he would never have selected such a frivolous woman to be amongst the first to serve King's Betrothed.

She bowed, and he nodded in response. "Welcome, my Lady Dara."

He wished he could seal his ears against her squeaky-voiced response: "I thank you, my Lord King's Second."

He smiled pleasantly but cast an anxious glance to the entrance as the second Lady entered the tent. The Page announced her: "The Lady Yadla." She too wore a crimson dress, with a matching waist cord of the same style as Lady Dara's and a similar hat, though hers was flatter and more flattering. She came in cautiously, one hand on the unmistakable swell of her belly.

"Lady Yadla, I did not know you were with child." Jinil reached to help her.

The petite woman beamed at him, her green eyes warm, and shook her head, her light brown braid swaying with the movement. "Well, it has been several months since I saw you last, my Lord King's Second. No no no, do not look concerned! I thank The Powers I chose to come to the border for the homecoming. How fortunate that the decision led to serving our new Queen. Please do not worry about me." She laughed lightly. "No one believes me when I say this, but truly, I have never felt better."

"Then congratulations are in order." He smiled pleasantly, wearing his best Ambassador's face; he had hoped to enjoy her favors, if The Powers willed it. "When will you be joined?"

"After I see that our Lady King's Betrothed is provided with a handsome trousseau." Lady Yadla bowed her head and went to Lady Dara's side.

"The Lady Nalya."

The dreaded blond woman came into the tent. The mere sight of her made him want to call for a bath. He had hoped her three hundred miles away, at court. Or better, at her estate, nearly on the opposite end of Eskalind, six hundred miles distant by the major roads.

"King's Second." She gave him a pained smile, raising her maroon-sleeved arms and dipping in an exaggerated bow that caused her embroidered skirt to swell with air and poof around her slender hips. The rose-colored cord that wrapped tightly around her waist interlaced firmly over her bosom, calling immediate attention to her breasts. Not that they needed the extra enhancement. Her striped hat was larger than the other Ladies' combined. It looked ridiculous, nestled atop her pale locks like an oversized bird nest.

Once again, his years as an Ambassador served him well, and he spoke in measured tones. "I was told Lady Lasta was amongst the Ladies gathered to welcome our Lord. She was who I sent for."

"Alas, whilst she had planned to be here, she did not in the end make the journey from King's Halls. Broke her toe, I believe. And for a woman of her size, *that* is a serious injury." Nalya blinked, a blasé expression on her face.

Once he had found that expression humorous, endearing even. No longer. He silently thanked The Powers that their former affair remained a secret between them. If the King knew he had lain with a widow … well, it had been an honest mistake on Jinil's part. Not that that would matter: she had an entire estate to lose if word reached the King's ears. He spoke in a low tone. "My Lady Nalya, you will return to King's Halls."

"And my term of service will be over long before I arrive. And you will need all three of us to make dresses for the Queen if the Joining Ceremony is tomorrow. Especially since I have twice as many servants as they."

The other two Ladies glared at the blond.

Lady Yadla said, "My maids and I sew swiftly, my Lord King's Second."

Lady Dara piped in, "I made my sister's Joining gown in an afternoon." She bit her lip, as though uncertain what she had just said. "I made it by myself," she said. "It was plain, but beautiful, cut just right for her figure. How lovely she looked that day! And her little daughter is the sweetest. Yadla, I hope you have a daughter. Girls are a delight to dress!"

Jinil was amused by their sniping, and glad to find he was not the only one who considered Nalya disagreeable. "I trust you all have had a pleasant time together here at the border."

Lady Nalya narrowed her eyes.

Lady Dara snorted, then tried to disguise it with a coughing fit.

Only Lady Yadla replied with complete composure. "Your concern is very kind, my Lord King's Second." She turned to Dara and offered the taller woman a clean, pressed handkerchief.

Inwardly, he sighed. He found Yadla attractive, intelligent, and capable, a woman who appealed to both his mind and his senses. Unlike the King, who had made obvious his fondness for a statuesque and voluptuous bride, Jinil preferred dainty, delicate women like Yadla. Though in the end he knew his final lover would be determined by The Powers' Will, not his. An old worry surfaced, that he had found his wife in one of his lovers in the borderlands but had not known it, and that he had unknowingly fathered a babe beyond Eskalind's borders, leaving the child and its mother in what circumstances he did not wish to imagine.

He assumed a regal demeanor before his Queen-to-be's attendants. "My Ladies, you will attend Marna, King's Betrothed, furnishing her with a Joining gown and a trousseau. You will familiarize her to our Joining Ceremony customs whilst respecting the traditions of her land as well." He looked Nalya in the eye, steady and expressionless. "If anyone causes the King embarrassment or discomfort, they will be dismissed and a new term of service instated. In the stables."

She pursed her lips, then raised her eyebrows in a caricature of innocence. "Well, I for one am certain we *all* promise to be on our best behavior, then."

He wondered if that was a threat or a promise.

—————

Jinil reported to his Lady King's Betrothed's pavilion immediately after conferring with the three Eskalinder Ladies. His Lord's Hudikslander sat with her back pressed against a tall carved wooden chair, upholstered in burgundy fabric and decorated with walnut-colored tassels. Across from her rested an empty mahogany-armed folding chair with an embroidered canvas seat, last seen in the King's quarters.

To her side waited her undernourished Page, the lad's bony shoulders and elbows giving his tunic a pointed aspect. But a gleam of intelligence shone in his eyes, and his cheeks were no longer as sallow as the pitiable, scrawny waif who had begged to follow the King's men to Eskalind just a week before. The child clasped his hands behind his back in a classic waiting-to-be-of-service pose, the pair's posture reminding Jinil of amateur actors in a traveling players' show earnestly performing their parts. But King's Second recalled the uncertainty and loneliness he himself had felt thirty years ago as an orphaned peasant boy brought to Farlock King's Halls to begin his education, aspiring to fulfill the potential the Records Keepers believed he possessed. He trusted The Powers were at work again.

The Queen-to-be spoke. "You wished to see me, Jinil?"

"Yes, my Lady King's Betrothed." He bowed, and noted her bare feet on the brown carpet, and his jaw nearly sprang open in shock. *Surely she does not mean to offer herself to me? No, that is not the custom in Hudiksland. Then I must let her know, if I can speak to her alone.* Raising himself calmly, he said, "Your attendants have arrived, and I hoped to speak to you before you meet them."

"Good, I had hoped to speak with you as well."

"Certainly, my Lady King's Betrothed. What did you wish from me?"

"The King speaks highly of you, but I know little about you, and your family."

"Ah, the tale of my family is short, for there is no one but myself." King's Betrothed's gray eyes darted to her Page, then back to Jinil. She nodded for him to continue. "I was what we in Eskalind call a joining babe, which means my parents joined because my mother got with child."

Her Page leaned forward, and King's Betrothed spoke hurriedly: "In Hudiksland, this would not be spoken of at all. Are things different here?"

"Aye, my Lady. We believe that if a woman gets with child, it is a sign from The Powers that the lovers are meant to join." He thought she winced slightly at the word *lovers*. Thus he continued more delicately, "My parents both died not long after I was born, and as I had no other family, I was raised in a King's House. I believe in Hudiksland you would call it an orphanage?"

The boy by her side glanced anxiously at King's Betrothed. She inhaled slowly. "Yes, you are familiar with our customs. I wish to be more familiar with yours. Please, tell me how you came to serve the King."

The blond lad shifted on his feet as Jinil continued, mindful that talk of orphanages might be unsettling to a parentless borderlander child. "At the King's House, there was a Healer, a kind woman who gave me the best of care. She saw some promise in me and recommended me to the local Records Keeper, who in turn brought me to Farlock King's Halls, where I served as a Page until I was selected for Ambassador training. I later served as Eskalind's Ambassador in Kursak, Eastlant, Havadra, and Gergelt. One land at a time, of course." He smiled slightly, hoping this small attempt at humor might loosen their anxiety.

King's Betrothed nodded, gazing at him steadily. He read a touch of nerves in her gray eyes and strove to speak calmly, in a companionable manner. "When I returned from my last Ambassadorship, Farlock King designated me a Counselor. Not long thereafter, he died in battle, and Dalock King kept me in that position, later promoting me to King's Second." He bowed slightly. "I thank The Powers daily for allowing me to serve the Strange Kingdom, and our royal family, these many years."

Jinil hoped the pair heard the truth in his words, for he was indeed grateful for the path The Powers had laid before him, though as a young orphaned lad, he had doubted their benevolence.

"I thank you, King's Second," his future Queen replied. "In Hudiksland, only nobles may serve the royal family. Amongst the common people there are … whispers … that more able advisors might be found from beyond the titled circle."

"My Lady King's Betrothed, Eskalinders believe The Powers see fit to call people from all manner of circumstance to their best purpose. I can attest that my experiences and observations bear this out."

At this she smiled, asking, "Are you hungry, Jinil?"

"Aye, my Lady, thank you."

"Favik, go to the kitchens and fetch us fresh bread and sauces." The boy bowed and raced off eagerly.

"My Page has proven quite reliable and commendable." King's Betrothed pronounced the last word carefully, as though it were new to her. "I thank you for seeing the promise in him." She gestured for him to sit. "Were you going to say more about my Lady attendants?"

Jinil sat across from his Queen-to-be, folding his hands in his lap. "My Lady King's Betrothed, one of the noble Ladies was … unexpected."

"It sounds as though she is not entirely welcome." Her eyes hardened, as though she were preparing to do battle. It struck him how intimidating a woman of her size could be, even seated. There was an inner strength of will, something unbendable, in her. They sat a moment in silence. A horse neighed outside the red fabric walls of the pavilion. "You need not tell me if you do not wish to." Her tone was offhand. "I heard the warning in your voice. I assure you I can handle her."

At this, Dalock's Second smiled. "I have no doubt of that." He continued his speech in a quiet voice. "My Lady King's Betrothed, I would have you know what manner of Lady she is, and also that her behavior is extremely unusual in Eskalind." His future Queen displayed not the least hint of curiosity that he could detect, but indeed an expression worthy of an Ambassador to Havadra. "The report I received whilst we were still in Hudiksland told of four Ladies at the border. When I sent my request for three to attend you, I omitted Lady Nalya, whom I found unacceptable. But in truth, there are only three Ladies here at the border with us. Given the press of time and the shortage of seamstresses, I am afraid Lady Nalya's skills, and certainly those of her entourage of servants, are needed, though I wish it were otherwise."

"I see." His Lord's future wife tilted her head slightly. "Is she joined?"

"Lady Nalya is Acta Sua, or head, of her noble house. In truth, she is the last of her house, a widow without any family. She has no children; her husband died in the same battle as the King's father." He lowered his gaze for a moment. Now twice in the same conversation he had made mention of that lamentable day.

"That was eight years ago, I am told?"

"That is true."

"In Hudiksland, a widowed noblewoman is expected to re-join, even if she is elderly. To build family alliances and such."

"Our ways are different, my Lady King's Betrothed." Aware that he was educating her in the customs of his land, Jinil unfolded his fingers and spoke in the gentle, soothing tone he usually reserved for breaking ill news to his King. "We do not believe in re-joining, or taking lovers once a spouse has died."

This time he was certain she winced at the word *lovers*, but she merely said, "I see." There was a minor squint about her eyes, a slight blush on her round cheeks. "That must be difficult for some. Especially the young."

His voice was fervent when he said, "My Lady, in Eskalind we believe it is how The Powers mean things to be, that there is one specific person meant for each of us." Here he did not mention that he himself was nearly forty and had not found his wife. Perhaps The Powers were punishing him.

As if They prodded him onward, he poured out his story: "Unfortunately, Lady Nalya is the type of woman who willfully puts others in dangerously compromising positions. She took me for a lover before I discovered she was a widow. It poisons my heart to think on it." He lowered his eyes, whispering, "She was meant for another, had joined with another, then shared her bed afterward with me. It is unforgivable."

"Hmm."

He raised his brow to find her expression neutral, but a flash of something in her eyes. "Your pardon, my Lady King's Betrothed."

"No need, Jinil King's Second. I can see plain that this is painful for you to relate. I thank you for your trust and confidence. I know that some things occur in one's life that one is not entirely accountable for; circumstances are often against us." The Queen-to-be's expression was sad, distant even, as she gazed past him at the tent's entrance.

"It is true, my Lady King's Betrothed."

"I hope the tutor our Lord King says you are arranging for me will thoroughly inform me of all your customs. There is much for me to learn, and I would be a worthy wife to my husband."

He felt a mixture of chastisement and admiration at her forthrightness. "Please consider me your servant in these matters as well."

King's Betrothed nodded. "I thank you." Her movements and the modulation of her voice reminded him of how Dalock King said the same phrase, but there was another element at work. He was not certain what it was, but he dipped his head solemnly.

When his Lord's beloved spoke next, her tone had lightened to one of camaraderie. "Now, Jinil, I must say I appreciate your warning, and explanations. Tell me, are there any other customs a woman of Hudiksland should be aware of as she makes her way in the Strange Kingdom?"

King's Second felt as though The Powers smiled on him by granting him such an easy opportunity to mention her bare feet. He shifted slightly in the folding chair. "By your leave, there is one item the tutors may find too delicate to tell you." He glanced at her toes. She raised an eyebrow. "My Lady, I am well aware it is not the custom in your homeland, but in Eskalind, when a woman bares her feet to a man, it is a sign she would take him as…" Normally he would have said "lover," but in deference to her clear discomfort with the term, he said instead, "As her intimate companion."

"Oh." She swallowed the sound as she made it and looked away. Her freckled cheeks flushed deeply. "Then I will certainly reserve my feet for the King." Her toes hastily retreated under her skirt.

"Of course, my Lady King's Betrothed. I thank The Powers that Dalock King has found his Queen. His mother was much loved and is much missed."

"I thank you." She smiled, but still a touch of anxiety clouded her manner.

Her Page entered the tent, bearing a tray with a knife, small loaves of bread, and sauces. Another boy followed carrying a portable table, which he set between them. He left as King's Betrothed's Page placed the food tray on the table.

"Bring my shoes, Favik. Lord Jinil, I thank you for your counsel." She sawed into a loaf for her guest, and Jinil pondered how the gesture of slicing bread for a guest was one of informal hospitality and fond comradeship amongst the nobles of the Strange Kingdom. A class which he, though King's Second, was not truly a member of. But he thought it best to refrain from any more lessons in customs at the moment.

"I was hoping to speak with Dalock in private tonight. Do you think that can be arranged?"

"I will see to it, my Lady." He reached for the nut-studded slice she offered, a hint of cinnamon hanging in the air.

"I thank you." Her Page presented her with a pair of worn, slipper-like shoes. King's Betrothed ringed her finger around the opening to ease each onto her foot.

Jinil directed his attention to the contents of the bowls and sniffed pointedly. "Ah!" The nearest one, a thick, fresh, green-looking concoction, carried a slight scent of mint, with a trace of the chicken-roasting herbs. He glanced back at his Lord's Lady to see her pleased face at his enthusiasm.

"Now, my Lord King's Second, if you would try these sauces and tell me which you like best."

He grinned, hoping she had a hand in making them.

Chapter Eighteen—Three Ladies of Eskalind

Marna paced alone in her tent, waiting for the introduction of her attendants. The conversation with Jinil had unsettled her. At first, she had been shocked by his admission, in front of Favik, that his parents had joined because his mother got with child. Then all the talk of lovers made her think he was flirting. She wondered why Eskalinders talked of such private matters openly, though perhaps King's Second had only meant to be forthright with her in private quarters. King's Betrothed knit her hands, aware of the slight slickness of nervous sweat on her palms. She thought she heard female voices nearby, perhaps the noble Ladies approaching. The edge of her mouth tugged downward as she wondered how many of their families were plotting for Dalock's throne.

Favik interrupted her musings as he scrambled into the tent. He stood tall by the flap, announcing in as solemn a manner as his young voice could manage, "Your attendants, my Lady."

She unknotted her fingers and smoothed her plain skirt.

The younger of Dalock's Pages, Moril, poked his head through the fabric and whispered to her Page. Favik replied in a sharp, annoyed voice, "No, I am able!"

"All right!" Moril disappeared, and her Page resumed his dignified stance.

One by one, three women entered her tent, their eyes lowered to the carpet. They wore red gowns of fine, smoothly woven material, with shimmering cords at the waist and crossed across the chest, and odd hats. Very odd, floppy hats, with striped patterns in Dalock's colors.

Marna studied them in this brief moment of stillness. One was with child, thus not Lady Nalya. The tall, dark-haired woman's shoulders bowed forward meekly; thus Marna doubted she was Nalya either. That left the elegantly thin blond, who cleared her throat in an obvious attempt to gain attention. King's Betrothed smiled, waited a long moment, then spoke. "Welcome, my Ladies."

They raised their eyes and looked at her. The flaxen-locked Lady gasped; the others wore pleasant expressions, though the tallest one's eyes enlarged slightly. Instantly provoked, Marna challenged the light-haired woman. "Is something amiss?"

The blond eyed the future Queen's form. "We may not have enough cloth."

King's Betrothed summoned her most superior tone. "You must be Lady Nalya." She enjoyed the tight, sneering sound at the end of the woman's name.

With a tone of equal superiority, the blond replied, "I am."

Favik piped out each Lady's name. "The Lady Yadla of the House of Wenil, Farlich King's Friend." The woman with child smiled and lowered her gaze.

"The Lady Dara of the House of Naymil, Merlich King's Friend." The tall woman opened her mouth as if to speak, and a squeak escaped. She placed a hand over her mouth and hastily bowed.

"The Lady Nalya, Acta Sua of the House of . . . , um . . ."

Moril's voice whispered through the fabric walls, "Adril!"

Favik continued smoothly, as though he had memorized the title since he learned to speak. "Of the House of Adril, Narlock King's Friend." The Ladies bowed in unison, though Nalya bent less than the others, and she did not have the excuse of being with child. She narrowed her eyes at the lad, who had the hint of a grin at the corners of his lips.

Everything about Nalya reminded Marna of the haughty court Ladies in Castleton, who sent their servants into shops before them to turn out the townsfolk so they could peruse the goods without fear of dirty peasants stepping on their silk shoes.

Lady Yadla spoke. "My Lady King's Betrothed, we are most honored to make your acquaintance, and we thank The Powers for this opportunity to serve you. But let me ask your pardon." She bowed, an abbreviated gesture given her condition, and raised her kind green eyes to King's Betrothed. "Our time to prepare is short, and we must decide upon your trousseau and Joining gown." She rested her hands over the slight bulge of her belly.

Lady Dara added, "As soon as we received word of the King's betrothal, we sewed a sleeping robe for you. And we began some skirts. Will you need riding pants? I know they are not the custom in Hudiksland, and did I mention the sleeping robe we made?" She tilted her head at the end of each utterance, and her dark braid rose and fell each time she did this, making a sound like a whisk beating frothy egg whites. "Oh, and fortunately we do have much cloth. I had it sent from my estate, which is nearby. Perhaps you will come visit with the King? And I have some sample designs for your gowns. And of course, you may use our gowns and hats as models too. But maybe you have new ideas for us? I love your bodice's style, with the scooped neckline!" That prospect seemed to excite her.

"I thank you. A bodice would be nice. As time is short, no hats for the ceremony. Let us begin," Marna commanded, hoping she sounded imperious to the snippy blond Lady, and that they would not press her to wear silly headgear.

The next hours passed in a blur of bolts of soft, finely woven cloth, enough fabric to uniform an army, unrolling before the Queen-to-be. Her new attendants showered her with drawings of dresses in current fashion, outlined in dark ink and colored inside with reds, browns, and occasionally white.

"My Lady King's Betrothed, will you carry Lorarent or Persica for the ceremony?" Dara asked.

Marna puzzled a moment, unfamiliar with the terms and embarrassed about her ignorance. "What is the Eskalind tradition?"

"Well, that depends. Are you with child?"

Marna started at the question. She bit back her initial response with a short, "No." She had hoped to sound calm and queenly.

Dara smiled blankly. "Oh, then Persica would be customary, my Lady?"

Yadla interjected in a tired tone, "Yes, Dara, Persica is the tradition."

Lady Dara giggled. "Then it will be Persica for our Lady King's Betrothed and Lorarent for you, Yadla!"

The future Queen pondered what to make of Dara's question and response whilst the Ladies wrapped measuring ribbons around her hips and bosom, scratching the results onto tan-colored writing sheets and chattering back and forth.

Yadla regarded the marks. "Are you certain these numbers are right, Lady Nalya?"

"I did measure her twice."

The petite woman shook her head. "Dara, please measure her waist for me."

Nalya sniffed. "I told you I already did it twice."

The taller woman cinched the ribbon around Marna's middle and squeaked, "Thirty-eight dots."

"Lady Nalya, would you have our Lady King's Betrothed faint from a too-tight gown on her Joining Day?" Yadla snatched the burgundy-feathered quill and angrily scratched out the wrong number. "Recheck them all, Dara."

"Hips fifty-three dots, bosom is … forty-nine."

"That sounds more like it."

Marna watched their interactions with a mixture of curiosity and amusement as Yadla rose and held yet another bolt of crimson cloth next to Marna's face. She shook her head, retrieving another, this one shaded a warm red. "Your pardon, my Lady King's Betrothed, but would you consider that this is not a befitting color for you?"

Nalya interrupted. "I favor it. It matches her hair."

The expectant mother continued speaking to Marna. "My Lady King's Betrothed, your hair has lovely red highlights, yet these colors do not bring them out." Yadla turned to Marna and lowered her eyes. "Your pardon, but would you consider brown, as a more suitable shade near your face?"

The King's soon-to-be wife nodded as Nalya chirped, "But we do not have enough rich brown cloth, and the bodice and blouse of her gown must be very fine fabric for all to see." The Acta Sua of the House of Adril sat with a flourish, fanning her scarlet skirt wide around her legs, prominently displaying the floral patterns stitched in the hem. "Pity we have no time to embroider something pretty."

Dara rolled her eyes, whilst Yadla retorted, "Lady Nalya, I am certain there is brown cloth."

"Where? I do not see it."

"That is because you are sitting on it!"

Marna suppressed a laugh. Nalya tucked a dainty foot under her skirt, heaving a sigh, her bountiful bosom straining the cords criss-crossing her chest. Perhaps her figure had attracted Jinil to her. The Hudikslander smirked, for a moment wishing Nalya gone so Yadla, Dara, and she could speak freely and learn more about one another in a companionable setting.

King's Betrothed knit her fingers, her thoughts turning darker, and hoped she would be able to at last speak to her husband-to-be this night.

Chapter Nineteen—A Secret Revealed

Jinil answered his Lord's call to meet at the King's pavilion. Dalock King sat at a small table, in one of only two chairs in the room. A surprisingly unornamented bed rested off to one side. Dalock's Second turned his head to pointedly survey the room, and the Lord of Eskalind said, "I sent everything else to Marna's quarters."

"A little bit more everyday, I see."

The King gestured for his Second to sit. Jinil's elbow grazed one of the small bronze chalices on the table, and he reached to steady it, thankful he had not knocked over the decanter.

"Yes, my Second. My well-intentioned endeavor must end if I am to have any furniture left."

"Perhaps a more equitable distribution after the Joining Ceremony tomorrow."

"Ah, all into one pavilion." Dalock King spoke with relish. "Soon, we will be back in our own quarters, in our own Halls." He glanced at his small cot. "I miss my big bed." His grin widened.

"Soon, my Lord." Jinil could not help but chuckle, grateful for his King's playful mood of late.

His Lord smiled, his eyes losing a bit of focus, as if he were engaged in a fond daydream. "Soon, yes, thank The Powers." He pulled away from the table. "I want everything to be perfect for my Marna."

"The arrangements are well made and in capable hands, my Lord."

"Good. Good." Dalock King quirked one side of his lopsided mouth, an expression of silent, anxious consideration. Jinil realized his Lord must be nervous on this, the night before his Joining.

"All will be well, my King."

The younger man turned his brown gaze to his Second, gave an unconvincing nod, then looked away. "I have been meaning to speak to her about our Joining Night. I do not know her status." He stood to pace the bare canvas floor, devoid of its usual resplendent carpets.

King's Second cleared his throat. "Ah yes. I recall our earlier discussion about where to quarter King's Betrothed, as her land is one of the many kingdoms where it is expected that the husband has had prior experience, but the wife has not, and relations do not take place until after the Joining Ceremony."

His Lord snorted. "I never understood that. Where do they suppose the men get their experience with women?" He shook his head, as though talking to himself. "So foolish. I am glad our ways are different." The husband-to-be continued pacing. "Well, I will have to ask her and go from there, let her know our custom is different, that it is no matter if she has lain with a man before." He halted his back-and-forth amble of the pavilion and stood straight, giving the appearance of a man who has made a firm decision and is ready to forge ahead. Looking at his Second, he asked, "Is our business finished?"

"*Our* business, yes." Jinil could not resist a slight grin.

"Then I am off to talk with her." The King returned to the little table and lifted the bronze decanter. "Um, spot of wine first, Jinil?"

———— • ————

Dalock made his way to Marna's pavilion, the stout torches along the path casting swaying light and shadows around him. "Jinil, why did you let me drink so much?" Then he remembered he had left Jinil behind. His Pages trailed him.

"My Lord." The Guard at her door bowed as he recognized his King.

"Hullo, Damil! Announce me."

The Guard tapped the fabric wall, and Marna's Page poked his blond head through the flap. "Announce the King, lad."

Dalock waited a moment, then was ushered in. The Page departed the tent.

"Hullo, Marna." He realized he was trying not to slur.

"Are you all right?" His bride-to-be furrowed her brow. She wore a soft-looking caramel-colored sleeping robe with a burgundy sash. In the candlelight, the highlights on her long, loose hair flickered vermilion, seeming to dance around her head.

The King blinked. "I had a bit of wine with Jinil."

His beloved smiled, coming closer to him. "It smells good." She closed her eyes.

"You smell good too." Dalock reached for her. His betrothed's eyes opened as he drew her close, the many candles reflecting in those gray sparks like a portal to another world. He cooed with pleasure.

She traced his ear with deliciously warm fingers, asking, "Is it really only a few more hours until we'll be joined?"

Perhaps breaking with the traditions of her country and spending the night with her husband-to-be might be within her consideration, after all. Then he remembered what he had come to ask and inwardly winced. "Marna, there is something I need to ask you."

She pulled away, her expression serious. "Yes, and there is something I must tell you if you are to be my husband." His intended folded her hands before her waist.

The King smiled. "I know in your land there are certain restrictions on a woman's behavior, prior to her joining, but that is not the custom in my land."

She looked astonished. "What do you mean?"

"Well, it may surprise you to learn that in my land, we accept physical love between unjoined couples as a natural part of life."

"You … think it is all right?"

"Yes!" Enthusiasm punctuated his voice, and he watched her consternation with wry amusement. "Your eyes are most pretty when you are confused." Marna shook her head, and wanting to allay his bride-to-be's bewilderment, he charged ahead. "Actually, I am glad you have prior experience." He saw her lips tense as though she would speak. Given her suddenly pale and drawn countenance, he felt like a gigantic oaf, but he aimed to keep his tone merry and jovial. "I am sorry, Marna, maybe I assumed, but I thought you were trying to tell me that you had lain with a man before."

"I have. Once." She looked away, the muscles in her neck standing out. "But it was not by my choice."

Dalock's light mood evaporated. "What?" His mind surged with this unexpected information; he could barely sputter out words. "Someone? Was it Malik?"

"No, I could have … gotten away from him, I think." Her voice was bitter and low. "It was King Hudik's son."

Dalock felt as though he had galloped into a stone wall. "Prince Humik? I thought him a good man!"

"No, not him." Her brow furrowed, her face flushing pink. "His younger brother, Prince Huprik."

In his shock, he blurted, "How?"

She looked at him, gray eyes glassy with held-back tears. "I know, he looks like a weakling compared to me, but he …" She lowered her chin, and he could see only the crown of her head. "He had a knife." She paused. "And his rank."

Dalock felt a searing rage expanding in his chest. The thought of that vile man taking his Marna, with a weapon, using his status to do so— He bit his teeth.

"Oh Dalock, it was three years ago, when I was still living in Castleton. Father and his apprentices were at market; I was home alone." Marna spoke in a rush, as one finally unburdening herself of a tale long restrained. "The … prince came to examine a sword Father was making for him."

Suddenly he recalled Narnik telling him that the reason she had come to live with her sister's family was because she had insulted their king's son. He knew he could bear to hear no more. "Stop, Marna, please." She caught her breath, reached for his hand, and squeezed, her fingers cold and damp.

"You will not want me now." Her voice was wan, stretched.

"No." He pulled her close to him. She sank in his arms, her head lowered against his chest.

"Shh, love." He pictured Prince Huprik's smug face at King Hudik's feast and felt his heart freeze as a thousand ways to torture the man flooded his mind.

———

Favik watched the King leave his Lady's tent, the King's brown cloak swirling about him in his haste. His manner was different from what the boy had seen before; it reminded him of the way his father would hold himself after speaking with the landlords. Favik shook Moril awake, then waved goodbye to him and Trevil as the two other Pages sleepily stumbled after their master. Then he brushed his hair from his eyes and scrambled to his Lady's tent.

She sat on her bed, staring at the fancy embroidered wall coverings. "My Lady?"

She did not respond. "My Lady?" he asked again, louder as he approached.

She turned to him, her expression distant, as though she did not really see him. Her eyelids were puffy. The boy puzzled over this, but hoped it did not show on his face. "Are you all right?" He was uncertain if it was proper to ask, but he wanted to help.

Shaking her head, she buried her head in her hands.

"My Lady!" He knelt by her feet. "What happened? What can I do?"

She said nothing, and not being able to see her face, he could not tell if he was making things better or worse. "Did the King hurt you?" A protective anger gripped him.

His Lady's voice was strained. "No. No, Dalock is a good man. A wonderful man."

"Good! If he had been mean to you, I would not want to serve him." He spoke boldly; the idea of anyone mistreating his Lady burned his heart.

She raised her kind face to his, and he was relieved to see a fond light in her eyes, as though she had read his mind, knew his heart.

"Thank you, Favik." Despite tears still clinging to her round cheeks, his Lady smiled and hugged him firmly. Her touch softened his growing fury. He closed his eyes. For a moment, he forgot that he was in her warm arms and instead thought himself back home, in his bed, waking in the sheltering embrace of his father after a nightmare. He had wondered if he would ever feel that comfort again.

The boy croaked a whisper, finally allowing his long-held anguish to overflow. He did not mean to let the words slip from his mouth: "I wish you were my mother."

"Oh, dear lad!" She held him a while longer, kissed his head, then released him. She wiped both their tears with careful fingers.

"I will follow you, my Lady," Favik pledged, his voice soft and solemn. "To whatever end."

She bestowed upon him a welcoming smile that lit her entire face, so warm and different from the false grins of the nobles who visited their farm on collection day.

"Thank you, Favik. I'm better now." She kissed his forehead, and he felt as though a weight had lifted, as though at long last The Powers had granted a respite from the hardships besetting his short life.

"We should get some sleep."

"Yes, my Lady." He rose and went to his blankets by the tent's door with a sense of purpose in his heart. Nestling into his pillow and covers, he watched his Lady blow out the candles. *I will be the best Page ever for her. And someday I will be her Knight.*

He drew the blanket tight around his crossed arms; it almost mim-icked the warmth and reassurance he had felt moments ago.

The late hour found Jinil at a small desk in his tent, a cluster of nearly spent candles at his elbows, reading the scroll before him. Sleep never came easily, and he thanked The Powers he did not need much of it. While the King's business filled more hours than a day held for most men, Jinil saw to his assignments, then read for pleasure whilst others warmed their pillows.

Many years ago, during his Ambassador training, the other diplomatic Apprentices nicknamed him "Candle Killer," a jest warranted by his long nights in the King's Library. Indeed, he had memorized nearly as many of the tales of the Strange Kings as the knowledgeable but unorganized King's Librarian Beril, a man who clearly spent more time reading the volumes in his care than filing them. Wading through the accumulations of loose parchments, papyrus sheets, scrolls, and The Powers knew what else jumbled on teetering shelves, in voluminous baskets, and even on the floor—in the King's Library, which should have been the glory of a realm free of civil strife and power struggles!—just thinking about it heated his face with aggravation. It was no wonder that as Chief Counselor, Jinil had since established a small, well-organized collection of best-loved volumes in his own pristine quarters. A small step before the great plunge, for once the King was joined and distracted with his wife, Jinil planned to see the Librarian earning his keep by putting his domain in order. If The Powers willed it, of course.

A rustle and a swift exhalation brought his attention to the younger of the King's Pages, entering his tent.

"My Lord Dalock King summons you to his quarters straightaway," Moril panted. His swollen eyelids bespoke a sudden awakening to perform this urgent errand. "The King seems … upset?"

"Then let us be off." After dousing the candles, the pair hurried to the Strange King's pavilion while the dark-haired boy answered Jinil's inquiry as to what was amiss.

"I do not know what happened, my Lord King's Counselor! I was talking with Trevil and the new Page when I fell asleep outside King's Betrothed's tent, then I was shaken awake. I ran after the King, but he shouted to fetch you." The lad gulped. "He was very angry. I wondered if I had done something wrong. I did not mean to fall asleep!"

King's Second pondered what this might mean; he doubted it had anything to do with Moril's nap. He withheld a sigh of disappointment and wondered what plan of The Powers now unfolded.

They arrived at their master's pavilion, and Moril held open the flap for Jinil to enter. He found his Lord standing with his back to the entrance, uncharacteristically; his broad shoulders were held high as though he were about to pounce unseen on prey. The young ruler wheeled to face his man, burly arms crossed over his large chest.

Reading restrained fury in his King's narrowed eyes, Jinil bowed cautiously. "You sent for me, my Lord?"

"I spoke with her." Dalock King's voice was honed but controlled. "She was taken."

Despite all his training, Jinil started at the news that King's Betrothed had been raped. His first thought was to wonder when this horrible event had occurred, his next, how his sovereign would punish the attacker. Given the tension in the air, he ventured only an apology, in a low and sympathetic voice. "I am extremely sorry to hear that, my Lord."

Neither man spoke for a ponderous moment, till the younger man broke the silence with a roar. "Go on, ask me who did it!"

The Chief Counselor considered how best to defuse the King's rage, but before he could reply, the enraged sovereign spat, "It was Prince Huprik! And he used his rank—" His voice closed around the words as though someone had him by the throat.

King's Second watched with compassionate patience as his ruler unburdened himself, yet inwardly, Jinil wondered how this might change his Lord's plans.

"Do not doubt that the man will pay, though the wages be three years late." Dalock King spoke in a cold tone, full charged with malice. He paced toward his confidant. "My first thought was to call for my horse and ride to King Hudik's quarry and challenge that loathsome, supposed son of a king." Jinil nodded solemnly. "Before my parents' deaths, I would have. By The Powers, I would have."

Jinil waited, surprised again by this revelation. It was the first time the young King had ever spoken of that day, yet, as often happens, one tragedy recalled another.

"Chief Counselor, we will devise a plan, you and I. Involving this … abominable royal. A plan that his brother, the Crown Prince, may well find to his satisfaction."

It was as though The Powers struck Jinil over the head. In a flash, he saw his King's intent: use the rivalry between the two princes of Hudiksland to eliminate King's Betrothed's assailant. While he, of all men, appreciated the King's warmheartedness and comradeship in times of truce, he knew that once provoked, Dalock Strange King could be unleashed into a berserk apparatus of war, lethal to all who stood in his path, and untouchable by anything short of the Will of The Powers. Thus, the Chief Counselor found it difficult to mask his relief that his headstrong King would not slay the Hudiksland king's son in a public challenge of arms that would undoubtedly generate tremendous discord between the allied nations, at least as long as Hudik King sat on his silvered seat.

Jinil also wondered what formidable followers might support Prince

Huprik over his elder brother. Angling his head in a humble manner, he asked, "My Lord, you would solicit Crown Prince Humik in this endeavor?"

Dalock King tucked his crooked chin closer to his crimson-tunicked chest, a look of sharp cunning upon his asymmetrical features. "Humik suspects his vile brother of plotting for the throne. From what I saw, the worm has an unnatural interest in their sister as well. Scum." He gave a half cough, half snort of a sound. "The Crown Prince will, I suspect, be helpful in resolving this to our satisfaction."

"If Humik's rival to the throne were eliminated, it would prevent a war of succession when Hudik King dies." Jinil nodded, breathing slowly. "Have you settled on a plan, my Lord?"

"Do not conceal your pleasure in my restraint."

At this Jinil gave a slight tilt of his head in acknowledgment of his Lord's perceptiveness. "My King is a man of mature thought."

The younger man met his steady gaze, then the corner of his mouth twisted into the beginning of a grin, but his eyes remained steeled and intense.

"Let us have this matter settled swiftly and efficiently—but by sly and secret means, as the wretch full deserves. We have a Joining Ceremony to prepare for tomorrow."

Favik poked his freshly scrubbed blond head into Marna's pavilion as her Ladies arrayed her scarlet-skirted Joining Gown about her nut-brown velvet slippers. The excited lad bounded into the spacious room, a newly sewn chestnut linen tunic draping long and straight above his cherry-colored breeches. "He's coming! The King is coming!"

"Well, delay him, you silly boy; we are not ready yet!" Lady Nalya pulled at the front of her Lady's hem, her blond head bobbing dangerously close to Marna's knees.

The soon-to-be Queen regarded her white-clad attendant with unkind thoughts, considering that if the annoying woman made one more ill-favored remark against Favik, then she and Malik would have something in common—knowing the displeasure of Marna's knee. But the thought of her former suitor brought a touch of sadness to her heart. It recalled her family's absence on this, her Joining Day to a man whose love and concern still startled her.

Her throat tightened with stoppered tears as she pictured her youngest niece Lena's toothy grin when Dalock played hide and seek with the girl, who had squealed with pure joy at his games and silly faces.

A reassuring pat on the lacings at the back of her fitted chestnut-silk bodice returned her to the present moment as Yadla's calm voice said,

"Nonsense, Nalya. Our Lady King's Betrothed is dressed, and she looks beautiful."

"More beautiful than anything!" Favik grinned as though he had been offered a plate of Marna's roast chicken. He bowed, then dashed back outside.

Lady Dara stepped before the bride as Nalya skulked away with her arms crossed over the snow-colored fabric of her gown. Marna hoped she would spill a very dark sauce upon it. Dara beamed and tilted her head as she said, in her up-and-down tones, "Oh, how stunning your look, my Lady King's Betrothed! And the sleeves came out perfectly even. This brown is a perfect color on you. Quite perfect! And lovely! I think you are beginning a new fashion!" Marna managed a slight smile.

Favik interrupted her thoughts as he whispered from the doorway, "The King is almost here!"

Outside the tent, the excited buzz of many voices grew as men and women hailed their Lord with glad shouts and whoops. Marna fought the urge to wring her hands. "How many people are out there?"

"Lots!" called her Page.

Yadla stepped closer, handing her a long sprig of beribboned flowers of a pale yellow hue, while Dara tucked a few strands of Marna's long, loose locks behind her ears. King's Betrothed glanced at the small table nearby, where little crumbs of bread and empty sauce bowls remained from the morning meal. "Is there time to call for more bread?"

Yadla shook her head, and she and Dara moved to their prearranged places on either side of the bride and reached for her crimson train. "Shall we, my Lady King's Betrothed?" Yadla's voice was patient and kind.

Marna nodded at Favik to pull aside the fabric door. A bright shaft of sunshine illuminated the opening, as though a thousand candles shone onto her path. She blinked for a moment, then stepped into the warm light, finding herself strangely comforted and calmed. Outside, Dalock waited for her with a grin that spanned the distance between his ample ears. He held out his slender, strong fingers, and she stepped forward and took his hand as cheers and rowdy shouting swelled the air around them. Marna blushed from all the attention but held her head high.

Dalock's firm grip steadied her nerves, and they walked side by side, past the clamoring, smiling people lining the dusty yellow path. Unlike the rather uniform appearance of pale Hudikslanders, there seemed to be no clear physical trait that characterized the crowd as Eskalinders, save perhaps that the majority had dark hair. Everyone was clad in at least one garment in the King's colors, and nearly all were waving small strips of red, white, or brown cloth on little sticks. Behind her, Marna's Ladies carried the long length of her skirt, with Yadla and Dara holding the sides and waving to the gathered people, and Nalya, as previously arranged, at the rear.

The Joining party progressed through the spirited camp toward a clearing upon a slight green hill, where Jinil waited, attired in a long two-colored linen tunic, half red and half brown. He grinned at the pair, but another surge of anxiety plagued Marna's chest as she realized the moment was at hand and all eyes were upon them.

Her husband-to-be whispered in her ear as they approached his Second, "I wonder what Jinil is so glad about?"

She turned to him, wondering what he meant, till she saw his jesting grin. The bride decided to play along. "He looks almost as happy as when he tried my roast chicken."

Dalock chuckled softly and kissed her hand, a fond and loving look in the brown depths of his gaze. "My Marna."

The pair stopped before Jinil, who raised his hands for the gathered assembly to quiet—which did not happen. He cleared his throat and gestured more broadly. Still the crowd buzzed animatedly. Marna flicked a petal of her Persica blooms with her thumb. "Were the ale tents set up too early?"

Dalock turned, facing the crowd, and his voice boomed forth with command tinged with mirth. "Good people! Would you delay your Lord his wife?"

Tittering laughter and scattered applause broke across the assembly. Gleeful shouts of "To the King and King's Betrothed!" and "Hail!" rang out.

Dalock faced Jinil. "Begin, my man." He winked at his love. "*We* can hear you."

His Second proclaimed, "We live this day in Legend unwritten and unfolding, a tale we will tell in the days to come to those absent today, the tale of the moment of the joining of our one hundred and twenty-fourth Lord of Eskalind, Dalock King, Son of Farlock King and Treya Queen of Eskalind, to Marna, Wernik's daughter, of Hudiksland."

At the mention of her father's name, Marna nearly jumped. The bride's cheeks flushed with embarrassment, yet no one else seemed to react to her very common status. An anxious glance at Dalock revealed his manner had not changed, though he must have sensed her anxiety, for he squeezed her hand reassuringly.

Jinil continued, and the crowd quieted a bit. "I call each of you to witness, in this, the two thousand eight hundred and eighty-sixth year since the founding of Eskalind." Someone blew a faltering horn, which was answered with annoyed shushing.

Dalock's Second faced the couple in turn. "My Lord, my Lady. By the Will of The Powers, I declare you joined!"

"That's all?" Marna said—just as her husband encircled her in his arms and kissed her passionately, nearly whisking her from her feet as the crowd went wild, roaring and whistling, stomping their feet in a frenzied display of joy that shook the earth. Dalock released her, and she could not help but laugh with unfettered delight till he bent down to, of all things, lift her straight in the air!

She looked down at him in amazement as he clutched her legs through her skirts with one arm, her bottom resting against his wide shoulder as he raised his free hand in the air and shouted, "Marna Queen! Marna Queen!"

Men and women exuberantly repeated his call, and as their Lord paraded his wife through the crowd, small girls whirled around them, bepetaling the air with King's Flowers, the white blooms swirling about the rejoicing royals and seeming to rise and float of their own accord.

It was many, many hours later and well into evening when Marna at last beheld the interior of her candlelit tent again as her Ladies gathered to prepare their Queen for her Joining Night.

Yadla led her to a soft, cushioned chair, though it could have been the hardest seat in the Kingdom and the exhausted bride would not have minded. How her feet ached from dancing and parading about. She massaged her wrist. "I think I met every last citizen of my new home, and had my hand kissed by every male old enough to walk!"

Yadla chuckled lightly and brushed the Queen's long tresses with a bronze-handled comb. "Ah yes, I am told Eskalind is unusual in how the nobles and commoners intermingle. Here, no one thinks it amiss that my betrothed is a Sergeant who was raised in a King's House."

"Oh Yadla, you should be the one sitting, you must be very tired."

"No no, I am well, my Lady. It was a beautiful ceremony. Such a happy day."

"And a delicious feast too!" Dara hiccuped. The three women laughed lightly, carefree and joyous, till the new Queen of Eskalind realized how relaxed and comfortable they all were. Someone was missing. She looked at the pair of Ladies. "Where is Lady Nalya? I have not seen her in hours."

Yadla placed the comb onto a small table. "Her term of service ended at sunset, my Lady."

"Ah." Marna stood up. Yadla gave her a knowing look, her green eyes mirthful, as Dara unlaced the back of bride's bodice and whispered, "Thank The Powers!" The Ladies tittered together as they assisted her out of her Joining clothes, the bride glad to be rid of the beautiful but stifling attire. The darker-haired Lady bent to retrieve the scarlet skirt as Yadla brought the Queen's loose-fitting sleeping robe to her.

"I doubt I will wear this long!" Marna stifled a giggle, but it came out sounding like a sneeze. Despite a flutter of nerves, she looked forward to getting to know Dalock … better.

Lady Yadla arranged Marna's hair lightly on her shoulders, stepped back, and smiled up at her new Queen. "Such a beautiful bride!" She tilted her head, and the King's Wife read her question.

"Call my husband, I am ready."

Marna could not help giggling at her attire: red riding pants, stitched by Dara and Yadla from soft linen cloth. A slight breeze lifted her hair as the horses trod onward, and her caramel-colored skirt billowed over the back of her saddle like a fat pillow. If only the back of the blouse did not scratch. She had chosen a poor day to wear it for the first time. In terms of fineness, the patterned texture of the velvet fabric outrivaled all other garments her Ladies had sewn for her. Yet whilst the new Queen would look her best upon her first arrival at King's Halls, she would not be comfortable.

At her side, Dalock rode, gazing at his land with fond eyes. "Husband," she called, "are you pleased to be home?"

"I am. I was just thinking how alone I felt when I left here last, months ago." He brightened. "No longer! Now, how is my dear wife faring?"

"Well, and pleased to be upon horse rather than in a jostling carriage." Marna neglected to mention the other drawback of the carriage ride: Dara's ceaseless chattering. "I do miss speaking with Lady Yadla, since she left to return to her estate and her betrothed. But I also missed the fresh air of riding in the open."

Her love nodded. "I am glad Yadla made a good companion. Shall I recall her to King's Halls after her child comes?"

"Oh no, I would not want her moving her family on my account. Dalock, I was grateful to hear she too is joining for love."

He chuckled. "That is the way of things here."

"Is it also the way of things for a noblewoman to join after a child's conception? Jinil told me about joining babes, but I thought it was only for the lower ranks."

He shrugged. "Many of my royal forefathers were joining babes. It is the way of things here in Eskalind." He inhaled as though the essence of the country were in the very air. "Marna, we are almost at my Halls. I made a bit of a detour to give you the best view. Ride with me to the crest of that short rise?"

"All right." Following his lead, she urged her gelding after him. Dalock stopped his mount at the peak of the slight hill and waited for her with an expectant expression in his fond brown eyes.

"There is your new home," her royal husband said, nodding to the fields below.

On the plain, in the distance, an immense brown structure sprouted from the earth. It appeared to be made of a single piece of light brown stone, but looking closer, she realized it was smaller rocks mortared together and painted. Connected to the building on its far left rose a round tower, ringed with many long windows near its crest. The main part of King's Halls was punctuated with windows of rounded or arched shapes, some clustered together as though to light grand rooms and others more spread out in a manner that made it difficult to discern their function.

Around the entire building ran a short wall that a horse might easily jump, and it echoed the color of the rest of the structure. Beyond the wall, on the far side of King's Halls, a village sprouted, though she could not discern details other than a quantity of small buildings edging a cluster of canopied tents. A great courtyard stretched away from King's Halls in her direction and ended in an arched gate wide enough for several horses to pass through at once. A terrace overlooked the courtyard, bordered with short columns and traced by dark wooden archways topped with battlements.

Something moved past one of the arches, and Marna realized it must be a person, and thus this structure must be larger than she had first realized. Yet nothing resembled a castle, save for the big tower and the battlements, which seemed oddly placed.

"I know you will enjoy the gardens, but they are on the opposite side. See the wide, round tower? With the windows at the top? That is your chamber. And mine is opposite it, on the other side of the tower, facing Braanya Queen's Market," Dalock said.

"That, that is your castle?" Marna's voice was elevated with shock. "It looks like a huge … house?"

Dalock laughed. "Eskalinders have not needed fortifications since the ancient days, my Queen. See those rocks over there?" He pointed to the left of the large edifice, beyond the tower. "That was once what you might call a castle. We call it a quarry. It was built by the second King, Heedlock King, nearly three thousand years ago."

She glanced at the ancient foundations, blackened and crumbling, no more than an abandoned pile of rocks, then back at his Halls. "But how do you defend … *that*?"

Dalock grinned at her clear consternation. "I do not think I have seen you wear that face before." Marna scowled. "Or that one. You see, since the days of the First King, The Powers have protected all lands within our borders. That is why we aid in the defense of the border kingdoms."

"The First King joined with one of The Powers; Eskalinders defend rather than destroy; the King does not have mistresses … This is indeed the Strange Kingdom." She laughed, turning to her husband. "I am glad we have already lain together. Otherwise, I would be concerned that there would be something unusual to *that* as well."

Dalock attempted a neutral face, but a jovial light shone in his brown eyes. "I could arrange …"

"Tease!" she accused with a smirk.

"I will work on that. The teasing." The King no longer hid his mirth. Leaning toward his bride, he cooed, "The sooner we get there, the sooner you will see your quarters."

"Good! Then I can be free of this itchy clothing." Marna reached to scratch her back.

"Do you need someone to attend you?" False innocence played on her love's face, no less endearing for her having seen the expression many times in the past weeks.

The newly joined woman guffawed, shaking her reins with both hands and spurring her horse ahead. "Race you!" she called, glancing over her chestnut-clad shoulder with a saucy smile, just in time to see Breena surging into a gallop against the fair wheat fields, the horse's dark eyes glaring with steeled purpose as though she charged an enemy in battle. Dalock's hearty laughter belied his mount's antagonistic expression. Marna thrilled to hear his fond voice as she crouched close to her gelding's neck, the wind coming so fast she found it exhilaratingly difficult to breathe.

The King easily passed his wife, giving an unself-conscious whoop as he raced by. Dalock steered Breena away from what appeared to be the main entrance, angling instead toward an open gate on the far left side, near a set of brown-tiled, low-roofed buildings that had escaped her notice before.

A twinge of gratitude fluttered in her chest at not entering through the larger, more public gate. Marna followed Dalock's route to a small courtyard, halting her horse at the entrance as she spied her husband standing aside Breena and lovingly patting the mare's neck. A lanky younger man with a startled expression in his close-set eyes gathered the reins. A few people carrying ladders stood halted, whilst a seated group had paused in the act of tying garlands of King's Flowers. Everyone wore the same expression as the stable hand—utter surprise.

A Guard, helmed in bronze, stepped toward the King, thick leather boots shuffling on the straw-strewn cobblestones. "Welcome, my Lord! Your pardon that all is not in readiness. The reports told of a later arrival."

The gangly lad, his face the picture of concern, said, "And you come alone!"

"I am not alone." Dalock turned to Marna, as though he sensed she watched and waited. "You see, here follows your Queen." He clapped his hand on the youth's shoulder, then walked to his wife. "Marna, was that a fair race?" His voice rose in cheerful, skeptical amusement, laughter shining in his eyes as he gathered the reins from her. "Calling it after you started?"

"Oh hush." He tossed the reins to another stable hand as she reached for his arms. "You outmatch me!"

"Ah, in racing horses." Her husband squeezed her waist as he lifted her from her steed. "But not in other matters." Gathering her into a close embrace, he murmured, warm against her ear, "Welcome home." The King's Wife detected a catch in his voice, as though her beloved fought a sob. Trying to forget that they stood in public view, she curled her arms about Dalock's back, hoping to comfort him against any secret sadness shadowing this homecoming.

Dalock purred against her hair, "Are you with child already?"

Startled at this unexpected question, Marna backed away from his embrace. "What?"

Her husband patted her belly, which was cushioned with the folds of her skirt that had gathered at her waistline when he withdrew her from the saddle. "Ah, it is your gown." He smiled, but she thought she detected a distance in his eyes. Or rather, an expectation.

Stepping back, Marna fiddled with the skirt to free the hem to fall to her feet. "Perhaps I am." The new Queen gave a demure smile before playfully squeezing his firm arm and, speaking in a throaty whisper, said, "Or are you making a suggestion?" Dalock laughed. It pleased her to hear warmth in his tone.

"My Lord, welcome!" A man with dashes of gray in his dark locks approached from a tall side door. His face was lined, but his brown eyes sparkled with affection and a near-boyish alertness. "And my Lady." He bowed. "It is a glad day, our King safely returned and"—he glanced at Marna with a welcoming smile—"joined to a beautiful Lady."

Dalock clasped his man's arm. "I thank you, Chamberlain. Would that my father and mother were here to greet us."

"Aye, my Lord, they would be most proud."

The King nodded, but again Marna noticed a distance in his gaze. The Chamberlain continued, "My Lady Marna Queen, I have known the King since his Naming Day—"

At this her husband interrupted, laughing in a tone of fond exasperation. "Mardril, come, come! No stories of my foolish younger years now."

"Aye, my Lord, I'll oblige you!" The older man chuckled, seemingly more to himself than to the newly joined couple. He raised his green eyes to his young Lord, suddenly all duty and propriety. "But I must delay no longer and report that an urgent message from our Ambassador to Kaymif arrived not long ago. I was in haste to send a Swift Rider to you."

"Ah, my Ambassadors are masters of timing, are they not?" Dalock glanced to his wife, who wondered at the meaning of yet another Ambassador's letter. "Marna, my love, I must attend to this missive immediately." Here she read a hint of resignation in her husband's manner. She nodded, while committing to memory the new word she had just heard. *Missive. Rhymes with dismissive, which is something these letters never are, except Dalock must dismiss himself whenever they appear.* To The Powers, she wished she could read, and be of more use to him.

Mardril's polite voice interrupted her thoughts. "Here is the letter, my Lord." From his caramel-colored tunic, he withdrew a folded parchment of nearly identical color, sealed with two blobs of red wax.

The King grasped the envelope. "Have Jinil sent to me when he arrives; I will be in the Council Chamber. See my Queen to her quarters so she may rest from our long journey." Tucking the correspondence into his tunic, he undid Marna's pack from her horse's back and handed it to Mardril. Then he reached for his wife's hands. "I will come to you as soon as I am able." He took her arms, drawing her close to his warm gaze. In an alluring tone he whispered, "Then I will show you the baths." He leaned to kiss her lips, then at the last moment nipped her nose. She laughed as he waved goodbye.

The new Queen continued climbing the curving stone stairs that supposedly led to her chamber. "Mardril, how many more stairs?" she called behind her.

"We are almost halfway there, my Lady."

"Halfway?" She inhaled slowly as she marched on. "Is there a kitchen at the top?"

"No, my Lady. We can call a Page to bring bread and sauces if you require food, my Lady."

She hung her head. Her back tingled from the increasingly itchy gown; her eyes squinted in the bright light pouring through an elegantly arched window in the curved wall to her right. Across from the window was a carved wooden chair cushioned with red velvet trimmed with nut-brown tassels. Marna eyed the tempting resting place but continued her upward march.

On they trod. "It's been nearly one hundred stairs," she muttered.

"Only a few more, my Lady."

At long last she spied a stout door with glimmering, sword-shaped, coppery hinges. It was closed. A plain earth-colored cup rested near the wide threshold, as though set down in haste. "Does this door lead to more steps?"

"No, we are here, my Lady. Please let me pass." She did so, and the Chamberlain held open the door. The King's Wife entered her quarters, and found herself grateful to be ahead of Mardril so he could not read the surprise on her face. The room was larger than her father's forge and Werna's house combined.

On her left, a few deep gray stone steps led to a wide, raised platform with a betasseled, crimson-curtained bed, festooned with easily a dozen shimmering bronze-beaded cushions. Each pillow was of a unique design and shape: slender crescents, bulbous ovals, pointy stars, stout loaves—all were outlined with polished yellowish-brown pearls or sparkling beads. Surely a fortune had been spent on the bed coverings alone.

Continuing beyond the ornate resting place was a wall of rounded stones, inset with a door of hammered bronze, patterned to resemble lines of swords, each about a hand's breadth in length. The handle was carved of a clear-jeweled red stone and set in the shape of what she now knew to be a capital *D*. The handle cast a ruby-colored glow about the door. Marna inhaled as calmly as she could. "What a spacious and well-appointed room." She nearly clucked to herself with pride at finding use for two recently learned words. "But where does that passage lead? More stairs?"

"To the King's Chamber, my Lady." Mardril straightened. "Only King, Queen, and King's Son—oh yes, and his wife too, if he has one—may pass through this door. By long tradition, since this house was built."

The Hudikslander Queen of Eskalind nodded, stifling a snort that such a structure might be called a house, and wondered if Dalock's room could possibly be as large as hers. It really ought to be bigger, but perhaps not as fussily furnished.

"I will place your bag upon the bed," Mardril said as Marna continued her visual tour of the room. She surveyed the lengthy tapestry that ran along the wall. A pair of handsome horses grazed in the threaded field, the bordering edges trimmed in red and brown patterns. On the far side of the wall was yet another metal-clad door. Beyond it, diamond-paned windows edged the opposite, rounded wall of the tower, which was broken in the center only by a fireplace, made of water-smoothed rocks, in the middle. A series of long pillows for sitting, or perhaps sleeping, abutted the wide ledges.

Her circuit of the outer edges of the room complete, Marna returned her gaze to the bed. At its foot rested two trunks. Across the rug-covered stone floor was a chestnut-colored couch, facing the fireplace and flanked by scarlet-upholstered wood chairs nestled at its sides like Advisors leaning close to their Lord. To the right, a long table edged with carvings stood surrounded by eight chairs. Between this table and the main door was a smaller table with a little mirror resting on a red lace scarf.

She glanced back at the second door, whose purpose remained a mystery to her. "And that door?"

"To the Queen's Garderobe."

The word was so odd, she reacted without thinking. "Gard-eh … ?"

"A necessary, my Lady. With a washroom."

She wondered if that meant it was also a room for bathing, or for washing laundry. Though confused, she nodded, half wanting to ask more, half feeling foolish for her ignorance.

Mardril sighed, a wistful look on his features. "This garderobe is a marvel of the Kingdom, my Lady, for it has running water."

Her curiosity piqued, Marna sensed her opportunity. "Really? I must see it. Would you mind?"

The Chamberlain gestured with a slight bow. "As you wish, my Lady."

Marna stepped across her new room, her stair-tired feet sinking gratefully into the soft rugs. She opened the door to find a long, narrow room, ending in two windows of similar size to the ones in her main chamber. Fresh, lavender-scented air flowed from one of the ajar windows, and just outside, a bucket hung from a pulley.

Just before the other window, inside the room, was a dark, odd chair with a hollowed-out seat that looked a bit like a mixing bowl. A pipe ran behind it and up to a ceramic box, from which dangled a long-handled chain. The new Queen puzzled this from the doorway and advanced into the small chamber, passing a bronze washbasin similar in design and craft to the one in her tent, though instead of resting on a tripod stand, this bowl was mounted to the wall, and it had a thin column of pipe exiting the basin and diving to the floor. She halted her steps by a small table with an ewer that was at the basin's side.

Across from this small washing area was a dominating bronze tub large enough for two people of goodly size. Hollowed, arch-roofed niches in the surrounding stone walls gave small spaces for short candles and larger spaces for folded cloths and sprigs of lavender in little ruby-colored vases.

"How do you find it, my Lady?" The Chamberlain stood at the entrance to the small room.

Faced with the luxury and oddness of the room, the King's Wife ventured a question that she hoped would not reveal the depths of her ignorance. Careful not to address her comment to any particular feature of the room, she faced the older man and raised an eyebrow. "Mardril, this is indeed a marvel, but how does it work?"

He smiled, inclining his head, the crinkling about his eyes hinting that he had been asked this question before. He gestured at the chair near the window. "The lavatory functions on an ingenious system, invented by the King's grandfather, Farlich King. Ah, that is a long and amusing tale." Mardril cleared his throat as if reminding himself to continue. "The cabinet above the seat is filled with water, and when one releases the chain, water flows down the pipe, into the bowl, flushing away to the pipes in the floor, which exit far down the tower."

Marna leaned toward the strange chair, noticing that it was not contained, but had a hole at the bottom. Her eyes widened slightly as she comprehended what the man meant—it was an outhouse with flowing water. "Fascinating," she said with the utmost sincerity. "Are the … garderobes elsewhere in King's Halls like to this?"

"No, my Lady, the tower garderobes are unique. The others are more, mmm, old-fashioned." Mardril raised his head slightly, a suggestion of a pleading expression in his eyes. "Though there has been talk, over the years, of adding them to other parts of the building."

"Then this is reserved for the use of the King and Queen?"

"And their guests. It is a long walk down the stairs, my Lady."

"I can imagine that I will have many guests."

"Aye, my Lady." Mardril eyed the chair wistfully, as one might when departing from an old friend when hope of a future reunion is in doubt.

Marna clasped her hands together and leaned forward, a gesture that, unfortunately, caused the fabric on her back to irritate her skin. "I thank you for the tour, but must attend to a few matters now."

The man backed out of the room with a bow, and the new Queen followed him into her spacious quarters. "My Lady, shall I send for the Ladies of King's Halls to be introduced and attend you?"

"Yes, please, and see to it that my Page, Favik, is shown the way here when he arrives." Her throat clenched around the words as the annoying prickling sensation on her back increased.

"Very good, my Lady." With that the Chamberlain departed, closing the main door soundlessly behind him.

The Strange Queen surveyed the room, uncertain what to explore first. Giving in to her first impulse, she rushed back into the garderobe and eyed the mysterious chair by the window. Hesitantly, she approached it, then reached decisively for the chain. A whooshing sound surprised her as a torrent of water rushed into the bowl, spiraled about, then vanished down the hole. She laughed. "Oh, Werna will never believe this!" Marna yanked the chain a second time, and more water rained into the bowl, roiling like a forgotten pot of broth over a roaring fire, dancing up into the air and splashing her skirt. "Oh!" She backed away, feeling a fool. "Well, at least it is only water."

Removing the skirt, she fluffed it over the washtub, glad that her riding pants remained unharmed by the strange chair in her fancy outhouse. "Please dry quickly. I can't meet my Ladies in riding pants!"

Deciding to change into her old skirt, she left the garderobe and headed toward the crimson-curtained bed, where her pack rested. On the last wide stone step, she tripped in her haste and sprawled headfirst onto the embroidered coverlets, sending several of the beaded cushions skittering onto the floor.

Marna pulled herself upright. "A fine Queen I make. And this itchy blouse will be the death of me!" The Hudikslander unlaced the front of her bodice and flung it aside, feverishly scratching at the buttons. Pulling the fabric over her head, she turned the blouse inside out, noting the ragged seams that had caused her distress. "Ha! Lady Nalya's handiwork. I should have known." Marna dropped the troublesome garment, kicked it away, and retrieved the pack that stored her old blouses and skirts. "I hope Favik will bring my other dresses before the Ladies of King's Halls arrive." Pulling the worn, but comfortable, cotton blouse over her head, she exclaimed, "I will not stand for irksome clothes!"

The Queen removed her fine riding pants, replacing them with the better of her old skirts, then plopped onto the bed and, once satisfied with the firmness of the mattress, studied the room.

In a dark corner, not far from the bed but screened from the main door by a black curtain, rested a small piece of furniture. Straining to see it in the shadows, she finally recognized it as a cradle. "Oh, what a gloomy place for a babe. I wonder when it will be filled, and how many times?"

Comfortably ensconced on the bed, she studied the dark wooden form. "A Queen's duty is to make sons, so make them I must." Marna raised her eyes to the crimson fabric stretched across the top of the bedposts.

"I am far older than Werna was when she joined. I will not mother as many children, thank The Powers." The new Queen traced the pattern on a pillow, and her rough skin caught on the delicate fabric. She pulled her hand away. "May They protect me as They have Werna. I hope not to suffer Mother's fate."

She inhaled slowly, feeling her ribs sink into the mattress. A strange sensation filled her body. It was as though she were being subsumed slowly into the mattress, but she was not herself, she was Dalock King's mother, and his father's mother, and each of the Queens of Eskalind in succession unto the first to reside in this chamber. Each of them lying with their husbands here, bearing their children here, some dying here.

Marna pulled herself upright and walked the several paces to the largest table. She ran a finger over the deep, rounded carving that edged the table. It depicted horses chasing one another, so true to life one could discern the wind flattening their forelocks. A bronze platter occupied the center of the table. The new Queen imagined elegantly clothed Ladies and exotically dressed visitors from foreign lands seated around the wooden slab, chatting about politics, fashion and jewelry, kingdoms and customs she had never heard of, and using words strange to her uneducated ears. Anxiety gripped her stomach at how much was expected of her.

"I should call for some food. Then I will feel better." Looking around the chamber, uncertain what she searched for, she finally paced to the main door and opened it. No one was outside.

She sighed. The King's Wife closed the door behind her and followed the long curve of the stairs. Near the bottom, she heard a rustling, like a fast-flowing river. Entering the window-lined corridor, she saw a group of about seven women, dressed in red shimmering dresses, hurriedly approaching. It was difficult to discern individuals as they rushed forward, but their hair varied from dark to light, and in each case was fashioned into a single braid hanging over silken, hazelnut-colored dress cords that crisscrossed over the chest. Perched atop their heads were silly brown and red striped hats, similar to the ones worn by her Joining Day attendants when she first met them. The smooth, fine fabric of the women's gowns flickered in the sunlight and the window-cast shadows. One noticeable characteristic they shared with the ladies of court in Hudiksland: each and every one of them was elegantly thin.

"Why did they not tell us that our new Queen had arrived?"

"Aye, we could have been ready to greet her properly!"

"Will Lasta be coming to the Queen's Chamber too?

"Of course not, she cannot make the stairs."

"I wonder if Dara be with her."

"Vaynya, watch your elbows!"

"How does my hat look?"

They coursed past Marna, nearly flattening her against the wall. One Lady looked down her long nose. "Out of our way, girl."

It had been a long time since anyone called Marna a girl.

She imagined them at the top of the stairs, with a closed door and no word from inside to greet them, and smirked.

The women hastened up the stairs to the Queen's Chamber, their chatter echoing along the corridor. Vapors of perfume peppered the air in their wake, and the Hudikslander stopped and sneezed. Continuing with her mission, she stepped into a bright beam of sunshine, only then spying one last woman belatedly dashing after the others. The sight stopped the King's Wife midstep, for she had never seen anyone like this woman before. Her skin was dark brown and smooth, her features delicate and exquisitely proportioned.

The new Queen had heard tales of dark-skinned peoples before. Once, as a small girl, she had stood on tiptoes in a crowd, unsuccessfully straining to see such an oddity, a diplomat from far foreign lands, in Castleton. But this woman's skin was not black like coal or even midnight, as the rumors told. Rather, her coloring carried a hint of bronze in its depth.

Like the other women of court, she wore her long, straight tresses in a single braid draped over her left shoulder. In her long-fingered brown hands, she fussed with a piece of fabric banded with the King's colors. "Ridiculous hat!" She bunched the cloth into a ball, shoving it into a pocket in the folds of her crimson gown, where it bulged in a comical matter, bouncing over her knees as she ran.

As she passed plain-clad Marna, the last of the Strange Queen's future attendants acknowledged her with a nod and kind expression in her dark eyes. Then a puzzled look knit her smooth brow and her lips parted to speak.

Still frozen in the shaft of sunshine, the new Queen lifted her finger to her own lips and bestowed a crafty smile, one worthy of Narnik when he outsmarted his older brothers. The dark-skinned woman tilted her head, just as one of the Ladies called from the stairs, "Saralya, hurry!

We are waiting for you."

The woman responded in a frazzled voice, "Coming!" She bowed her head low to Marna.

The new Queen grinned and followed her nose to the kitchen.

CHAPTER TWENTY-FOUR—A VISIT TO THE KITCHEN

In the King's kitchens, the head cook paced the stone platform overlooking her domain. "When's the new girl arriving? Today by noon, they said, and it is already half-past." She was a wide-hipped and heavyset woman with, despite her most recent comment, a pleasant and cheerful manner. Cook adjusted her lopsided kerchief and pointed at a line of women scrubbing vegetables below. "Ayda, dear, you must poke the potatoes in the middle before they are roasted. There, there, that's the way."

An anxious-faced boy scrambled up the short set of stairs and held a pan before her. She dipped her stout fingers into its sticky red contents and tasted the sauce. "No no no, dearie. Too sweet for the traditional recipe." The boy looked about to cry. "Start again, my dear, third time's the charm. You'll get it." Cook patted him on the back and sent him on his way. Looking up, she saw an unfamiliar face at the main doorway, opposite her platform. "Ah, the new girl, at last! Come here, dear." She beckoned.

———

Marna waded past the chopping tables and pots belching steam, toward the Cook, who waved her up the stairs at the far end of the cavernous kitchen.

The older woman smiled pleasantly. "Welcome, dear! I am most happy to see you. What pretty hair you have." She touched Marna's arm, a warm expression upon her plain features. "Best to wear your hair up in a kerchief in my kitchen though."

Marna smiled as it dawned on her that the poor woman thought her a kitchen helper. "Now, you look a good cook, dear, with meat on your bones! I'm glad to see it. I can never imagine a thin cook capable with sauces and such." She led Marna down the stairs, along the aisles, pointing out the different stations and activities. "One must love one's wares!" Cook continued rambling. "I like sturdiness in my girls, though you are more woman than girl, I'd say."

"I like your plain talk."

"Aye, that's all you find here, my dear." She grinned and drew Marna to her side as a man carrying a huge bowl passed them. "We leave the sugar words for them noblefolk." She laughed. "But not the King, he's a fine man, just like his father; loves his horses, no flatteries for him, no no." She smiled with approval. "Have you seen him, dear?"

"I have."

"Well, I do go on and on. There is a feast to prepare, and not just any feast, but our Lord's Joining celebration. How wonderful he's found his Queen! I hope to The Powers that she likes my cooking." Cook swiped a finger on the edge of a bowl of a reddish sauce that a sad-faced boy was stirring. "Perfect, Vinil! I knew you would get it." The dark-haired lad beamed. "Now tell me your name, dear."

"I am Marna, King's Wife."

The cook blinked. "You ... are?"

The Queen nodded.

"Oh, my Lady, may The Powers forgive me!" She dropped to her knees and put her thick hands over her face. A group of boys chopping vegetables stopped in midstroke and watched.

"An honest voice rises above a din of fools."

"My ... my Lady?" The older woman lowered her hands, her face bewildered and flushed.

"An expression from my country, though it is seldom heeded." Marna bent toward her. "Stand up, my good Cook." The King's Wife helped the Eskalinder to her feet. "Please, there is no need for forgiveness."

"Oh, my Lady! My tongue runs away from me. How can I ever…"

Marna raised an eyebrow. "Leave the sugar words to the noblefolk."

At this, the beginning of a grin tugged at the woman's broad mouth. "Aye, my Lady, I see your meaning."

"Now, I need a bite to eat. And show me where you keep the chickens."

Chapter Twenty-Five—Many Unfamiliar Things

In Dalock's dark-beamed Great Hall, Marna sat by the King's side at the high table reserved on such special occasions for the Strange King and Queen. Her fingers traced the bronze threading embroidering their table covering. She surveyed the room, hoping to The Powers she would not spill something damaging to the handiwork of the luxurious cloth. Down the five steps at her side, two wings of banquet tables stretched the length of the long room. She could not discern a pattern to the seating, for Lords and Ladies draped in rich fabrics sat alongside Healers in their plain red apron dresses, Attendants from the King's Baths broke bread with two russet-skinned merchants from foreign lands, and Chamberlain Mardril had a stablehand by his side. It amused her to see that some of the chastised Ladies had changed their hairstyle to mimic hers, exchanging hats and thick braids for loose locks flowing down their backs.

Pennants bearing Dalock's emblem of a red sword on a brown field hung from the ceiling, whilst talk and laughter filled the air as the assembly celebrated their Lord's joining and safe homecoming. The new Queen wore her brown-bodiced Joining gown with a garnet beaded necklace that the King had presented to her when they toured the baths. After their pleasant time soaking together in the hot water, she had wanted nothing more than the quiet of her new chamber, but duty called, and hopefully a delicious meal too.

"Try this sauce, Marna," Dalock encouraged. "It is unusual."

"You have sauce with everything." Other guests were using their little pitchforks to dip pieces of food into the sauces. "Even whole bread." A man dunked a loaf into a large hammered copper sauce bowl. His companions laughed and downed more ale, their voices echoing from the high ceiling.

She turned her attention to the middle of the room. Between the long tables resided a smaller table populated by people garbed in green and yellow, at great odds to the displays of Dalock's brown and red, and the white and red for the First King, that attired those at the long tables. "Dalock, is that table in the middle for charity?"

"Hmm?" He had just shoved a large heel of bread in his mouth, but managed to speak. "No, traveling players."

"Traveling players?" It made no sense, for the actors sat drinking and speaking conversationally with one another, making no effort to talk over the boisterous courtfolk. Every once in a while a word or two would reach her ears, but that was all. They exhibited natural expressions and mannerisms, not exaggerated like the players in the market at Castleton. One could easily mistake them for common people going about their business, which at this moment appeared to be, fittingly, a feast or a tavern scene. But Dalock's tray-bearing servants watched the actors warily, hurrying around the players' table as though afraid of them.

"Oh good," Marna's husband said. "One of my favorites." He pointed his knife at the actors. "Marna, watch this part!"

A woman wearing a straw-blond wig poured ale for a red-faced man from a broad-based ewer, using both her hands to steady her earthenware jug. The man leaned back, leering at the rear of her skirt, then pinched her bottom. Suddenly, another of the actors leapt onto the table, brandishing a sword, chasing the bottom-pinching man away. Marna started, but no one else paid any attention, save the King and a few others. The serving woman put down the vessel, placed her hands on her hips, and peppered her champion with angry words.

"Well done!" Dalock stomped his feet, laughing.

Marna turned to ask what the story was just as Jinil approached and leaned to whisper something in Dalock's ear. The King looked troubled. "I will be right back, my dear." He stood and left with his Second, leaving Marna alone at the head table.

Feeling conspicuous, she broke a piece of bread and dipped it into the sauce she favored most. It was an ashy green, with a smoky taste and the pungent scent of an herb she could not identify. Glancing at the Ladies, she fought a grin, remembering the look of horror on some of the Ladies' faces at their formal introduction. Her eyes fell to the one who had acknowledged her in the hallway. Saralya. It pleased her to find the woman gazing back at her with a shared, conspiratorial smile.

"A drink to our new Queen!" Jinil's voice called over the crowd. Marna turned to see him standing before a table at the far end of the room, a chalice aloft in his hand.

"To our Queen!" male voices echoed. Not certain what was expected of her, the bladesmith's daughter smiled graciously at her guests. "I thank you."

It must have been the right response, as all the men emptied their cups. Dalock found his seat next to her again, slipping his arm warmly around her back.

A stout woman whom she did not recognize, clad in a chestnut-brown linen gown trimmed with sparkling red stones, limped slowly to Jinil's side. He offered her an arm, and she steadied herself.

"Who is that?" Marna whispered.

"Lady Lasta, seniormost of the Ladies of King's Halls," her husband murmured in her ear, then he playfully nipped her earlobe. She bit her lip at the intimate gesture before such a large gathering. Across the Hall, Lady Lasta raised her goblet and spoke in a clear alto. "A drink to our Lord the King's safe return!"

The female guests and the Ladies of King's Halls raised their goblets, cheering, "To the King!"

"I thank you," Dalock said as the women drank. He placed a gentle hand on Marna's arm to stay her from reaching for her chalice.

Lady Lasta looked at Jinil, raising her gray eyebrows slightly, and the pair spoke in unison, "And to King's Son, when he comes."

"To King's Son!" everyone shouted. Dalock whispered to Marna, "Now we both drink, or they will think you are with child." She hastily reached for her polished bronze goblet, nearly tumbling it over as she grasped the rounded gemstones decorating its sides, aware that all eyes in the crowded Hall watched the foreigner from Hudiksland. But Dalock smiled fondly at her, and they tilted their metallic cups to the lofty ceiling. The King's Great Hall boomed with the stomping of feet and spirited shouts of "Hear, hear!"

She brought a crimson napkin to her lips, whispering to her husband from behind the cloth, "I hope I do not disappoint them with daughters." Her beloved turned to her, and for the briefest of moments, his eyes widened and his lopsided lips pursed in an expression she would have found comic were it not for her uncertainty as to its meaning. "Did I do something wrong?"

"Later, my dear." His expression softened and he patted her leg, making no effort to hide the gesture, which again shocked her, given the number of people present who would no doubt notice. "Ah, here comes the main course."

Marna looked to the Hall. Serving men entered, bearing large platters heaped with the chickens she had helped Cook roast. Inhaling slowly, she studied the crowd's reaction. Everyone peered at the platters with puzzled looks. A serving man stepped toward her and Dalock. He gripped one of the little pitchforks they used for eating, although this one was larger than usual, and placed a half chicken on Dalock's plate and another on hers.

Dalock beamed with anticipation. "I will have two halves." The man obliged. "I was glad to hear of your kitchen adventure," her husband whispered to her. "Soon our guests will know true happiness: Marna's roast chicken."

She indulged his eagerness with a smile but noted expressions of disappointment or puzzlement on their guests. Only Jinil, seated at the far end of the Hall, grinned like the King. He too signaled for a double serving.

The servants distributed the chickens to all the company. A few Ladies called for sauce. "I did not make a sauce for the chicken," Marna said quietly.

"Mmph." Dalock's mouth was stuffed with the roasted meat. "It does not need a thing." He turned his attention back to his plate, the first bird already nearly a carcass.

Having satisfied herself overmuch on delightful samples of sauces and moist cakes during her kitchen trip, Marna picked at her meal, watching the gathered company. Some stared at their plates as though uncertain what to do. Others cut into the chicken without enthusiasm. They tasted their first bite, and their faces lit with surprise. Then they sawed into the meat with vigor, shoveling more into their mouths.

"More chicken!" a large man called to the servants, and they rushed to fulfill the command. Those who had refrained wondered what the fuss was about and nibbled tentatively. Soon they motioned for more food as well, and the only sounds in the Hall were the patter of the servers' feet scurrying from one guest to another, the plinking of chicken onto plates, and satisfied chewing.

Marna smiled. She glanced at Lady Lasta, seated at the far end of the room.

Lasta caught her eye, pushed her chair away from her table, and stood. A grin graced her broad lips, her cheeks rosy and cheerful.

"My King and my Queen, Lords and Ladies," she called. A few looked up from their plates. "My sister, our King's Cook, tells me our Lady had a hand in our delicious meal this evening," she began. That got everyone's attention. They turned to Marna, who wondered how it was that the head Lady at court was sister to the Cook.

"Another toast to the King's Wife," Lasta proclaimed.

"To Marna Queen!" shouted their guests, some rising to their feet.

Others banged their cups on the red-cloth-covered tables, or stomped their feet. The noise grew to such a din, Marna wanted to cover her ears. She stood, and the crowd quieted with anticipation.

"I thank you," she began. She looked at Dalock, his brown eyes warm with love and pride. She placed one hand on his shoulder and reached for her chalice with the other. "May we have many more feasts together."

"Hear, hear!" Dalock roared, rising to his feet. They toasted one another and drank, while the assembly cheered. Then the King kissed his Queen, and for that moment, any doubts Marna held about how she would fare in this unfamiliar land fell away, and she knew only joy.

"Hullo, Marna," her husband called from the doorway that linked their chambers. He wore his brown locks loose, the tips of his ears protruding endearingly amidst his mane. A crimson robe, tied loose at the waist with an embroidered, dark-honey-colored belt revealed an enticing bit of his well-formed chest.

Marna faced him, standing in the middle of her candlelit room clad only in a caramel-shaded velvet sleeping robe, her freshly brushed hair falling long over her shoulders. Her love came toward her. They faced one another a moment. "It was a delightful feast," she ventured.

"And delectable." He took her hands, bringing them to his lips. He inhaled, his expression rapt. "Mmm, those are the chicken-roasting herbs."

She laughed as he closed his eyes, kissing her fingers with delicious slowness, one by one. "Dalock ... Dalock ... there was something you meant to tell me, yes?"

"Mmm," he purred against her skin, his lips traveling to her wrist.

"At the feast? There was something you meant to tell me, about something I had done wrong." She withdrew her hands.

His eyes flew open. "What? Oh. Here, Marna, let us sit." Her husband gestured to the chestnut-colored couch before the lit fireplace. They sat together. His voice low, he spoke in an almost whisper, "I have often thought of us here together, drinking wine and talking about our day before the fire."

Marna smiled without parting her lips, waiting. When he did not continue, she raised an eyebrow and tilted her head, the only sound her hair shifting across the soft fabric of her sleeping robe.

"No, Marna, I am not forgetting what I meant to tell you. And I am not stalling either." A nearby candle fizzled. He looked at it.

"Dalock…" She elongated each syllable.

He turned back to her, took her hand, and murmured, "It concerns what you said at the feast. About not wanting to disappoint our people with daughters. What I have not told you is that the King cannot have a daughter. He always has a son. One son. And no other children."

Marna blinked. This made no sense. It was impossible. There must be something she did not know, some secret passed from one Queen to the next. If only she could read!

"I hope this is not a great disappointment to you," he continued in a rush. "I saw how dear your sister's little ones are to you, Marna, and I imagine that you might want armfuls of children." Here he hesitated, his demeanor that of a new man shyly come a-courting. "But our son will be our sole child, as I was, and all my fathers, since the Second King."

He kissed her hand, looking at her with such a pleading, waiflike expression that had she not been entirely confounded, she would have gathered him into a firm embrace. Instead, she stammered, "But, Dalock, what if, what if… The Powers forbid… something happened to the babe?" The thought of possibly losing a child forced the breath out of her for a moment. A tear coursed her cheek.

Her husband leaned closer, lightly brushing the moisture from her face. "Dear Marna! Do not worry, our son will be protected by The Powers until he has his son, and that will be a long time from now." He smiled slightly, a hint of melancholy in his eyes. "Remember when we spoke in your pavilion, and I told you I enjoyed the unjoined King's Gift? That I cannot die until my son is conceived?"

She nodded, but thought better of telling him she had thought it a pure jest.

"When I was a lad of four, I fell from that window, right there." He pointed to the window adjacent to the fireplace.

The Queen sat upright. "But that is a drop of well over a hundred feet!"

"Aye. The Powers protected me. I landed on a pile of hay that no one recalled stacking there. My only injury was the lopsided face you see before you now." He grinned, as if for emphasis, and she could only nod in mute response as she wondered what to believe of this strange tale.

"I am sorry, Marna, that I did not tell you all this before, that I have forgotten to tell you many things. But I know, I know The Powers meant for us to be together. Sometimes I forget you are new to our customs! You must understand, in some ways, I feel you have always been with me." Dalock stroked her hand with his beautiful fingers. "I forget that it has only been a short while we have known one another, my dear."

"My love, I would that we always speak plainly with one another…"

He knit his brows.

"Shh." She touched his forehead, and he closed his eyes as though her touch were a balm. "I did not mean that as a scolding." He opened his eyes as she replaced her hand on his long fingers. "But, Dalock, you must understand this is quite strange to me. I wonder if there is something that your Queens have done to prevent further children, some herbs or…"

"No, Marna, it is just the way it is with the Kings of Eskalind, thanks to The Powers. One son, one heir, a clear line of succession." He smiled, and she was glad he found nothing offensive in her words. "You are ever my practical love. And once we have tutors for you, you can read all the Queens' chronicles and see for yourself, hmm?"

She raised an eyebrow. "So you are telling me that once we have our son, you will still come to my bed?"

Now they both smiled. "Of course," he said, with a perhaps too-eager grin. She leaned to kiss him. Her husband took her in his arms, grazing her cheek with light kisses. "You are not disappointed?"

Marna laughed. "That I must go to childbed only once?"

"Aye."

"No. I am glad, really." Though he nearly filled her vision, the King's Wife looked to the bronze ewer atop the low table between the couch and the fire, and when she spoke again, her voice sounded far off, even to herself. "Since I was fourteen, half my life, I have helped my sister with her children. I even attended at some of their births, back and forth from my father's house to her home. While I love them, I feel . . ." She gazed back into his brown eyes. "I feel there is something else for me here, besides mothering our ch— . . . our son, and loving you. I cannot explain it, it is a sense I have." It felt odd to admit it, but it was truth. She watched for his reaction, hoping she did not disappoint her husband with her own strange statement.

Dalock smiled. "I knew you to be a richly Gifted Lady," he said. "The Powers have more plans for you."

She shifted slightly in his arms. "Would that I knew what they were."

"We will live each day and see what comes." He drew her close for another delicious kiss, his beard softly tickling her chin.

"What about the nights, Dalock?" she teased. "We cannot forget the nights."

"Oh yes, we must find a way to occupy ourselves at night." He leaned to kiss her again.

"I cannot imagine what we will do." She stroked his long brown hair. In the candlelight, she could see glints of red in the dark strands.

"Hmm," her husband purred in a low voice, reaching an arm under her knees.

"What are you— ah!" Marna yelped, laughing as he hefted her into his arms and carried her to bed.

Chapter Twenty-Seven—The Scroll Merchant's Daughter

Jinil, King's Second, approached the Guard outside his Lord's private chamber. "Is the King within?"

The man nodded and opened the door. Jinil entered, but saw no sign of his young ruler. The door to the garderobe was slightly ajar. "My Lord?" No reply. Jinil glanced at the closed door that connected the royals' quarters. When he exited the King's generous room, the bushy-browed Guard regarded him with a chuckle in his eyes. "With the Queen again, hmm?"

"Perhaps. Send for me when our Lord returns." King's Second paced down the stairs. Reaching the last step, he paused a moment, regarding the first dozen of the numerous stairs that led to the Queen's Chamber. Many years had passed since he had last ascended those steps, when the King's Mother resided at the top. Then Jinil was a new Ambassador, freshly returned home to make his first reports to Treya Queen, governing in her lofty tower whilst her husband was away at war. How high and distant she had seemed to the awed young man, breathless from his first climb up the stairs, his skin prickling with nervous anticipation and sheer desire to impress his Lady. He felt an odd sensation as he gazed at those dark steps. Perhaps it was reluctance to make the trek upward with no guaranteed result that stayed his feet.

Then the thought that his Lord and his Lady might be at table, and thus accessible, propelled King's Second, and he ascended the Queen's stairs.

At the midway point he heard a slow, rhythmic sound, like breathing. He stepped quietly. In a small alcove, Jinil found the source of the noise: a woman, dressed in fine red silks, slumped in a chair, and snoring. Her black hair framed a smooth, dark brown face that most men would find lovely to gaze upon, though at the present moment her mouth dangled open like a drunk slurring for more ale. An open scroll tilted in her hands, and near to her red slippers rested a basket of neatly stacked scrolls.

He smiled to himself, certain the woman would not wish to be disturbed from such an unflattering repose, and advanced up the steps.

"My Lord King's Second." The Guard next to the Queen's door bowed slightly. "Our Lady Queen asked not to be disturbed. I'm sorry you made the trip up here."

Jinil nodded and spoke quietly. "No matter. I seek the King. If you know him to be available, send for me."

"Yes, my Lord King's Second."

Jinil walked away. When he reached the sleeping woman, he tiptoed past, noticing a strange light on her face that moved as he passed by. He paused until realizing it was sunshine coming through the window opposite her chair and reflecting from the parchment in her hands and onto her face. The scroll slipped a bit from her sleep-loosened grasp with her every breath, threatening to soon escape her delicate fingers. He stood a moment watching this, half wondering why he did not move along.

The scroll dropped, and Jinil bent to catch it just as the woman reached to do the same. Their heads collided and he reeled backward for a moment, mindful not to topple down the stairs.

The woman spoke. "Ow, what happened?" She squinted up at Jinil, her eyes narrowed by the bright sunlight. Both held their heads where they had met.

"You were dropping your scroll. We both reached to catch it at the same time. Are you all right?"

"I think so." She peered at him. "Who are you?"

He stepped to the side, lowering his hand so she might see his face.

"Jinil, King's Second. And you have not been at King's Halls long, my Lady Reader to the Queen."

She stood and bowed, a hint of a smile on her lips, perhaps at his deduction of her position. "I never thought to be so fortunate as to be called Reader to the Queen. My parents named me Saralya."

"We both hold positions at King's Halls without King's Friend in our names. How did you come to serve with the noble Ladies?" He smiled pleasantly. As King's Second, he had full right to ask such a question, yet he did not want her to feel this was an interrogation. Now that she was awake, the pleasing proportions of her face and gleam of intelligence in her dark eyes intrigued him.

"To make a short tale of it, my local Records Keeper ruled that for my family service, my skills would be best put to use at King's Halls. I learned to read as a very young child, and know all of our histories and Legends by heart, though of course different authors relate the tales in their own manner."

While curious why she must serve for her family, Jinil found it too easy a question. What he enjoyed most was that she acknowledged the subtleties of the various Legend Writers. Most people knew the popular tales, yet few could quote and compare the eloquence of Eskalind's best authors. Perhaps further discussion on this topic was in order. Then again, they had only just met. "You have not been at King's Halls long."

"It's true. I arrived whilst the King fought in Hudiksland."

"How do you find life here?"

With only the slightest of pauses, she replied in a steady, calm voice, "I'm used to a quiet life pursuing knowledge."

King's Second pondered whether in her reply he read distaste for the aimless activities common amongst some Ladies of court. To his mind, these past years without a Queen rallying her attendants' energies toward worthy goals had yielded slim accomplishments. Jinil also considered whether her quiet life might include a lover, though something in her tone made him think not. "Then reading to our Lady must suit you."

"It does, my Lord King's Second. Reading the Legends of our Kings can't be called work." Her voice was honest and clear; King's Second could find no fault with her. He decided to risk a mischievous question.

Glancing up the stairs, he asked in a playful voice. "Do you think we will see King's Son within the year?"

Saralya lowered her chin, looking at him with a sparkle in her deep brown eyes. She spoke with restrained mirth. "We know The Powers alone may answer that, my Lord King's Second."

"Of course, my Lady Reader to the Queen." He grinned, glad she had enjoyed his flirtatious comment.

A door creaked open, and the Queen's voice rang from the top of the stairs. "Guard, send for my Reader."

"Aye, my Lady." Footfalls approached.

"Ah, you are called," whispered Jinil.

"Then I must go," she said. "And perhaps the King may have need for you soon." Again that light in her eyes.

"It seems our duties coincide."

Saralya smiled and bowed, then made her way up the stairs. He watched her ascend, the silky swish of her gown powerfully hypnotic, his duty to report to Dalock King temporarily forgotten as he hoped their pleasures might in future coincide as well. Once she disappeared from view, he breathed deeply, resolving to visit the Records Keepers' folios kept at King's Halls and discover what he could about her family and circumstances. His nearly disastrous affair with the widowed Lady Nalya had obliged King's Second to learn as much as he could about any woman's past before considering a liaison. The fact that Saralya was called to serve for her family demanded investigation as well. Female service was highly unusual. There must be a reason.

But the King sent for Jinil before he could exit the corridor to the royals' quarters, and the pair spent hours in council. A letter from Eskalind's Ambassador to Havadra reported that Havadra's childless king lay ill with a potentially fatal fever. His brothers each sought the throne, and while the elder stood as the recognized heir, the younger gave hints of usurping his brother's position. Eskalind might need to lend its armies to stop a civil war in the desert kingdom by the sea.

Dalock King grumbled, glancing at the door to the Queen's Chamber. "By The Powers, I hope it does not come to that. To leave again this soon. And for Havadra, of all the borderlands."

Jinil distracted him with the latest news of the Hudiksland plan, which always gained the King's full attention, and required careful maneuvering of messages and coordination of actions. Thank The Powers, his newly joined ruler was pleased with their preparations on the matter, and King's Second marveled at his Lord's restraint and strategizing. The young ruler had grown much since he assumed the throne. Jinil felt a glint of pride at his progress, much as an older brother might on guiding a younger sibling's maturation.

Many hours later, instead of repairing to his quarters after council with his Lord, Jinil detoured to the King's Library, ensconcing himself, amidst its chaos, in the recent public records of the citizenry. As King's Second, his position allowed him to petition the Records Keepers for their official documents, but not wanting to call their attention or questions to his task, he sat stoic as a stone under the sculptor's hammer and endured the process of sifting through bundles of incongruent records.

After wasting a solid inch of tapered candles, and more than a few silent curses on the Librarian's mismanagement, tidy stacks of papyrus sheets attested to his efficient sorting of the records he perused. How long they would maintain that order, only The Powers could guess. Turning to a basket of jumbled scrolls, at last Jinil's eyes encountered the name of Saral, a prosperous Scroll Merchant and Copyist in the southernmost part of the land. Saral was recorded as being the widower of a Guerland woman, with little use of his legs since a terrible incident in his boyhood, and thus unable to fulfill his citizenship service duty to his country when he came of age.

Jinil tapped his chin, pondering why, if Saral was a Copyist, the

Records Keepers did not enlist him as an assistant in their offices to fulfill his Eskalind citizenship service obligation. Then he noted the date. "Ah, 2850, when there was an excess of Records Keepers across the land." It was also the year of Jinil's birth and Naming.

Thus the Records Keepers decreed that one of Saral's children would serve in his stead. It was a provisional form of citizenship, but not uncommon in such circumstances. Later, Saral joined with his Guerish wife and parented a sole child, a daughter, whom they educated on par with a King's Historian. *Saralya.* He thought the name just as his eyes alighted onto it. A Records Keeper dictated that Saralya was to serve at King's Halls for five years when she came of age, at sixteen, but the year prior, she and her mother journeyed to Guerland.

Here Jinil leaned away from the record, wondering if Saralya had sought to avoid her obligatory service to the King by leaving Eskalind to reside with Guerish relatives. Reading further, he found that on the return journey a year later through Havadra, violent marauders attacked their caravan. Her mother and many others were brutally slain; Saralya was unable to cross back into Eskalind for months.

A Records Keeper must have agreed that this was a horrific event, as an unusual five-year mourning stay was granted on Saralya's service on behalf of her father's obligation. Thus the Scroll Merchant's daughter with a love for quiet scholarship arrived at King's Halls to serve for her father just as the King returned from Hudiksland with his bride. Perhaps The Powers had a hand in these strange events.

His eyes followed the graceful curves that spelled her name, fascinated with their harmonious appeal. Jinil considered how young she was—nearly fifteen years his junior—and the possibility that she had traveled to Guerland to shirk her duty to King and country. But Saralya returned, suffering the terrible loss of her mother en route, and The Powers only knew what depth of troubles she had experienced before crossing the border back to Eskalind.

The King's man rolled the scroll closed and placed it on the shelf where it should have been stored.

After a few pleasant days mostly immersed in his Queen's company, Dalock regretfully returned to his usual schedule for managing his land: council meetings, briefings, and the inevitable ill-timed Ambassador's letter. Yet his duties felt lighter, for at the end of each day, he shared the evening meal solely with his beautiful wife, sitting on the couch in her quarters or his, recounting their days for one another.

It did not surprise him when she outpaced her reading tutor's expectations, nor when the man requested an assistant to lighten his load, as the Queen insisted on longer lessons. When Marna herself asked for a third tutor, and that in addition to having a newly arrived woman at King's Halls serving as her Reader, Dalock could only comply with a smile. In truth, he had expected no less from his Gifted Queen. One night he watched her copying a text onto papyrus, her lips tight with concentration, and he thanked The Powers for leading him to her.

Yet his thoughts and his heart turned colder when he recalled that her life had not always been so, protected inside the borders of Eskalind, guarded within his Halls, snug in his nightly embrace. The younger prince of Hudiksland must pay for his foul deed, and pay dearly. Dalock King exhaled slowly, controlled and conscious of the anger rising from his gut. Letters had been sent, his Ambassador informed. His plans were laid, the trap would be set; he need only wait till the time was ripe.

———

Midmorning sunlight angled through the glass panes into the Queen's Chamber. Marna did her best not to sigh audibly as her Ladies Dara and Vaynya once again pinned her hair with beads and jewels.

"My Lady, this side is done. I do not believe it could look more lovely!" gushed Vaynya, with such confidence Marna almost believed her for a moment.

"This new hair style is much more fun than braids!" Dara's singsong voice roiled up and down, grating on Marna's nerves worse than dueling hammers in her father's forge. With a flourish, Vaynya handed Marna a mirror.

The Queen had seen swords give a firmer likeness. She ran her freshly manicured fingers along the beveled red stones framing the dull glass. Her skin felt tight and sticky from the hand lotion. "Yes, it is pretty," the King's Wife managed, without enthusiasm. She glanced at Saralya, who sat in one of the comfortable window seats surveying a large, bulky scroll, her eyes darting from line to line.

"My Reader," Marna called, aiming to keep her voice light despite her annoyance. "Please read to me."

"Yes, my Lady." The Queen's Reader fumbled as she twisted the lengthy parchment to its beginning.

Marna waited impatiently. Scrolls struck her as a clumsy and unruly apparatus. There was a sharp pain on her head. "Ow!"

"Oh, my Lady, I do apologize!" Vaynya fell to her knees and bowed, her long nose angled to the floor. "I will be more careful, my Lady, I do promise."

Vaynya's supplication annoyed Marna more than the injury. "Perhaps a style involving less pinning is in order." Vaynya nodded, smiling with her teeth, eyes anxious. Dara looked as crushed as though discovering a dark sauce had deeply soiled a favorite gown. "Lady Dara, perhaps you could create a plainer but pretty style for me."

Her attendant jerked upright, suddenly joyful once again. "Oh, I would enjoy that, my Lady! Lovely but simple. Yes, I can do that!"

Marna motioned to Saralya to read.

"This is the tale of Heedlock King, son of the First Strange King, and how he found his wife."

The Queen sighed, melting into the pleasant, soothing tones of her Reader's voice, yet her thoughts ran to finding a better use of her Ladies' time than tedious grooming rituals.

Marna Queen surveyed the cavernous King's Library. Teetering scroll shelves, in fading, chipped coats of paint, rose to the dark ceiling. Piles of parchment of every color, and scrolls too, sprawled at her feet, covering the flooring to the extent that she could not tell if the underlying surface was wood or stone. "One would find more order in an unsorted laundry basket," she muttered.

"Over here, my Lady, the herb lore volumes." Beril, the Master Librarian, beamed, leading her to the only section of neatly stacked scrolls. "I am told you will enjoy these." He stood next to one of the towering wooden cabinets, a slight bend of expectation in his thin frame as his Queen waded to him.

Marna heaved her red skirts over a stack of parchments in a variety of washed-out hues, reminiscent of faded flower petals. Their edges ruffled as she passed over them. A faint cloud of dust rose from her path. It prickled her nerves that in the King's well-ordered household, the Library looked as though ransacking pillagers had attacked it long ago, and was never tidied since. "Beril, is it always this disorderly?"

His proud expression fell into one of pinched concern. "I… it has been many years since we have had a King, or Queen, my Lady, who found much interest in the Library. Our tales, yes, certainly, but not the Library itself. And I … I am only one man, I don't even have an Apprentice…"

"Then perhaps my Ladies, and Saralya and I, will assist in setting it to order."

"Of course, my Lady." He looked to Saralya as if pleading for help.

The Queen elongated her vowels, choosing her words carefully. "I have especial interest in seeing the chronicles of the Kings. And their Queens."

"Oh yes, my Lady, they would be over there." Beril gestured to a large cabinet, in the back of the room, its facing carved with a tree and latched with a metal lock intricately wrought to resemble two leaves with undulating edges.

"Do you have the key, Master Librarian?"

"Um, well…"

The King's Wife raised an eyebrow, and the Librarian hastily fumbled with the clanking chain tethered to his belt. The trio plodded toward the imposing cabinet.

"This is quite old," Saralya remarked as they stopped before the towering scrollboard. "From the reign of Trelich King, I believe. His emblem was a tree and two conjoined leaves, and there, in the grooves are traces of paint in his colors, orange and red. Though it is faded."

"Yes, my Lady Reader, you know our history well." The thin man nodded approvingly, the keys clinking between his shuffling fingers as he searched for the right one.

Marna felt a mixture of pride in her Reader's abilities and envy in that she found herself lacking. "But why is this cabinet locked?"

"These are the chronicles meant only for the King and his immediate family, my Lady."

So this is where the Queens' secret to birthing only sons lies. She strove to conceal her anticipation but could not help leaning forward. Dalock King's Wife bit her lip, hoping she could read well enough to learn what she needed to know.

The Master Librarian interrupted her thoughts. "Or did you seek the public chronicles, my Lady?"

"No, this is what I am looking for."

Saralya reached to stroke a set of hinges fastened at waist level. They also were fashioned to look like twin leaves, with soft, ruffled edges that curled and elongated along the sides of the cabinet. Becoming annoyed with the clanking of the keys in the Librarian's hands behind her, Marna busied herself by examining the strange lock. "My, what cunning craftsmanship. I can't even tell where the key fits. My father would be impressed." Just as she touched it, the lock fell open in her hands. Saralya gasped.

After her initial shock, the new Queen fixed the Master Librarian with an arched eyebrow. "It seems there is much disrepair that needs to be set right here."

Beril cowered under her irritated gaze, dropping his handful of keys. They fell with a yank and swung on his belt chain like a thief at the gallows in Castleton. "Yes, yes, there is, my Lady."

The King's Wife briskly brushed the reddish rust from her hands.

"My Lady?" Saralya's voice was meek and uncertain, sounding more like a young girl than an educated courtier. "Might I … touch the lock?"

Marna nodded, releasing her hold on the two halves of metal now dangling from the imposing cabinet's handle. Her attendant stepped forward, reaching with slender fingers to touch the metal. The pieces recoiled for an instant and then conjoined, as though an invisible hand had fastened them. The trio jumped, and the Queen swore aloud. "By The Powers!"

Her Reader turned, dropping into a deep curtsey, dark brown eyes gazing reverently at Marna. The Librarian simply stared, the bottom of his dry lips quivering.

Saralya spoke. "My Lady, this is a moment of Legend! I've read that only the King or Queen can open certain locks. I now recall that Bravna Queen opened the lock of Trelich's cabinet whilst she was but a young girl, and that is how it became known that she would be Queen one day."

The new Queen grasped the lock again; it separated in her trembling hand. "Oh!" She stared at her open palm, trying to reconcile the image and cool touch of the two pieces with the thought that they should be one.

"P-perhaps," began the Librarian. "Perhaps now we know why there was no key?"

Dalock King's Great Hall echoed with the sound of the royal household chattering over the long tables at their communal dinner, but for yet another night, neither the King nor the Queen supped amongst them. Jinil contented himself with his meal, bantering pleasantries with his tablemates, who came and went or lingered as mood or duty prescribed. To his side was planted Safnil, a Groom with a talent for horse care and for eating slowly, but not for human conversation. The young man's brown eyes trespassed the border of his plate only to survey a new sauce bowl placed between the men by a serving woman.

Across from Jinil, Cook sat with two of her new assistants alongside, crumbs the only occupants of their plates. All wore brimless red hats, fitted close to the head and framing their faces with a cheerful ribbon trim. "Now, dears," Cook instructed her charges, "when we place our plates on the dirties tray, pay especial attention to what remains on the other plates. That's one honest way to tell which dishes and sauces did not please." Gathering her own plate, she stood, winking at Jinil. "My Lord King's Second." She and her workers tilted their heads to him, then her attention was drawn behind him. "Sister!" Cook called. "We are leaving; you may have our seats." Her assistants departed, one nearly colliding with the King's Page Moril, who darted in front of her.

"I thank you, my thoughtful sister," Lasta's resonant alto replied. "My toe is much healed, but I am grateful for a shorter walk and a warmed seat." The heavyset Lady came into view and patted her sister's arm as Cook made her leave. Jinil reached for a bread basket, plucking out a nut-crusted roll that smelled of toasted walnuts. The elderly noblewoman called, "Come, dear, sit by me."

Jinil raised his eyes to find Saralya across from him, her long, lovely locks brushed behind her back. She helped Lasta into her chair and then sat. A servant placed clean plates and utensils before the pair. "Thank you," offered the half-Guerish woman as the Lady peered about the table, eyeing the sauce and food bowls.

"Dara," Lady Lasta called, leaning forward and rubbing her hand as though it pained her. "Do pass that vegetable bowl before you. Those are my favorites."

Jinil studied the Queen's Reader whilst she spooned sauces onto her plate, her fingers deft and delicate. Another servant deposited cups of wine before the newly sat pair.

Lady Dara's high-pitched voice squeaked, "Lasta, did you hear? I was just telling how the lock just opened in the Queen's hands. Why, Saralya was there and saw it herself! Saralya, tell her the tale! Oh, Lasta, she did tell me, but only after Vaynya and I asked her about five times." She giggled, beaming as though she had discovered the prettiest ribbon ever created at a market stall.

Lady Lasta proclaimed in her sonorous tones, "You are speaking of the lock on Trelich King's cabinet? I recall when the King's Mother, Treya Queen, opened that cabinet for the first time." The elder Lady reached for a a sauce bowl. "The talk of these Halls for days!" Though she chuckled, her eyes misted, and when she spoke a moment later, her tone was tinged with a widow's memories. "Why, it was not long after my Lord husband and I were joined. Ah, to be newly joined again." Lasta's usually merry face creased with melancholy. She ladled a thick red sauce onto her plate, and one could almost see a sigh in her actions.

After a quiet moment in consideration of the seniormost Lady at court, Lady Vaynya, never the most tactful of women, asked—in a light voice confident of its ability to lift everyone's mood—"When will our newly joined royals appear before us for evening meal again?" Vaynya glanced to the Soldier seated next to her. "Should we wager? Now, I do believe Saralya would know. She has the Queen's confidence, does she not?"

"Saralya!" yelped Dara, her long neck straightening as she rose in her chair to glance over heads at the Reader. "Oh, what say you to Vaynya? Will we see the King before us first? Or the Queen? Or, oh! Both?"

Jinil lightly traced the smooth flesh of the scar intersecting his beard, waiting to see how the Scroll Merchant's daughter would handle the gossip's question.

"Mmph." The Queen's Reader pulled an empty fork away from her lips, puffing her cheeks. Jinil nearly guffawed at her ploy.

"Oh, let us not bother her when she is eating!" squeaked Dara. "It certainly is a delicious meal, even if it is not the Queen's chicken." The dark-haired Lady looked startled, then swiftly added, "Lady Lasta, do pass my compliments to your sister, our wonderful Cook."

"I will, but please do pass that vegetable bowl."

Dara complied in a flurry of apologies and nods that sent the red stones in her dangling earrings bobbing like a duck on a wind-blasted lake. Then her conversation adopted a new turn, and then another, so that neither she nor Lady Vaynya troubled the Queen's Reader any more at the communal table. Jinil caught Saralya's lovely eyes for a moment and lifted his mug from the table in a subtle salute. She nodded, tracing her fingers around the rim of her cup, a soft smile gracing her delicious lips.

For once, an Ambassador's letter from Havadra brought good news, at least for the Strange Kingdom. In the King's quarters, Jinil sat across from his Lord's small dining table, listening as Dalock King read, "The king of Havadra, Esthmirs, lord of the desert, ruler of et cetera, et cetera..." His brown eyes scanned the papyrus for the end of the lengthy formal title. "We know this, get to the point! Ah, here: 'Died in this first month of the year 2887, passing his fever to his younger brother, lord of—' By The Powers! Another paragraph of titles." He flipped to the next sheet, nearly dipping the completed page into one of the bowls of sauce clustered by his elbow. "Ah, he's dead too."

"The younger brother?"

"Aye. Which leaves the middle brother, he of many more titles…" He shifted to the next papyrus. "Esthofts, the new Havadran king, lord of the desert, and so on, and so on."

Jinil picked at a rough herb lodged between his front teeth. "Both the Havadran king and his second heir dead in the same letter."

The two men glanced at one another. "Poison," they blurted in unison.

Dalock King shook his head, reaching for a stubby slice of roll from the bronze-wire bread basket, then immersing it into a bowl of Queen's Recipe sauce. "The Havadrans are ever true to form." He stuffed the morsel into his mouth. "Mmm."

King's Second replied, "Yet Esthofts was the designated heir, and his rival's death may avert another civil war."

"True. May The Powers hear me, I am glad our ways are different." The Lord of Eskalind slid the letter to a bare spot on the wooden slab. "One King, one son, no question as to the succession for nearly three thousand years."

"Thank The Powers," Jinil replied. His Lord nodded, turning his head toward the diamond-paned windows lining his chamber. King's Second wondered if Dalock pondered when his own son would come. Though joined only a few months, there was no lack of effort on the royals' part. He kept his smile to himself.

"Well, my man, I have also another letter, confidential, straight from the hand of Humik, crown prince of Hudiksland. Now that is an interesting read." The new husband pushed away from his private dining table, leaning back in his chair with a creak.

"Aye?" King's Second watched his ruler closely.

"Humik's men have word that his younger brother has approached various nobles in his cause of supplanting the crown prince when Hudik King dies. But the lout is not very good at acquiring allies. Prince

Huprik attempted to … take a powerful noble's daughter." A slight sneer edged the corner of his mouth. "Claimed he thought her a serving girl."

Jinil shook his head, noting the cold demeanor that hardened his Lord's features. Under normal circumstances, he would have criticized the Hudiksland prince's idiocy in neglecting the obvious differences in attire in his land between women of rank and those who lacked noble alliances. "The aggrieved noble sides with Humik against Huprik, my Lord?"

"And many others do as well."

"This works to our benefit."

The King sat silent a moment. Then he spoke low and calm. "I will do it myself."

"My Lord?"

His eyes narrowing, he cut a glance to Jinil. "Kill Huprik. We will arrange it with the crown prince; when the time is right, I will journey there myself and slay the scum."

The Chief Counselor sucked in a slow breath. By The Powers, he sympathized with his Lord's desire to personally punish the Queen's attacker, but should King Hudik discover that Dalock King was behind the death of his younger son … At the least, a tricky diplomatic crisis would ensue. Though given King Hudik's weak health, the shock of his youngest son's death might end him as well. Jinil pondered too the likelihood of Hudiksland nobles supporting Eskalind's meddling in internal affairs that did not involve an invading army. Doubt clouded his thoughts, and he muttered, "As you wish, my Lord."

The King eyed him skeptically. "Jinil, a ride would be good." He stood, his man echoing the action.

"My Lord, our meeting with Ambassador Hornil is not until just before dinner. It promises to be short; he wishes to query you before departing to his posting in Kursak."

"Good, that gives us enough time. Come, let us see how the world looks from horseback." Dalock King grinned, but there was no smile in his eyes.

The two men traipsed wordlessly down the many stairs, passing out of King's Halls, toward the stables, each steeped in his own thoughts. Clear sunshine greeted them out of doors as workers trundled past bearing straw and saws. "Safnil!" the King called to the Groomsman with downcast eyes. "See our horses readied." The man muttered something that sounded like an affirmative and a "My Lord."

"Stay a moment, Jinil. I want to see if I can catch my wife's attention from here." The men paused on the dusty yellow dirt of the stables' forecourt, looking to the uppermost window on the Queen's side of the royal tower. The King placed a hand over his eyebrows, squinting to view the ring of windows encircling the top. "You must see what Marna has done with the Library. She and her Reader have worked wonders."

"I will, my Lord." The thought of the Master Librarian at last working for his keep uplifted Jinil's mood. Perhaps he was wrong to worry about the Hudiksland Plan.

"Ah, look, Jinil, there she is, by the two open windows." Dalock King waved; his Queen waved back. Jinil stepped behind his Lord, watching.

The King blew a kiss. The Lady of Eskalind smiled, her hand fluttering a goodbye whilst turning away. A slender red sleeve, ending in a dark brown hand, reached to close the window. *Saralya.* Jinil brought his hand to his forehead, as though he needed to brush away a troublesome lock of hair. The hand in the window stilled. He gave a slight lift of his hand. Saralya responded with a quick flit of her fingers.

"Jinil, did you see her?" the new husband asked. "She went to the other window."

He was uncertain for a moment whom his Lord meant, and he resumed a detached, diplomatic expression. "I did not notice."

"*You* did not notice?" Dalock King turned to his Second. Scrutinizing Jinil's face, he quickly turned back to the windows, catching sight of the Reader as she closed the second window.

"Ah-ha! Jinil, my man, you are caught." He thumped his Second on the shoulder and chuckled. "When did she show you her feet?"

Surprised at his Lord's deduction, Jinil exclaimed, "I have not seen her feet!" A trace of unexpected wistfulness tinged his voice.

"Yet, I wager!" His Lord winked. "I see that look in your eyes." They laughed together, continuing their steps to the stables in a jovial mood. Then the King touched his arm lightly, murmuring close to his ear, "If you ever feel for a woman how I feel for my wife, you will understand why I will continue with my plan, no matter the consequences." He stared straight ahead as though saying nothing of any importance, but in that moment Jinil sensed a resoluteness in the King's manner, a firmness, as though it were a tangible thing between them, with a will of its own.

After his Lord dismissed him for the evening, Jinil entered the King's Library, marveling at its transformation. Atop each stack, new labels written in a smooth, graceful hand and deep red ink named the general contents below. These scroll tags dangled in neat order, their titles turned outward for quick identification. The wooden floor gleamed with fresh polish, the musty pall of neglect banished, replaced with a slight tinge of mint.

King's Second could not resist a subtle grin.

Gleaming brass candelabras illuminated the dark wooden tables, their tops bare and dustless. Three Ambassador Apprentices, not far from their final assessments, sat together, studying their scrolls. One scratched at his new-grown beard. They nodded in deference to the King's man as he occupied the table adjacent to them.

The Master Librarian approached Jinil. "Here are three of the volumes you requested, my Lord King's Second." Beril carried himself stiffly, as though mindful not to irritate an injury. The Librarian placed the scrolls on the table, made a grimaced bow, and left.

Jinil unrolled the lengthy parchments, careful to give long attention to the sections that did not interest him prior to reaching his goal: a detailed map of a forest in Hudiksland, not far from Marna Queen's family's home. Enthusiastic whispering by the Apprentices redirected his attention, their musings far too animated to be simply discussing their studies. Shooting a look of warning reproach, he saw their attention directed at the doorway, where Saralya stood bent in hushed conversation with Beril.

One of the young men murmured, "An exotic beauty."

Another, in undertones, "She must be from Guerland."

The third purred whilst fondling his beard. "I would do more than admire her feet if she showed them to me."

"Silence is expected in the Library," King's Second intoned in his most authoritative voice.

"Your pardon, my Lord King's Second." The Ambassador Apprentices ceased their commotion but kept solid watch on the object of their desire.

The Librarian, suddenly bright-eyed and as attentive as if one of the royals were in his presence, nodded with vigor at the Queen's attendant. "Yes, my Lady Reader, I just replaced it on the fourth stack on the left. Shall I assist you?"

She murmured a reply that did not reach Jinil's ears and turned to make her way alone toward the shelves.

A look of sudden realization crossed the older man's face. "And do mind the scroll bags on the floor!"

Just as Beril spoke the words, Saralya lurched forward. Her arms flailed and swiped a few scrolls from a shelf as she tumbled to the floor. Scrolls rolled in every direction, haphazardly clanking upon the floor, unfurling like pennants whipping in a breeze. Jinil, the Apprentices, and the Librarian all rushed to the young woman's aid, bounding past chairs and tables and leapfrogging the uncoiling parchments.

The Apprentice with the fresh beard reached her first. "My Lady Reader!" He touched the smooth silk of her sleeve as she raised her head. Saralya looked more startled by the attention than by her fall. "Will you forgive me? I should not have left my bag here."

"Why *did* you leave your bag there?" growled Jinil, inserting himself between the prone woman and her would-be suitor. The Apprentice backed away like a chastised pup. Jinil offered her his hand. "Are you all right, my Lady Reader?"

"Yes, I think so." She took his hand. He gently raised her to her feet.

She gave him a weak smile of reassurance.

With a glare at the Apprentices, Jinil stated, "You three, clean this up. Libraries are not meant to be hazardous places." They crouched, hastily retrieving the scrolls and their sacks, rolled the fallen scrolls back into tight coils, then skulked to their seats. He turned to Saralya again, realizing she still held his hand.

"The Queen … tells me you have a library of your own."

He saw in the warm glow of the candles that her eyes glistened a deep, dark brown with just the barest hint of gold in their depths. "I do."

Before he could invite her to see it she asked, "Do you ever accept visitors?"

"Rarely, but I would be honored to invite you."

"The honor is mine." If his heart skipped a beat, he was too pleased to notice.

Jinil turned to the Librarian, feeling more kindly toward the man than ever before. "Beril, keep the volumes I requested in reserve," he ordered, and then he led Saralya to his quarters, not for the first time silently thanking The Powers they were nearby. He gestured to the Guard at the door to leave them alone as he ushered her though the doorway into the candlelit chamber. He closed the door just in time to see Saralya nearly trip over his bed.

"Oh! What has gotten into me? I am not normally this clumsy." The Queen's Reader smoothed her dress as she stood, her eyebrows rising in bewilderment.

"I'm sorry, it is a narrow room for a bed. This area was intended to be the receiving room or library, but I rarely entertain, and I needed the larger space of the main chamber for my volumes." Jinil motioned for her to continue along the stone-walled passage, lit with shield-shaped sconces of thin, translucent jasper. "There are swords on the wall on the left…" He hoped she did not mind his caution as she walked toward his library, but he did not want to interrupt their time alone with a call to the Healers.

"My, this is a lovely reading room." The Queen's Reader admired the towering shelves of carefully organized scrolls that lined the walls of the spacious room. A desk and writing chair sat just to the left of the doorway, and an upholstered chair, wide enough for comfortable reading and sleeping, rested under the vaulted window on the right. "You have the Sea Copy of Jasbad!" Saralya exclaimed, reaching, but pausing before she touched the red-coral-knobbed scroll lying unfurled on the reading chair.

"You have heard of this scroll?" He was impressed she knew not only of the obscure author but also of this exquisite volume, capped with carved coral from the seas of the far south, near Ofsha.

"Aye, I searched for it in the King's Library." She bent for a closer look at the illustrated parchment, pearly ink glimmering on its dark surface. "I always thought it odd that Jasbad's work, which speaks much of gardens and the abundance of the land, found favor in the courts of the sea nations."

"Ah yes, gardens." He felt ridiculously pleased with her assessment of the author and recited his favorite passage as she stroked the scroll knob. "'Though my heart feels certain, my tongue cannot yet name the name.'"

Saralya glanced at him, a spark in her eyes, as they finished the phrase in unison.

"'Thus I carry its bloom unspoken within the garden of my thought.'"

They gazed at one another, and a warmth blossomed in his chest that thrilled and simultaneously calmed him. Even the air between them seemed to shimmer as he studied those dark orbs revealing a startling depth, a window to a mirror mind, to an immaterial presence that beckoned him to recognize himself in different form. "I have thought of that line often, of late."

"I have as well." Her voice was shy, but serious. She glanced at the floor, and stepped out of her slippers, her bare brown feet peeking from underneath the red hem of her skirt.

He touched her cheek.

"Shall I stay?" she asked.

"Please."

"You look glum today," the Queen observed from her window seat. As her Reader entered the Queen's quiet chamber, the distinct sadness of Saralya's expression contrasted with the infectious joy of the past few weeks since she and Jinil became lovers.

Saralya said nothing, her eyelashes aimed at the floor as she paced to the Queen. Marna's Page Favik shut the chamber's door behind him, leaving the pair alone.

"Come, what is it? I would cheer you if I am able." Marna patted the soft fabric of the crimson cushion next to her. Her Reader sank heavily by her side.

"There is nothing you can do, my Lady." She fidgeted with the faded purple ribbons that bound the green-knobbed scroll in her hand. Tears stood in the Queen's attendant's eyes. "It seems… I am not… with child."

"This makes you sad?" Saralya nodded, wiping her eyes with a burgundy-colored handkerchief. "My dear," began the Queen, hoping to distract her companion, though by now she knew this odd custom of her new country. "Help me to understand. In my homeland, an unjoined woman with a lover would weep with joy at this news." She touched Saralya's arm lightly. "Tell me how it is different here."

Her Reader straightened as though reading a Legend scroll to a formal gathering of all the Ladies of the court. "Eskalinders believe that if a woman gets with child, it is a sign from The Powers that the lovers are meant to join."

"But if no child follows, the couple will not join?"

"Yes." Saralya spilt more tears, which she quickly dried. "Unless they both feel the union is right. I had hoped..." She inhaled slowly. "Jinil is unlike any lover I have ever had. He can quote all of our greatest chroniclers at length; he safely traveled the borderlands, and many of the outerlands, he tells wonderful tales about them; he is handsome and tender..." She shrugged into her handkerchief.

"There. Now do not weep. It is clear what you must do." The Reader looked at her Queen, who winked. "You will have to try again. After all, the King and I have not given up in this matter."

"But that is different, my Lady. You ... you know you will have a son, someday."

Marna grinned at the woman's surety. Saralya was a scholarly woman, possessed of an immense education her Queen envied, yet even she believed that strange tale.

"Well, my dear Reader, I would not have you sad. We will see what comes, and if it is any comfort to you, I will ask The Powers to grant you and Jinil a child soon."

Saralya's dark eyelashes fluttered with suppressed tears. "Oh, my Lady, thank you. Thank you for asking The Powers on my behalf!" She grasped the Queen's hand, pressing it to her forehead in gratitude as though her wish were indeed granted. Marna started slightly, but smiled, hoping she did not show her surprise at this fervent display. All she had done was utter a common Hudikslander phrase. She would most certainly ask The Powers every day after this!

Never in the full year since meeting Dalock had Marna felt this tongue-tied.

From across her chamber, her husband pled, "Why do you not wish to go to Kursak? It is only a bit over two weeks in a light carriage. We will have our trunks packed and sent ahead to make our journey faster, perhaps ride part of the way for speed." Dalock paused, but she did not reply from her window seat, her eyes occupied by the trembling fire in the hearth. "Marna, it is a coronation, but you act as though it were a battle!"

She shot him a steely, warning gaze. He softened, stepping toward the long table, resting his hands upon a chair back as though pulling the seat away to allow her to sit. "I have a better idea. Kursak's seat is close to Hudiksland. We could visit your sister, see her family on the return home. It would only be a week's travel." He smiled. "We would stay as long as you like."

By The Powers, she did not want to admit to him she was angry at Werna, but she was. Every letter she received from her sister contained yet another request for help. In the early months of her Queenship, Werna asked for helpers, then for builders for a larger house. Now that was completed, her latest appeal was for horses. It irked Marna that not one letter contained thanks, only more requests.

"Kursak would be honored to have us *both* in attendance."

She chewed her lip.

"Are you unwell? Is that why?" In her husband's voice she felt his hopeful inquiry, whether she was finally with child.

Aggravated, words at last came to her, and she flared, "No, but Dalock, I would not delay my studies for travel." She heard the truth in her words as she spoke them, as though her mouth revealed a part of her thoughts unreachable until this moment.

"Have Saralya read to you in the carriage." Dalock's voice hinted at the unraveling of patience.

"And have the poor woman ill from the motion? I think not," Marna countered, watching his temples redden with frustration. How well she knew him now. He should understand she would not be swayed. "I would not have you unhappy," she began, "but realize, I must stay here, continuing my education, without the interruptions a long journey brings."

"You feel compelled to remain here?" The King's voice rose with each word.

Marna raised an eyebrow at his demanding manner. "I do, my Lord." Ice frosted her voice.

"Do not call me that!"

"I will when you use that tone with me!" the Queen shouted, standing, incensed with his insistence.

"Mar—" Dalock stopped himself. "As you wish." He thudded to the adjoining doors open between their chambers. His back to her, he stood in the doorway, announcing as if addressing a Soldier awaiting instruction, "Jinil will accompany me, leaving you in command at King's Halls during our absence." He departed her quarters, closing his door, sliding the iron latch to shut it tight with a clank of restrained force.

Marna exhaled loudly, shook her head, and crossed her arms. "So that is how my husband behaves in a quarrel. Petulant at not getting his way, giving orders." Staring hard at Dalock's latched door, she muttered, "At least we were joined over a full year before it happened."

Shutting her own door, she threw the bolt, and addressed the wooden barrier as though it were her husband. "Is my being in command here a punishment?"

The Queen charged to her main door, flinging the handle toward her with such quick force, the Guardsman on the landing started as it swung on its hinges. His eyes darted into the empty room, and before she could speak, he dipped his head, asking, "Shall I call for your Reader, my Lady?" He raised his eyes to hers.

The Lady of Eskalind nodded and closed the door, proceeding to pace a furrow in the tea-colored carpet whilst her thoughts ran in circles. Knitting her fingers, she plodded to the King's door, and stopped. The Queen quivered a hand to the ruby-jeweled handle. The muffled slamming of a door sounded on the other side, likely his main door. She withdrew her tentative fingers. "Acting like a child!"

She turned to her writing desk, crowded with bronze bowls overflowing with fruit, small pots of sauces, an untouched bread basket, all awaiting the King's and Queen's pleasure. The switch in roles of the two tables in her chamber was further exhibited at the dining table, where loose parchments and coiled scrolls lay scattered or stacked as though a person of two minds, one prone to order and the other to chaos, had arranged them. "I was right; I must continue my studies now. I have made much progress." Raising her chin she paced to the window, eyes to the lazy clouds overhead. "Maybe I will call for Favik and give him another lesson."

Her main door opened. Saralya entered and bowed, avoiding the Queen's eyes. "Come, Saralya," Marna called, moving to the long table and sitting. "I will read this scroll and hear your corrections." She picked and picked at the silken ribbon tied about the scroll. Finally it released.

"Yes, my Lady." Her Reader drew a chair next to the Queen. "Which tale is it?"

"Narmlich King, who, it says, had great difficulty finding his wife. Hmm." Marna scanned the parchment; its original deep violet color had faded along the edges to a pleasing lilac. In the shimmering green ink before her, she was gratified to see no unfamiliar words.

"Might you read a different tale, my Lady?" Saralya's tone was constrained.

Marna turned, finding her Reader glaring at the tapestries. "Was it something I said?"

Her attendant shook her head with a quick motion. "No, my Lady, something Jinil said. Many things that he said!" Her Reader rose, then sank back into her chair, a range of emotions revealed in her tensed features. "I finally asked him, and he will not join with me!" Saralya blurted, her voice uncharacteristically unsteady. "After all we have said, shared… he will not. I cannot believe it!" She looked at the Queen, dark eyes alight, then glanced at the floor whispering, "How can he not see we were brought together by The Powers? I came to court, he returned from a long absence, both of us without lovers, and …"

Marna could not catch the words through the descending whimper of her Reader's voice. She lowered her scroll, placing a sympathetic hand on her companion's arm. Saralya drew a long breath, seeming to calm herself, then blurted, "My Lady, how can he not see it?"

"I thought the two of you well matched! Is there no hope then?" Instantly the Queen wished she had given her utterance even a moment of consideration.

Saralya shook her head. "Oh, I don't know! He wants to be a father, The Powers willing." The young woman hung her head. "There is still a chance I might be with child." She raised her dark eyes. "And then he would join with me."

"Would you want him after this … ?" Marna silently thanked The Powers for stopping her tongue before she said "rejection."

Her Reader nodded. "Then it would be clear we were meant to be together. My Lady, I love him." Tears formed in Saralya's dark eyes. "I was not a joining babe, yet my parents joined. Since I followed, The Powers made clear my parents were meant for each other." She sniffed. "If only… if only Jinil would give us more time."

Marna pursed her lips, wondering if her companion recalled her

Queen's promise to ask The Powers to send a child. Before her, Saralya wept into a vermilion-colored handkerchief, embroidered with the King's emblem, edged with his initial. Marna looked away.

"I'm sorry, my Lady, that I am in such a state," Saralya whimpered, steeped in her grief, oblivious to her Queen's troubles. The dark-haired woman dropped her heavy head onto her Lady's velvet-clad arm. "I thought Jinil … was the one."

"There, there, dear Reader." Marna patted Saralya's hair as tears of her own welled, blurring her vision. "We do not know what The Powers plan for us, yet we must carry on. Look, you are a beautiful, intelligent woman; I am certain you will find happiness one day." She stifled the comment that her regard for Jinil had dropped like a stone flung from her tower window.

Her companion nodded half-heartedly, raising her head. "Thank you, my Lady." She darted her handkerchief to her smooth cheeks, patting a dripping tear. "Please, please do not think me ungrateful. I thank The Powers every day for allowing me to be your Reader. Ever since I was a small girl, I knew I must one day serve on my father's behalf. I dreaded it for years." Saralya glanced at the Queen sheepishly. "But I'm truly glad to be in your service."

Marna managed to pull her lips into a smile. "I thank you, my dear Reader. It seems we have each experienced a difficult day."

The Queen tried to vanquish her creeping doubts, yet she and Saralya were helpless to change their circumstances, like two prisoners locked in a tower. "Here, let us call for tea and cakes. A bite to eat and a lesson completed will shift our minds to better thoughts." It was not the first time she had uttered a wish aloud, hoping the words would make it true.

———

After Dalock's departure, Marna found sleep came uneasily. Worries cascaded across her thoughts swifter than butter melting on bread fresh from the oven. How she would respond if request for military aid came from a borderland, if she would ever get with child, even notions as mundane as offhand utterances being misinterpreted or maligned. One night, restless with anxiety, she crept from her bed, hastily donned two sleeping robes, and made the long trek down the thick stone stairs, alarming the Guards with the bright light emanating from her candle.

Politely shunning their offers of assistance, the Queen trudged to the darkness of the King's Library, holding her candle aloft like a beacon as she approached the tidy shelves of scrolls, uncertain what volume might claim her attention. Thoughts of visiting the kitchens for a quick bite were snuffed when a muffled shuffling sounded behind her. She spun, to see no one, just the cabinet of Trelich King, magnified in the candle's glow. Stepping toward it, she placed her free hand upon the lock, which parted for her fingers. Opening the heavy door, Marna peered inside, finding at eye level a gold-knobbed scroll resting lengthwise along the shelf, in opposition to the other volumes, which nestled one atop the other, their knobs an array of engraved metals, sculpted woods, and shaped stones.

"Perhaps this one will be a good read." Grasping the scroll, she tucked it under her arm, closing the door and reaching for the lock.

Again the shuffling sound. "We cannot have rodents!" she breathed, angry at the thought of any creature consuming the private records of her husband's ancestors. Opening the cabinet again, she found the contents completely repositioned, all scrolls lying parchmentwise in neat stacks, except for one—with, yet again, gold finials. The Queen peered into the cabinet, eyes roaming, searching for some explanation.

"My Lady?"

She turned, finding the Librarian behind her, feebly shielding his eyes from her candle. "Beril, you startled me."

"Your pardon, my Lady, I saw the light and came to find who was trying their hand at the cabinet."

"Others try to get in?"

"Before the King joined, I think every young woman in these Halls tried her hand when she thought no one was looking, hoping the cabinet would open and prove her King's Wife." The Librarian chuckled softly.

"I get more sleep these days, as that matter is settled, thank The Powers."

"And yet upon our first meeting, I questioned you about a key."

"Aye, and my apologies for not owning up immediately. It was not a test. The Library had …" Beril glanced at the neat stacks of scrolls. "It had gotten beyond my control, it seemed to untidy itself the moment I looked away, and I had no Apprentices or helpers to assist. When we met, I feared what you would think of me, and all other thoughts went astray. I am in awe of you, my Lady, for no one else living besides Dalock King can unlatch this cabinet."

Marna nodded, a bit pleased that Beril considered her the true Queen, but uneasy with the thought of other hands trying to pry into the secret cabinet of the Kings and their Queens. "I heard a strange sound coming from the cabinet when it was closed. When I opened it the second time, the scrolls had changed position." She gestured to the gold-tipped scroll in the cabinet. "This scroll was nowhere to be seen, yet now it is lying in front of all the others."

The Librarian nodded, his long chin a sharp point in the harsh light. "Treya Queen told me the Cabinet of Trelich displays the scroll a royal most needs at the present moment, as directed by The Powers." Beril bowed forward, and for a moment she feared he would burn his forehead on her candle. She pulled the flame away. "The Powers must mean for you to read this scroll." He squinted at the twin cylinders. "Gold was one of the colors of Treya Queen and Farlock King. Perhaps it is her scroll?"

The Queen shook her head with certainty. "Their other color was sable, and this parchment is too light. It could not have faded that much. Though in this light, it is hard to distinguish colors." Marna reached for the scroll and placed it under her arm, uncomfortably adjusting the other scroll already resting there.

"My Lady, please, allow me to fetch you a scroll basket."

She closed and locked the cabinet. "No thank you, I will simply sit over here and read for a while."

"Certainly, my Lady." The Librarian bowed again and shuffled away across the wooden floor.

Marna Queen placed her candle on a nearby table, laying the scrolls in the pool of orange light reflecting off the freshly polished wood. Untying the stiff velvet ribbon from the first scroll, she spread the the cylinders apart to read from the beginning. Words in shimmering gold ink, quilled in an uneven but legible print, greeted her.

The Chronicles of Merva Queen, by Her Own Hand.

"Ah, Dalock's grandmother. Her quilling is only slightly better than mine."

Or, A Tavern Keeper's Daughter Finds Herself Queen of Eskalind, and How She Coped; Written as a Conversation for Future Generations of Our Family.

"What an odd start. I forgot she was a Tavernier's daughter. At least I can read all the words." Marna chuckled lightly at the amusing bits of the former Queen's tale. "My, she writes as though relating to an old friend." Over the hours, the candle shortened as Marna immersed herself in Merva Queen's tales, feeling she had discovered a new companion.

Chapter Thirty-Three—Visiting Royals

Despite the plodding ride through Kursak, and a polishing by his Page Trevil, a slight dusting of Eskalind's yellow soil endured in the groove where the leather of Dalock's boots met the soles. He doubted anyone but himself would notice. He found comfort in this faint reminder of his faraway homeland across the many miles and days apart from his beloved Queen. At his side, Jinil waited, the two Eskalinders standing behind the large door that partitioned this cavernous foyer from the Kursak king's presentation hall. Dalock wished to The Powers that They would open a way for Marna to be here instantly to take his arm. Alas.

The striped oak and mahogany door ground open before the two men as the hall warden boomed, "Enter, Dalock King and Jinil, King's Second, Lords of Eskalind, our neighbors to the South!"

The Strange King grew weary of borderlanders always assuming Jinil was a noble, given his position. It felt like a taunt. Yes, someday he hoped to grant his Second title and land for his decades of loyal service, but it was too early in his reign to bestow such honors.

Then again, it had been ten years since he became King.

This sobering realization soured Dalock's thoughts as he progressed past Kursak courtiers, officers, and ladies, all clad in the long, belted tunics both men and women of that land wore, most in muted shades or whites and beige, enlivened by cotton- or metal-threaded embroidery tracing the cuffs and sleeves in vine-like patterns. All foreheads bent to the upraised fingertips of their left hands, Kursak's traditional gesture of respect. The only spot of bright color was the vermilion robes of his Ambassador, Hornil.

On the far end of the marble-banded floor, the twenty-third ruler to bear the title of Kursak stood on the dais, in the same attitude as his people. Midway through his third decade, he bore a weathered countenance, as though this event marked a long anniversary of a troubled reign. A step down from his position was a woman immediately recognizable from her graceful attitude as Princess Zala, wife to Crown Prince Humik of Hudiksland, and sister to Kursak's king. Instantly, Dalock recalled the sole time he met her previously, at the court of King Hudik, and the tender affection she shared with her husband. If only Marna were at his side.

The new ruler and his sister stepped to the floor, Kursak speaking in regal tones, "Dalock Strange King, our Ever Ally of Eskalind, most honored guest. Peace pledged to you."

"And to you, Kursak." As was the tradition of his land, the dark-haired man embraced Dalock about the shoulders.

Zala spoke in her melodious alto. "Lord Strange King, while I stand this day by my brother's side in the land of my birth, I bear a present for you from my husband, the heir of Hudiksland." She beckoned to a lad, who tiptoed forward, offering the Eskalinder a covered chalice wrought of sparkling silver traced with a pattern of *H*'s. As he accepted the cup, the princess held his gaze. "I believe you will greatly admire the crafts-manship." Zala reached to lightly tap the base of the cup. The intensity of her dark gaze and the gesture convinced Dalock that there was more to this bestowal than met the eye. His nod was formal and stiff, but he spoke warmly. "I thank you, princess. It is good to see you in health."

The corner of her full mouth twitched ever so slightly, and after bowing to the Eskalinder again in the Kursak manner, she and her brother turned and ascended the dais once more, facing the doorway for the entrance of the next guest. Dalock passed his present to Jinil for safekeeping as the door warden called forth, "Enter, Princess Huma, daughter of King Hudik of Hudiksland, our neighbor to the East."

The blond woman glided toward the narrow-eyed king of Kursak, the tight bodice of her light blue gown amplifying her bosom, her upturned face draped on both sides by a veil a few shades darker. Dalock recalled her dressing in his colors whilst she attempted to woo him at her father's court. Her colors today suited her light skin, for as she came to the dais's foot, her eyes seemed magnified and a rich, appealing azure.

Huma bowed before Kursak, brushing her sheer veil modestly over her revealing neckline, a gesture that drew attention to her curves whilst acknowledging that Kursak customs for women's dress were far more discreet than those of Hudiksland.

The new king acknowledged the princess with a nod and a tightening about the lips. His sister welcomed her husband's sibling. "*Peace pledged to you, Huma.*"

"And to *you*, saister." The women smiled at one another, but Dalock saw daggers in their eyes. As with most borderland royal courts, different feelings burbled under the prescribed pleasantries.

The Hudiksland princess coolly floated past the Strange King, with a brisk dip of her head, as the door warden bellowed forth the names of two princesses from Amkland, the land to the west of Kursak. Neither was likely beyond her teens; both were pale complected, their plain faces framed by honey-shaded locks braided into myriad thin ropes pinned in a mastery of twists and loops. Dalock could almost hear Marna's voice grousing about the waste of time and effort spent on their hairstyles. As the pair approached the dais, he noted the second Amklander was even less attractive than the first, with an unfortunate birthmark at the corner of her mouth.

Both greeted the Kursak royals with pleasant, cheerful voices that diminished the tension lingering from the exchange between Zala and Huma. The Amkish women were followed by the the queen of Nordak, Kursak's neighbor to the north, and her daughter, Hymeea, a blue-eyed beauty crowned with a glory of auburn locks. Both wore floor-length gowns of a milky color, overlaid with a diaphanous pearlescent fabric trimmed with white fur to lend them an ethereal appearance. Many of the Kursak courtiers watched with especial interest as the lovely Nordak princess glided past. Kursak himself eyed her with focused attention.

This marked the end of the entrance of the honored guests from the four lands ringing Kursak. The orderly distribution of the court melted as visitors and courtiers mixed together, seeking out confidants or making new acquaintances. A broad-shouldered couple from Eyfia, each cloaked in the soft gray wool of their land's famous sheep, waylaid a servant carrying a platter of short cups, and upon discovering the petite size of the beverage containers, relieved the man of the entire tray. Chuckling at the sight, Dalock made in the direction of the Nordak queen, whom he had not met before. He found her a genial, sensible woman and could not help but think that Marna would have gotten on well with her.

Whilst they spoke, another servant approached with a tray of dark wine and sweet juices, served in squat cups fashioned from several bands of metal.

"My father would demand ten of these to satisfy his thirst." Princess Huma reached across the tray for a cup. She procured two, handing one to the Strange King, who turned to offer it to the queen of Nordak, only to find the tide of conversation had swept her to another shore, leaving him marooned with the light-haired princess of Hudiksland.

"Your father is in good health, Princess Huma?"

She regarded Dalock over her cup as she tilted a small sip past her lips. "Yes, my Lord King, and I am as well. Thank you for your consideration." Huma smiled, gazing across the long room to where the Amkish princesses engaged in chatting with Kursak. "Just look at them. Could they be more obvious in their attentions?"

A wry grin tugged the corner of Dalock's lopsided mouth, recalling how Huma had presented herself, uninvited, in his bed. To his surprise, she noticed his expression and laughed lightly. "Yes, I suppose you do find that amusing." The twin blue jewels of her eyes glimmered at him.

"That time has passed; I am more mature in my dealings." The Strange King pondered her meaning whilst she adjusted a thick bracelet of oblong silver shapes, bulbous like seedpods, down her wrist. "I think Kursak prefers the ice princess."

"Ice princess?"

"Oh come, surely you know your geography," she teased, drawing her red lips into a pout. "Nordak, land of ice and the ice jewels?"

"Hmm." Dalock studied the interleaving pattern of colors on his cup.

"See! Follow his eyes." He reluctantly did so.

The queen of Nordak's daughter at that moment approached the Kursak ruler, and all his attention fixed on her, like a starving man brought a heaping platter of succulent delicacies.

Huma sighed. "Ah, to choose who one joins with. Only a lucky royal can make that choice. Would you not agree?" Her expression softening, she draped more of her long veil across her chest, as if shielding her body from unwanted attention. For a moment she appeared shy, vulnerable even, with the demeanor of a modest young woman seeking protection.

"Princess Huma," Jinil interrupted with a stiff bow, his hands still grasping the covered cup granted by her older brother. "My apologies for the interruption."

"Of course." Huma acknowledged King's Second kindly. Jinil continued, his eyes lowered, a signal to Dalock that his next utterance was not full truth. "I beg your leave, my Lord, but a letter from Marna Queen has just arrived; it is in your quarters."

"Yes, your wife! My sincere apologies, I did not congratulate you on your joining, Dalock King." She offered a slim hand to him. "I wish you much happiness."

"I thank you, princess, and shall make my leave now." With that, the two Strange Kingdomers repaired quickly to the commodious apartment set aside for Dalock King. Once ensconced and the solid doors firmly shut, Jinil placed the silver cup upon a round table inlaid with strips of varying shades of wood. "Your pardon, my Lord, there is no message from your Lady." His Second tapped the cup, which gave an unsatisfying, dull ring. "I believe this deserves our immediate attention; there is small latch inside the base."

Dalock nodded, picked up the cup, found it weighed less than he imagined, and turned it over. Seeing nothing extraordinary, he ran a finger along the inside, till his nail snagged on a small, metallic protrusion. Pressing it slightly, it released a catch, and the seemingly solid metal parted, revealing a hidden chamber. "Fine craftsmanship, indeed," the King murmured. Within, he found a slim coil of smoothed papyrus. That he handed to Jinil, who unrolled it carefully. "Well, is there a message?"

His man fought with the sheet, which insisted on curling back into a cylindrical shape. "Aye, my Lord, from Crown Prince Humik." Jinil crimped the unruly papyrus, forcing it to lie flat, then handed it to the King, who read in a low voice:

Lord Strange King,
I fear my brother Huprik's plots grow deeper the further we delve.
My wife and son have been poisoned with a potion of smoked Bane's
Root, which is not deadly in one dose, but grows in lethal potency
with each administration.

"A plot worthy of a Havadran," Dalock muttered.

Jinil pondered. "I thought Princess Zala looked well tonight." He shook his head. "Yet she must be ill with worry about her son."

"That despicable swine Huprik!" spat Dalock. He continued reading quietly aloud,

I hoped Zala and our child would be safe in Kursak but now have
reason to believe my brother has corrupted my sister, Huma, against
them. I believe she plans to poison them further at Kursak's coronation.
Zala and her brother know of this, and their every move is guarded.
I now know too well the mood of a man whose wife has been harmed.

"You are not alone," uttered Dalock in a cold voice.

A glance at Jinil revealed his Second staring at nothing, his green eyes unfocused. The Strange King cleared his throat.

The culprit is to journey to Fambay Forest on the morning after the new moon for a hunting expedition. There will be a close man, loyal to our cause, in his party. I will send directions, and a token by which he will recognize you.
All thanks and health to you, and to your family,
Humik, Crown Prince of Hudiksland

"At last the time draws near." Dalock dropped the note into the fireplace, watching fire curl the edges of Humik's missive. "Over a full year I have waited." The papyrus smoked, crinkling under the blaze's heat. In a moment, nothing remained save ash and cinder. Not for the first time he played out in his mind how Huprik would die, pleading for clemency. A cry that would go unanswered.

Yet this time Dalock thought too of his dear wife, miles and miles away, wondering if she carried their son. Perhaps this was all part of The Powers' plan—for him to die seeking his revenge, for his unborn son to grow up without a father.

Only a few ruling Strange Kings had known such a fate; all possessed wives who were capable governors in their husbands' absence. Marna was the definition of capable, though at times she did not see her own Gifts.

Still staring into the fire, he considered that it would be cruelty on The Powers' part to allow him to die seeking justice from his wife's attacker. But seek it he must. Dalock King sighed as he turned to Jinil. "I must quill Marna again, ask if she is with child."

For once, his Second looked surprised. "As you wish, my Lord."

Dalock plopped into the cushioned chair before his writing desk. "Have this note sent by Swift Riders." He hastily scratched his pen across the crimson surface of the thick papyrus, beginning with the date: *29th Day, 7th Month, 2887.* That much was rote; for the rest he strove to convey how he yearned for her and the expediency of needing to know her status. The door to the spacious chamber creaked open. Page Trevil entered with cautious footsteps, and Jinil intercepted the lad. The two muttered quietly for a moment, then Trevil dashed away.

Scrawling his name, Dalock blew on the ink, willing it to dry swiftly.

"My Lord, your Page informs me that the private dinner for the honored royal guests in Kursak's quarters has begun."

"Yes, yes, I know. I will attend. Once this blasted ink dries." The glossy brown sheen slowly soaked into the fibrous sheet, tauntingly slow. A tentative touch left no residue on his finger, and the anxious ruler folded and sealed the letter, pouring wax from a nearby candle over the fold. "Jinil, what do you think of Humik's latest news?"

King's Second glanced at the striped tiles rimming the fireplace where Prince Humik's correspondence had crisped to ash, then at the doorway. "I think one should keep a close eye on Princess Huma tonight."

"Me, Kursak, Princess Zala, Kursak's men, Zala's attendants ... tonight all of Kursak keeps eyes on Princess Huma."

"I believe she will relish the attention." Jinil's green eyes lit with cool mirth.

Dalock warmed to the banter. "And Kursak's other suitors will be beside themselves wondering at his lack of interest." They chuckled, though Dalock's turned to a cough from the acrid scent of burnt papyrus. "Ah, Kursak. What a strange tradition it is that he changes his name when he becomes king."

"I recall learning of that custom in my Ambassador's apprenticeship. I always thought it must cause great confusion among the historians, having all the kings named Kursak, and trying to keep the numbers ordered."

"Perhaps we should just call him twenty-three?" The Eskalinders laughed.

Not long thereafter, Dalock entered the private quarters of the newest monarch of Kursak, finding the other royal guests engaged in conversation in the commodious sitting area, brightly lit with candelabras and hanging chandeliers. The clusters of sofas, small tables, and upholstered chairs could easily accommodate two dozen guests.

Princess Huma sat chatting with the Nordak queen, while the three other unjoined princesses clustered about Kursak like young plants seeking the light of the sun.

Large bowls and trays of food rested on a long table to one side of the room, and male servants ladled and forked savory-smelling foodstuffs onto smaller plates, which were placed on low tables beside the sitting furniture. More Kursak servants, all men, passed by in their flowing tunics, retrieving and dispensing small, streaked cups of liquid refreshments.

Zala entered from a side chamber and greeted the Strange King, leading him away to sit with her on an unoccupied couch of striped fabric, framed with dark- and light-veined polished wood. Comfortably seated, Dalock reached for an empty plate from the nearest small table. Smothering the plate with a few forkfuls of grilled meats and vegetables, he asked, "How fares your young son?"

The crown princess smiled warmly, the gold-threaded embroidery on her high neckline sparkling in the brilliant candlelight. "Homik is well now, Dalock King. He was ill for a time before we journeyed to my homeland, but since residing in my brother's household, he is toddling and darting about, just as a wee boy should." Her light laughter belied the glimmer of moisture on her dark lashes; her pale cheeks colored slightly. "But tell me, do you find your quarters suitable?"

"They are very fine, princess. And my full compliments to your husband on the finely wrought cup." He wiped a bead of sauce from his lips. "How long will you stay in Kursak?"

Zala reached for a salver draped with green grapes. "I am not certain. It depends on many things." The princess glanced quickly at her saister. "For now, there is my brother's coronation to be attended to, and to be attended."

The Eskalinder laughed politely at her wordplay. A woman Dalock did not recognize entered the room, curtseying quickly to the gathered royals, a sheer veil in the fashion of Hudiksland ladies draped over her light-colored hair. She held her hands tight to her stomach, clutching a small blue box. A slight rattling sound came from her direction, perhaps from the box, or the chunky silver baubles about her wrists.

Huma called to her, "Ah, my maid has returned at last. Come, Tremika, I want to show the queen my mother's pendant." The slight but tall woman approached, hastily passing the box to Huma, who made a great show of unlatching the lid, while uttering, "My mother hailed from Nordak; this pendant was brought from there. She bequeathed it to me, as the sole daughter of our house."

The maid stepped away to stand by a wall while the queen of Nordak oohed over Huma's jewelry. "My, what a beautiful ice stone. A treasure."

The blond princess smiled appreciatively. "Thank you. I have always adored it. Would the other ladies care for a viewing?" She glanced at the young women gathered around Kursak, then to her saister Zala.

"Certainly," the queen's daughter replied, and gave a long look at Kursak before floating to her mother's side.

"I would love to see it," breathed the prettier of the Amkish princesses, rising from her chair and stepping toward Huma. As it seemed one sister could go nowhere without the other, her plainer sibling followed immediately. Even Zala rose, with apologies to the Strange King.

Dalock reached for the last strip of a grilled squash he favored, but it slipped from his grasp onto the floor. Reluctant to part with the tasty morsel, but a bit embarrassed to be eating off the carpet, he looked about to see if anyone had noticed. All the royal women stood gathered about the princess from Hudiksland while Kursak watched from his seat with arms folded and a grim expression, as though weighing evidence at a trial. Even the servants strained to catch a glimpse of the jewel in Huma's hands.

Given such a fortuitous opportunity, Dalock bent quickly to retrieve the errant tidbit. As he stuffed it in his mouth, he raised his eyes and spied Huma's maid Tremika intently fiddling with her sleeve over an unattended serving tray crowded with cups.

In an instant, he recognized the silvery object on her wrist: the same bracelet Huma had worn earlier that evening. His pulse quickened, for by The Powers, he caught a faint scent of smoke in the air. Springing to his feet, he marched toward the Hudikslander attendant. Tremika saw his approach and froze.

"What are you doing?" he asked in a low voice, eyes keen. The maid stared at him; a short, breathy sound came from her throat. "Give me that bracelet."

Tremika hastily unlatched it, passing the ornament to him without a word. A quick inspection revealed it was either the bracelet Huma had worn earlier in the evening, or a work of identical craftsmanship. There was a feature he had not noticed before: discreet latches on the underside of each oblong shape, one unfastened to reveal a small chamber, rimmed with wax. A dark drop glistened inside. A slight, pungent scent like a campfire lingered.

"Lord Strange King!" called the Nordak queen, the ice stone in her hands and her wide-eyed daughter at her elbow. "Do come see Princess Huma's lovely pendant. Your wife will want a full report."

"I am more interested in another piece of her jewelry."

Huma's face swung in his direction. Dalock disdainfully dangled her bracelet from a finger as she barked, "What?"

Before he could speak, Tremika ripped the silver chain away and dashed to the doorway. Two of the servants leapt to block her way. Spinning to face the room, she darted to the side as more men rushed toward her. Despite their civilian garb, they bore short blades, unsheathed from hidden scabbards, and the carriage of trained guardsmen. Huma's maid clasped the bracelet to her mouth, fumbling with the shiny links, feverishly licking the bracelet until the men grabbed her limbs. They held her still.

"*What* is going on?" demanded the Nordak queen, sounding every inch a peeved ruler.

Kursak rose, his small dark eyes glowering at Huma as though the will of his gaze would incinerate her. "This woman was trying to kill my sister."

"Oh," breathed one of the Amkish princesses.

"Oh," echoed the other.

Huma met his glare with her own, though the bottom of her ruby-hued lips quivered slightly.

Zala turned to one of the servants, ordering with a plaintive cry, "Go, see if my son is safe and bring him here!"

"I never harmed your little boy!" shouted Huma. "You think I would harm my brother's son?" She stood, lunging at Zala, who shrank in her seat as though the couch would engulf and protect her. Help came from elsewhere as servants and guards inundated the pair from all sides. Hands restrained Huma, shielding Zala, as the blond princess yelled, "Usurper! Before you stole my position, *I* was the lady of Hudiksland. Now Father will join me to some low-rank, fat lord. Let go of me!" Huma struggled against the firm-muscled arms holding her as they pulled her away. Her dark blue veil fell over her eyes, as though ashamed on her behalf. "Let me go! Call my ambassador!"

Kursak calmly ordered, "Lead them away."

"I demand my ambassador!" Huma cried as the guards lifted her and her maid, carrying them out of the room. Kursak placed a comforting arm around his sister's quivering shoulders, helping her to her feet, then leading her to a vacant couch to recover her nerves.

After the initial rush of elation from catching Huma's maid in the act, Dalock watched the spectacle with a heavy heart, even as little Prince Homik was safely reunited with his tearful mother. The dark-haired boy blinked large blue eyes alertly at the adults fussing over him, but what drew his attention was the shimmering pendant his aunt had abandoned on the table. Once liberated from the arms of his anxious mama, the wee lad toddled straight to the beckoning jewel. Hoisting it for all to see, he gleefully cried, "Mine!"

The Nordak queen responded, an eye toward Kursak, "Well, I do not think Princess Huma will need it anymore."

The new ruler patted his nephew's head as the youngster wobbled past his knees. "She has my pity, but not my mercy." Kursak rose, "Lord Strange King, a word?"

Chapter Thirty-Four—Perhaps a Worthy Invention

After what seemed an eternity, Dalock sent word to his wife of his safe arrival in Kursak. Marna dropped his message onto her desk. "He is still angry with me." Her eyes glanced at the papyrus again, half hoping to find a different message. "Written nearly a week ago. Asking again if I am certain I am not with child." A sigh escaped her lips.

"Yet he signs with words of love and longing." She looked out the window to the clear blue expanse of sky. "I should have gone with him."

The Queen glanced at the letter again, stroking the space to the right of her husband's signature, where his hand might have rested. "But I made my decision, I abide by it, and I must show progress."

She began an inventory. "My reading has improved; I no longer need Saralya's help with any words. I feel I've gained a fond companion in Merva Queen's scrolls. Thank The Powers for her reassurances that only one son will come of my joining with Dalock, though I am still not certain I believe it." She began to sigh, but stopped herself, lifting herself to her feet. "And Favik's lessons are coming along well. Teaching my Page what I learn speeds my progress and retention. Clever idea, Marna. No, the time spent is not lost."

She paced to her dining table, littered with wax tablets used to practice writing and stacks of parchment covered in Saralya's lovely quilling and awaiting assembly into handscrolls. Earlier her Reader demonstrated how to assemble them, the careful gluing of one edge overlapping another, sheet after sheet, rendering a cumbersome volume bound around a staff of wood.

"Tedious to make, tedious to use." More than once she had nearly ripped a scroll with frustration while searching for a particular passage. "There must be a better method."

Dalock's Queen turned her gaze to the scarlet-upholstered daybed resting before the closest window, brought for Saralya to sleep in this royal chamber during the King's absence. A neglected embroidery panel slumped against the crimson pillows, its bronze needle shimmering in the sunlight.

"I wonder which is more monotonous, scroll making or sewing?" Marna reached for the fabric, retrieving the needle. "What if I combined the two? I might stitch a fanciful pattern on parchment. Now what would be the use of that? A mockery of my hard-won education."

The Queen grasped the needle absently, poking its tip repeatedly into a blank parchment, tracing a pattern of a creeping vine. Despite its purposelessness, the activity lightened her heart. Carrying on, she enhanced the detail, creating long tendrils that filled the page. But when she lifted the top sheet to admire her silly work, the lower sheet adhered to the upper, for the needle had pricked through to quilled parchment underneath, binding them together.

"Well done, Marna, ruining Saralya's finely copied verse!" She gave a gentle tug to the top parchment, and the sheets separated with a slight effort. "Well, if I ever wanted to bind parchments together permanently, I would need to use thread." She paused. "Bind them together, with thread..." Squinting at the stack of some half dozen parchments that awaited gluing into scrolls, Marna reached for a coil of red thread, pulled a length, bit it off, and threaded the needle. Grabbing the parchments, she stabbed their left edge with the thin needle, pressing with a fingernail to drive the thread through the thick parchment.

"Bigger holes would make this easier." Her gray eyes scanned the room. On the low table by the fireplace, Saralya had left a carved bronze brooch with a thick pin, which Marna appropriated into an awl. She used her attendant's jewelry to puncture wider openings into one side of the stack of parchments, then swiftly laced the hollow spaces with stitches. Tying the thread in a knot, she leafed through the bound parchment.

"Well, this might prove useful."

Coronations in Kursak were lengthy affairs: days filled with feasts and ceremonies, nights filled with feasts and ceremonies, both indoors and out. Given the choice, Dalock preferred the fresh air of the outdoors to the increasingly annoying visual cacophony of stripes prevalent in Kursak decor. Thank The Powers the Kursaks knew no method of striping the sky.

No one spoke of Princess Huma's absence, though Dalock was amongst the few who knew the location of her current quarters: Kursak's prison. Her ambassador had indeed been consulted, and bowed to Dalock's testimony and assent to the charges against her. The story to be given to her father after the festivities was that she suffered fever, which would delay her homecoming, likely permanently.

These intrigues percolated beneath the jubilant gaiety, and the excuse of a Swift Rider arriving with a package from his Queen granted Dalock a welcome excuse to remove himself from the festivities. With Jinil at his side, they repaired to his quarters to discover a uniformly rectangular parcel. The anxious husband joked, "Well, I doubt she sent roast chickens."

"Perhaps King's Wife has discovered a process to preserve her specialty over the many days and miles." Jinil's wistful tone hinted that this would be a welcome invention.

His mouth watered at the thought, and wielding his short knife, Dalock cut the wine-colored twine binding the brown wrapper. Peeling away the cloth, he saw a thick sheet of cherry-hued leather, lightly embossed with his and Marna's initials. Atop it rested two envelopes in the King's colors, one addressed to himself in his wife's uneven hand, the second to his Second in script worthy of a King's Copyist.

"For you." He handed Jinil his letter, and slit the seal on his own.

Nothing in the room moved save the eyes of the two men feverishly scanning their letters. Mounting annoyance squeezed Dalock's chest, for he could find no response in Marna's letter to his query. He muttered, "Is she with child or not?"

"She is with child," breathed Jinil.

"What?"

"Saralya is with child, the midwives confirmed it!" The elated man gazed upward, his jaw dangling in wonder. "Thank The Powers! At long, long last. I have found my wife."

"Welcome news, Jinil!" The King thumped his Second on the back. "Better late than never, aye?"

Jinil grinned, the skin about his eyes crinkling. "'The earth is not enough to contain my joy.'" He reached for his scabbard, retrieving his short sword. The King, recognizing the familiar verse from Baavnif, held aloft his letter opener, and the two finished the line together: "'I will slice the sky to allow more room! Hee-ya!'" They lowered their knives in unison and laughed freely.

"Is the Queen with child?" a young voice squeaked. Dalock's Page Moril stood in the doorway, bearing a long encumbrance wrapped with gray cloth.

Wanting to douse any enthusiastic rumors before they ignited, the King replied, "The Queen's *Reader* is with child." He gestured for the lad to come forward.

Moril entered the room with wavering steps. His cheeks were flushed and shiny, his lips tinged purple. He grinned at Jinil. "Congratulations,

King's Second." Moril bowed formally, quite a task given the ungainly package in his arms, and hiccuped. "My Lady Reader is the most beautiful woman at court!" His clear brown eyes anxiously looked at the King. The Page clutched the cloth tighter. "Um, after the Queen, my Lord."

Dalock chuckled softly. "We know you mean well, Moril. Though you should *not* drink wine when you are on duty. Ever."

"I'm sorry, my Lord!"

"Good. Now what is that you are carrying?"

The dark-haired boy thrust the package forward. "From Hudiksland, for you, my Lord King." At Dalock's gesture, Jinil stepped forward to accept the item. He placed it on the table beside the article Marna had sent, thankfully covering most of the furniture's striped surface. Moril's cheeks flushed a darker crimson. The lad hastily bowed and left, to the amusement of both men.

"Let me guess what the Hudiksland package is," ventured Dalock in a bored voice. He walked to it and lifted the long parcel. "Heavy on one end, light on the other. Dare I say, sword-shaped?" He placed it upon another striped table.

But Jinil's attention rested on the neglected item from the Queen. "Do you know what this is, my Lord?" He scooped up the leather sheet, which revealed a stack of parchment sandwiched between another leather sheet. "A Records Keeper's binder?"

"Here, let me see." Dalock reached for the item, which slipped slightly from Jinil's grasp. The leather sheet flopped aside but that parchments stayed nestled inside. "It is all stuck together. And there is an inscription on the first parchment:

7th Day, 8th Month, 2887
To Dalock King:
Scrolls are cumbersome to use and to make,
They use enough glue to fill a lake,
Instead, with needle and thread,
Parchment bound is easily read,

Please have a look,
I call this a book.
With love, Marna Queen

He chuckled. "Ah, Marna, my dear wife, you may never be a Verse Master, but what strange thing have you made?" He flipped through the sheets. "Hmm, it is the tale of Farlich King and Merva Queen, my grandparents."

"A most romantic story."

"Aye. I prefer the players' version but am intrigued by this 'book.' Here, Jinil, read her letter. Tell me what you think." He slid the thin missive to his Second, and scanned a few leaves of Marna's invention, chuckling at the amusing misunderstandings that led to his ancestors' joining. "Hmm. It is like reading a letter—one simply flips to the next sheet."

"It appears we still do not know the Queen's status," his Second confirmed.

"No," Dalock closed the book with a thud. "But not knowing does nothing to alter my plans. Let us see what Prince Humik sent." He retrieved the bundle Moril had delivered, sliced the binding cords, and freed a scabbard from the cloth. Inscribed along its side:

Fair protection to the Bearer, a token of King's Will

"I need no token to prove myself," grumbled Dalock. "My own sword has killed better men than Huprik." Still, he grasped the patterned grip and carefully withdrew the weapon. It rang slightly from the action, like a faraway echo of its making. A thinly cut inscription ran along the center length of the blade:

Of fire and steel, Wernik made me.

"Marna Queen's father?"

"The same." He admired the thin, tapered edges of the polished blade, no thicker than a silken thread, evidence of the intense skill and care poured into the glimmering metal. The blade seemed crafted of an unbreakable intent, so potent the air about it shimmered. "I *will* use this sword."

"Then that is decided."

"Aye. Next we plan how I will journey to Fambay Forest alone and undetected."

Jinil cleared his throat. "My Lord, I thought it would be *we* who travel to Fambay Forest."

"That was the old plan, before we knew Saralya carries your child." He slung the blade into its scabbard, admiring the fluidity of the cool metal's fit into its polished sheath.

"Your pardon, my Lord, but I do not understand how that changes our plan."

Dalock laid the polished scabbard on the table. The sword covering's mirrorlike surface reflected the horizontal patterns in the wood and the ceiling above, as though the realm of Kursak had devoured the smooth silver of Hudiksland. The endless patterns of stripes the Kursaks admired was beginning to make his head hurt and his heart long to be rid of the place. When he spoke, his voice was dangerously quiet.

"Jinil, you are my Second. You know if I die in this endeavor, you will be needed to bolster Marna Queen through her rule till my son is of age."

"Your pardon, my Lord, but we have no indication that the Queen is with child."

"And no indication she is not!" He paced to a smaller table resting near the fireplace, its banded surface hidden under flat dishes heaped with comestibles. The vegetables themselves bore a pattern of lines from the metal grates the Kursaks used for cooking. The Strange King glared at the low fire. At least Kursak ingenuity did not extend to creating striped flames.

His Second wisely waited a long moment to break the uneasy silence. When Jinil spoke, he used his best Ambassador's voice. "If we were discovered in the act, and I too bore a token of Hudik King's fair protection, we both would be shielded from reprisal."

The King believed he understood his man's idea, and his own formed as though The Powers laid the path for him. "You are thinking of Marna's family, the silver medallion her braither owns. Their home is perhaps ten miles from Fambay Forest."

"Exactly." Jinil nodded, his green eyes keen, likely thinking his King and himself of like mind.

"We will journey to their home, borrow the medallion for you, perhaps some of their clothes as well, and rest a night there."

"Yes, my Lord, excellent!"

"Then it is decided." Dalock restrained a smile at Jinil's willingness, feeling a guilty pleasure at his stratagem. For he did not reveal his entire plan: to sneak out before his Second awoke, enlisting Marna's nephew Narnik to lead the horses away so Jinil would be stranded whilst he alone killed Huprik. Then he realized another benefit of the scheme. "And if my monthly Messenger and Scribe has visited my saister Werna recently, she may have more news about my wife than I."

Sadly, despite it being well over a week later when Dalock and Jinil arrived, Werna had no fresh news from her sister. As her youngest wailed in her arms, she admonished her braither that a nurse or two or three would be helpful with her large brood. "It is all too much, my Lord Braither, without Marna here to help. This new house is much larger, it needs more housekeeping, and now that we have more clothing and crockery, washing seems to take hours…" The babe cried louder, but Werna's list of needs continued, deaf to the child's pleas. Behind her, Palika watched silently, eyes downcast as though grieved by her mother's words and wishing herself far away.

Dalock offered assurances, that he would send a helper once he returned to his homeland. "At the moment, I need to find Narnik for a talk somewhere more quiet. I assure you, my saister, nothing to do with whisking him away to Eskalind." As though that notion brought to the surface all her former fears, Werna silenced her litany, cooing to the babe in her arms and meekly pointing the King in her son's direction.

Enlisting Narnik in his scheme proved to be Dalock's winning point. The ever-eager lad he'd known over a year prior had no less enthusiasm now, but his brain had caught up to his hasty actions, and he studiously plotted a series of events for waylaying Jinil when the appointed morning dawned.

Thus, after a pleasant day spent mostly roaming the vineyards in the company of his nayphews and nayces, the King absconded before first light to his assassination assignation.

Not trusting his prize mare Breena on this journey, a sturdy gray gelding from the family's recently well-stocked stable sufficed for his gallop to Prince Huprik's doom. A twinge of guilt bristled: his plan had included the Eskalinders cutting their hair short last night and shaving their beards clean away, for in the land of blond Hudikslanders, brown beards and dark hair would engender notice he hoped to avoid. Jinil would hopefully forgive his Lord's ploy, and the loss of his locks. Meanwhile, the bare skin on the King's chin felt cooler and lighter than the rest of his face, an odd sensation that kept him alert despite the early hour.

The sun rose briskly, cresting distant peaks to the northeast, obliterating their lofty tops with brilliant light, then crowning their western sisters' pointed heads with pale pink expanses that gradually shimmered into a glistening shoulder of firm stone. Dalock relished the natural beauty, not for the first time wishing his own land possessed such immensities. While The Powers had Gifted Eskalind with many natural features the borderlands would never rival, mountains were not among them.

Thinking back on his getaway, Dalock relished the details. He envisioned one day inscribing them into his personal chronicle, or telling the tale at Jinil's son's Naming Day celebration, ladling the details into the ears of future listeners, perhaps even their sons: the tale of how he outwitted his Second. Oh, the thought made him laugh, though he could not tell if the sting in his eyes was the wind or laughter's tears.

Thus the Lord of Eskalind arrived at the outskirts of the forest of Fambay, an ancient stand of towering pines and shady evergreens. Tethering his borrowed mount near a shallow stream and a bank of tasty grass, he traversed the mile or so of soft, pine-needle-strewn undergrowth toward the prescribed glade, passing nothing unusual except a few smaller red-barked trees marooned amidst the greenery.

Dalock tugged the close cap covering his head; it felt secure. Scouting from the deep shadows of the soaring trees to be certain he was first upon the spot, he spied the long, banquet-table-sized rock that marked this as the correct rendezvous point. Small, fragrant flowers clustered in tangled clumps about the pale granite slab, giving the place a pleasant aspect and sweet scent, a peaceful scene more worthy of a private picnic with his wife.

Completing his reconnaissance of the open green field, Dalock gathered a few palm-sized rocks from amongst the needled carpet of ground. Clutching his finds, he made for the thickest tree north of the glade. There he placed one stone atop the other against the far side of the stout trunk's brownish-orange bark. The signal rocks in place, he climbed a nearby low-limbed pine to wait.

As though The Powers smiled on his endeavor, the avenging husband had barely settled into his hiding place when three mounted horses trotted into the glade. All three riders bore the split standard of the sons of King Hudik on their tunics and saddles: one side outlining the silver crown of Hudiksland, the other the golden claw of their mother's house of Nordak. The telltale outline of a crown marked them as men of Hudik's younger son. Men employed by the heir of the royal house bore a complete crown on their standard. Dalock watched to see which of the two guards carried the full crown in his heart.

Prince Huprik sat slightly slumped in the saddle, grousing, "Why drag us here at such an unreasonable hour, Valik? I prefer hunting as an afternoon sport, not a morning one."

The man so addressed, long limbed and muscular, slid from his horse, tying the beast's reins securely to a low branch. "Your pardon, my lord prince. I thought the snares best checked early so the blood trail is fresher for the hunt." Valik motioned to the other guard. "Vermik, tend our lord's horse and ready a meal for him." He pointed to the table-shaped stone at the center of the glade. "That rock makes a good spot. Your Highness, rest a moment with food and drink whilst I gather the traps." Valik slung a limp sack over his shoulder.

Huprik glared at the rock as though it had insulted him. "I am more suited to a nap. Vermik, bring blankets." With a nodding glance over his shoulder, Valik wandered into the forest on the west side of the glade.

Dalock watched Valik disappear beyond view into the thick trees. Meanwhile, on the grass, Vermik spread a cloth for the prince. He paused a long moment, then hurriedly assembled a leather flagon, dark bread, and small, squat loaves of cheeses on the picnic rock. The sight of the appealing food made Dalock's mouth water, for in his morning haste he had neglected nourishment, or to bring food. To add insult, Huprik ignored the offered victuals. The prince unbelted his long scabbard, dropped it to the ground, and plunked himself onto the ground-strewn blanket, his back against the rock.

Something cracked in the undergrowth near Dalock. Valik approached the signal tree, carefully scouting its base. Spying the rocks piled atop one another, he breathed, "Thank The Powers." Raising his blond head, the Hudikslander squinted, slowly scanning the trees and low-growing plants. A twig scratched Dalock's cheek, but he did not flinch in his perch. Below, Prince Huprik's guard turned to face the glade, cupping his hands to his mouth. "Vermik! We've caught a big one. Come help me."

The lesser prince of Hudiksland lazily yelled, "I hope it is a large wench. I like the big ones!" With that, he flopped an arm onto the stone table, using his shoulder as a pillow. He closed his eyes.

Dalock silently positioned his blade, half wanting to abandon his hiding place and skewer Huprik, half wondering if he was the quarry. The second man crashed through the brambles. "Valik? Where? Valik, where is it?

The Strange King could no longer see Valik below, but heard him shout from closer by, "Over here!"

Vermik charged toward the King's tree, and a dark form leapt up beside him, swinging a black object that landed with a decisive crack on Vermik's neck. The man crumpled, falling onto his forehead steps from Dalock's tree.

Valik paced into Dalock's view, a stout branch in his hand. With a glance toward Prince Huprik's snores, he drew blade with his free hand

and skittishly kicked the prone man over. Vermik's head lolled at an unnatural angle from his spine, eyes open, dirt upon the whites. Valik exhaled. "May The Powers forgive me, I meant only to stun him!" He crouched to close the dead man's eyes, brushing a clot of soil from his cheek. "Alas Vermik, your only fault was your master." Valik dropped his makeshift club, retrieved something from his pocket, then fiddled with the pommel of his sword. Completing his mysterious task, he raised his head, asking in a low voice, "Will you not show yourself?"

Suspicious of what the man had just done with his sword, Dalock remained silent as Valik paced below him. After a few tense moments, the man muttered, "Then I do this myself." Valik swiftly sheathed his sword, retrieved his empty sack from behind a squat bush and returned to the signal tree. There he squatted to load Dalock's marker rocks into the pouch. Then Valik marched across the grass toward the prince, bent backed as though the sack bore a large, weighty catch.

Meanwhile, Huprik had rediscovered his interest in foodstuffs and was sawing at a pale, hard cheese.

Gathering that Valik intended to kill Huprik himself, Dalock surveyed the area for any remaining threats, then swung down from his hiding place to shadow Valik's progress, but from the trees. The guard wasted no time in approaching his vile master.

"What have you got?" mumbled Huprik through a mouthful of food as he faced his man. Valik dropped the sack with a clank on the grass near the prince and bent to untie the closure. "No wench *this* time," he grumbled, pulling the sack open to shield his sword arm whilst silently unsheathing his blade. "But I do have this!" Valik swung the weapon down toward his master, who raised his own scabbard with both hands to block the blow.

Valik's sword met the metal sheath with a sky-rending crack. The prince delivered a rapid kick of his pointed boots into Valik's knee and rolled away. The tall guardsman grunted in pain, whilst Huprik scrambled to his feet, pulling his sword free of its silvery housing. Valik turned to fend off Huprik, who darted close behind him, arching his blade across the blue expanse of sky and bringing the squat pommel onto Valik's back with a heavy thud.

Valik collapsed to the grass with a moan.

"Ally of my brother?" growled Huprik.

"Aye," answered Dalock behind him, holding aloft the blade of Wernik, Hudik King's armorer.

The lesser prince of Hudiksland spun round, panting, his blue eyes thin slits in the bright sunshine. "You call this a fair fight?" Huprik crouched slightly, long blade held away from his body, pointing at his new attacker. With his free hand, he gestured to Valik. "I was unarmed when he came at me."

The Strange King advanced slowly, his weapon held before him, the polished metal reflecting the green of the glade's trees at its sharp edges and the blue of the sky above. "My wife was unarmed when *you* attacked *her*."

"Your wife?" A moment of brief recollection shadowed his tan features, and Huprik drew his eyebrows closer together. "Are you the miller?"

Dalock made no reply.

"Or the baker?"

The King glowered.

"You are the tanner! No? The cook! Surely you are the cook, the cook from Hammerston? Or the cook from … Castleton?"

Dalock stood steady. "You are making this easier and easier."

"The cooper! I wager it, you are the cooper!" Behind him, Valik coughed. The prince tilted his pale locks slightly in the prone man's direction, muttering, "I thought I killed him." Yet his tone and expression brightened. "Or maybe *he* is the cooper." The prince bared his teeth in a grin better suited for bestowal upon a tedious courtier.

Prickling anger rose in Dalock's breast; the scum was toying with him. His usual battle plan in such a moment was to attack with all his fury. But he did not know if he still enjoyed the Gift of the heirless Strange King. Strategy must trump brute force. Another consideration was the extent of Valik's injury; perhaps he might figure in the fight. Calculating the distance between himself and his opponent, Dalock risked cutting his eyes toward the downed man. Prince Huprik seized the moment to leap forward and slash at him, shouting, "Have that, wheelwright!"

The King ducked, sidestepping away as though avoiding a hot fire, and caught the prince on the hip with the honed tip of his long blade. Huprik fell to his face on the grass, pivoted on an elbow to regain his feet, and wobbled upright with a panicked expression. He lowered his chin to assess the cut on his hip. Dalock seized the moment to charge him, ears thundering with the swift pumping of his heart. He slashed from groin to torso, slicing the prince's over- and undertunics, deep into the skin. Huprik dropped his sword, gagging, and fell to his knees, dark blood cascading onto his slashed clothing. His hands trembled as he brought them to his belly, trying to staunch the flow, hands slick with gore.

Raising his eyes to his slayer, he breathed, "Who, who are you?" The paleness of his face made his eyes appear larger, like a frightened child. Dalock's thoughts ran to little Prince Homik and how the creature before him had plotted to kill the wee lad and his mother.

"You will never know." With that, he placed the tip of his sword by the man's neck. Marna's father's inscription reflected the silver-edged collar of Huprik's tunic. The lesser prince of Hudiksland cringed, coughing. In that moment he seemed to age a lifetime, transitioning from a vigorous youth to a stricken, wizened old man wheezing for breath. "Huma?" he called, as though his sister were near enough to hear him.

Dalock paced behind him, blade tip hovering by the man's ear. He lowered it to rest on the cloth covering Huprik's shoulders. With slow, purposeful strokes, he wiped the blade's length clean. "You may die now," ordered the Strange King. A battlefield taunt from Baavnif rang silently in his head: "I would spit on you, were it worth the effort."

He walked away toward Valik.

As he reached the injured man, he heard Huprik fall with a dull thump behind him. Valik lay on his side watching. Though his eyelids were heavy, Valik regarded the prince's slayer with a slight grin and wet eyes. He made to stand. "Thank you, whoever you are, from myself, and from my sister."

Dalock crouched by Valik, offering an outstretched hand. "Your sister?" He feared the tale, given the dead prince's history.

With help, Valik unsteadily rose to his feet, inhaling deeply. "Aye, on my sword. Havnika's hair ribbons." He gestured toward his weapon, lying mute on the grass nearby, and bent forward, his hands on his thighs. Tied to the pommel of his blade, a pair of dark red cloth strips draped. "Her favorite color." The man coughed, a weak, breathy sound. "She died in childbed, birthing his child after he took her. My beautiful sister!" Valik's eyes swelled with tears. "If only I had been in Mother's shop when he came. I would have protected her." He balled his hands into fists, pulling himself to his full height with a grunt.

"I understand *exactly* how you feel." Dalock studied his clean blade, tilting it slightly, causing his faither's inscription to flash brightly. It seemed for a moment that the words were written in dark letters upon the sword. "Many are avenged this day."

"We must hurry away. There may be other men, some loyal to that creature," Valik glanced at Huprik's body, "who will search for us when he does not return soon."

"Agreed, but are you well enough to ride?"

"All the way to Kursak!" The former huntsman of Prince Huprik guffawed, a satisfied but bitter laugh. "After this, I should own a property there, though I would have done the deed for nothing but safe passage from Hudiksland." He retrieved his weapon from the ground, sheathed it. "Tell me your name and I will name my first son after you."

"It is best that only The Powers know." The prince's slayer gazed at the dead man.

"I understand." Valik limped by Dalock's side to survey Huprik's body, his lifeless eyes serving no purpose other than reflecting the beauty of the surroundings.

Satisfied the prince was finished, the King turned to his companion. "Peace pledged to you, Valik. That is the customary Kursak greeting."

"I thought you an Eskalinder by your voice," the future Kursak mused. "Peace pledged to you, stranger." The pair made their escape.

Chapter Thirty-Seven—A Strange Reunion

Saralya entered the Queen's pavilion, calling, "My Lady, will you not come outside for the King's arrival?" Glad shouting rang through the camp in the warm, late-Summer air.

Marna lowered her head like a chastened serving girl. "My Lord bid me to wait for him here." Her eyes did not stray from the carpets, but memories flooded her thoughts, of the fond look Dalock bestowed upon her as she walked across the border when she first came to his Kingdom. *He is still angry with me.* She paused, finding a lighter thought amongst the dark ones: that perhaps he sought to spare her a public reunion. The former Hudikslander glanced at the bronze plate near her elbow, empty save for a few crumbs. "Saralya, please send Favik to bring more sweet cakes."

"Would you like some bread and sauces also, my Lady?" her Reader asked. Marna could hear the worry in her voice. True, the Strange Queen had neglected substantial food ever since the journey to the appointed reunion spot, just as she refused her companion's suggestions to venture from the encampment and make the short walk to the nearby waterfalls and lake. No, she would be a dutiful wife and stay in her pavilion till her Lord came to claim or rebuke her. In the meantime, she would eat what she wanted.

Saralya's forehead wrinkled.

"Do not trouble yourself with me, my Reader. You must want to go to your happy reunion with Jinil."

"I would wait with you, my Lady, if it pleases you." Saralya placed a self-conscious hand to her lower belly.

Marna shifted her gaze away from her companion. She was only two months with child and already making that annoying gesture. The Queen said in a cold voice, "No, I would wait alone."

Without another word, and perhaps glad to be rid of her Lady, Saralya bowed and left.

Marna brought a hand to her face and slumped into a chair. A few moments went by, and she knew not her own thoughts. Favik quietly entered the tent and placed a fresh plate of cakes on the table, retrieving the empty plate and carrying it away as he left.

At least they both know better than to trouble me in this mood. Composing herself, she reached for the sweet treats and stared at the tapestries as she ate.

Suddenly, the tent flap flew aside, and Dalock's Page Trevil entered. "My Lady Marna Queen! Dalock King would have you meet him. Please follow me."

Marna sat straight at the unexpected intrusion. Trevil stood balanced in an erect and formal posture, seeming grown a hand's breadth taller since she last saw the fourteen-year-old lad.

"Just a moment, Trevil." Standing, she paced to the mirror on her dressing table. She slowly smoothed the garnet necklace her husband gave her the first night they spent in his Halls, then brushed a few morsels of cake from her bodice with a quick motion.

"My Lady?" Moril called as he entered the tent. Her husband's younger Page carried a brocaded cloth, of a rich brown color. "Dalock King bids you wear this." He handed it to her, and like Trevil, gave no greeting or indication that it had been two months since she saw him last.

Marna unfolded the fabric to reveal a stunning cloak, of a fine soft weave that made her fingers feel rough. "Oh my."

The boys grinned at one another and moved to assist her as she swept the fabric over her shoulders. "One last thing…" She reached for her cake plate, her fingernails brushing the engraved bronze, astonished to find it empty. The Pages tugged at the cloak's hem as the Queen realized she must have consumed the entire portion in a matter of moments. Shaking her head, she followed her husband's Pages outside.

As they led her through the camp, she bowed her shoulders, pulling her hood over her head to avoid the notice of the people. She spied Dalock's pavilion, set far away from hers. Now she regretted not walking outside with Saralya to make better note of her surroundings.

"This way, my Lady." Trevil gestured to several large black-flecked granite boulders lying amongst lush grass, a bit removed from the camp. A worn yellow dirt path wrapped along the right side of the giant rocks, and a lone small tree, its shimmering leaves the color of flame, stretched to the top of the tallest boulder.

Moril spoke. "You are to go ahead, my Lady." Trevil grinned as though he had won a wager.

Marna studied the slim path. The boys nodded and motioned for her to continue. Holding her head high, she threw back her hood. The Pages giggled. That annoyed her and gave purpose to her steps. She marched forward, following the trail around the boulders, their gray forms mellowing into an orange cast as the sun lowered to the horizon.

Coming around a bend, she saw a broad-shouldered man sitting on a smaller rock with his back to her. He wore a floppy, wide-brimmed hat and a tunic and breeches of plain, homespun fabric, much like a Hudikslander's attire. His posture was hunched, as though attending to an object in his lap. She stopped to glance around her, then caught the motion of him reaching with his right hand to pat the stone next to him.

Hesitantly, she approached his right side, recognizing what he held in his left hand: the book she had sent to her husband over a month ago. Then she knew his face despite the thin growth of new beard. It was Dalock!

She sat next to him. He reached for her hand, his eyes still on the book.

"Mmm, my Marna," he purred as he took her hand in his warm fingers. He closed the book, placed it with care at his side, and turned to her. "I need not content myself with this substitute for you now."

"Dalock!" she cried, emotion choking her voice. She threw her arms around him and pressed her face against his shoulder. He returned her embrace tightly, kissing her hair and neck, sending tingling sensations to her spine. After a long moment they loosed their arms and stared at one another. Each found it impossible to stop smiling.

"You are wearing the clothing you borrowed from Werna's, when we first met," Marna noted.

His grin broadened. "I am. I wanted to surprise you. And, I hoped you would recognize it."

"You cut your hair. For battle?"

"In a manner of speaking."

"But, you wore it long when I met you," she stammered. "That was just after a battle."

"Ah, but that was before I found my wife, when I possessed the heirless King's Gift." He lightly traced her cheek with a long finger. Reading her puzzled look, he continued, "To know no chance of harm until my son is conceived."

"Is *that* why you wrote asking if I was with child?"

"Aye, but your reply did not reach me in time."

Marna inhaled a full breath. "I thought… I thought…" She could not gather her thoughts, other than feeling immensely stupid.

"Shh," Dalock whispered, drawing her close again and kissing her. She lay in his arms awhile, cocooned against the warmth of his chest, her chagrin evaporating.

"May I show you something?" His dear brown eyes were serious.

She nodded and withdrew from his comforting embrace. Her husband stood, helping her to rise. Then he took her by the hand, leading her around the farthest boulder, where a fine mist danced in the air. Just as they rounded the turn, a sweeping view of three horseshoe-shaped waterfalls greeted them, the foaming jets of water plummeting from glossy black rock into a shimmering lake that reflected the pink clouds floating lazily overhead.

"By The Powers!" Marna swore. "It is magnificent! Beautiful!" The thunderous booming of the water crashing far below rumbled through the cliff face to her feet.

Dalock reached a steady, strong arm around her back. "This, right here, is the spot where my parents were joined." She turned to him, her mouth open but uncertain what to say. "Our people believe that great things begin here," Dalock said with an air of expectation. "They were very happy together." He kissed her hand tenderly, savoring the press of his lips against her chill skin, his warm eyes on hers. "And I am very happy with you."

Marna could not help smiling. "And I with you," she replied with her full heart.

Not two months later, in the eleventh month of the year, Marna sat at her desk in her quarters, her sister's letter spread before her. The Scribe's neat handwriting lined the sheet in even rows she could never hope to achieve. Her husband relaxed upon her couch, waiting for her to finish her tasks, unaware of the important news his wife waited to impart. But that thought did nothing to blanket the tingling sensation that had filled her body upon reading her sister's momentous tidings.

"The monthly messages from Werna's family arrived," she reported, studying her husband. "Of course you and I already knew of Princess Huma's death from fever in Kursak, and King Hudik's death. Very sad, but at least Crown Prince Humik's ascendancy to the throne bodes well for my homeland's future."

"Ah, yes. I still must watch myself to say *Humiksland* rather than *Hudiksland.*"

Marna nodded, distracted. She could not believe what else she had read in Werna's missive, and worse, or perhaps better, she wondered if Dalock had had a hand in it.

"What is the report of my saister's family?" he asked, sipping from his chalice, watching the fire.

"All is well with the children…" Her voice trailed off; she could wait no longer. "Dalock, she says Prince Huprik is dead. I cannot believe we had no word of it. Werna says he died not long before his father."

Her husband swirled wine in his bronze cup. "Hunting accident?" Dalock's voice betrayed nothing. He gazed at the goblet, tilting it side to side as though gauging its weight, his eyes keen as though it were an untested sword.

Marna studied his manner, thinking he knew more than he was telling. "Yes. Werna said it was a hunting accident."

A grim smile tugged at the higher corner of his uneven lips. "No one was more deserving than that scoundrel." The King used the voice he reserved for ill comments about the treachery of Havadrans.

Rising from her desk, she went to stand behind his couch. Placing her pale hands onto the soft fabric cladding his shoulders, she pressed gently. "Dalock," she dropped her tone to a whisper, "did our Ambassador to Hudiksland have a hand in this?"

The King raised his free hand to touch her fingers. "No. It was a matter I saw to personally." She gasped, reflexively covering her mouth with her hands. Her husband turned in his seat, facing her. With steady conviction in his brown gaze, he said, "Marna, no one will ever harm you again."

She blurted, "But when? When you went to Kursak?"

"Aye, a short detour from there." Her husband stood, placed his chalice upon the table, rounded the couch to her.

"But Dalock, will this cause a war with King Humik?" Fear for her sister's family's safety, were this to become known, added a note of panic to her voice.

He shook his head, his short locks bristly and odd-looking in the candlelight. "Twas a private arrangement between a King"—he lowered his crooked jaw ever so slightly—"and a former crown prince who wished to preserve his position, and his wife's and son's lives."

"Oh," was all she could manage. Her legs felt as weak as though she had been abed a month.

He reached to her, gently pulling her close, gazing at her as though she were his entire world. "Marna, I love you."

Tears fell from her eyes as she buried her head against his shoulder. "I know it," she whispered, and silently thanked The Powers, not for the first time, for sending her such a man. Breathing slowly in his secure embrace, she let spill her own surprise. "Dalock?"

"Mmm?"

"I am with child."

The seasons changed twice, though in Eskalind that meant little difference in temperature, merely that the trees lost their crimson and orange Autumnal cloaks, the bare limbs framing Winter's sky till the dark branches burst with pert Spring greens. All this time the royal family readied for the birth of their child.

Far below the Queen's Chamber, a training courtyard rang with the thrust and thwack of wooden and steel practice blades as Dalock perfected his defensive moves and techniques. Above in the tower, his wife muttered to her unpopulated room, whilst surveying the multitude of scrolls crowding her table. "I must have emptied the cabinet of Trelich King. Yet is there a chronicle anywhere that tells the Queens' secrets to birthing only one son? And every one of Dalock's foremothers who questioned if she would bear another child mentions that indeed, just a single son came of her joining."

Marna rested her fingers on the swell of her belly. "The Powers *must* have a hand in this. Perhaps they could speed up these final, interminable months before my child arrives." She laughed at herself. "First I worried if I would ever get with child, now I worry I will birth a daughter. Solutions drive fresh worries, as they say. I wonder how much more I would get done if I did not waste time on worry."

She reached for the final scroll resting on a chair, considering where to place it amongst the likely hundred upon the table. A knock sounded on her chamber's door.

"Enter! Ah, Saralya, would you help me?" Marna placed the coiled parchment precariously on her overladen table. The stout cylinder rolled away. Before she could halt it, dozens of scrolls cascaded over the table's edge, clattering onto the stone floor, rolling and unfurling onto the carpets as though eager to share their contents with the floor coverings.

"Oof!" cried the Queen, attempting to bend to retrieve them.

"No, please, my Lady, let me." Saralya rushed to her aid. She gathered the fallen scrolls while Marna gratefully stepped aside.

"I do not know what I would do without you, Saralya. I thank you," she sighed, settling onto the window seat. Saralya replaced the last scroll on the table and set about tidying them as Favik stepped into the room, announcing, "The nurses with your son, my Lady Reader."

"Oh yes, bring little Saril in," Marna said. Two women attired in plain brown dresses and kerchiefs entered the Lady of Eskalind's chamber. One carried a small red bundle, which she passed delicately to the new mother.

"I am most pleased our children will grow up together," the expectant mother said as Saralya cuddled her wee babe, his dark curls barely peeking over the crimson cloth.

"Yes, my Lady, for a while."

"For a while? Do you plan to leave King's Halls soon?" She aimed to sound conversational, but the thought of losing her closest confidant troubled her.

"No, my Lady," Saralya's expression was stricken. "I would stay as long as I may be of service."

"Saril is but a month old. Surely it is too soon to send him away for his education?" Marna wondered if this was her attendant's husband's doing. The Queen's regard for Jinil had never quite recovered after his initial rejection of Saralya. "I am certain we can find the best tutors for

Saril and my child, here at King's Halls."

"No no, I thought…" Saralya began, her eyes and manner the same as Dalock's when he had forgotten to tell her something, something important. Her Reader continued, "I, I thought that King's Son would be educated by himself, and kept alone. That is what the Legends tell." She gave the Queen an anxious look.

"Well," Marna began, just as a hideous squeal, disproportionate to wee Saril's size, split the air. "Dear babe!" The two women attempted to placate the child, the nurses fluttering to their sides. Then all emptied from the chamber except the Queen, who sat alone, pondering her Reader's words. "Another serious talk with my husband is in order. By The Powers, how many more of these 'surprises'?"

———

His wife bellowed—in a voice surely heard far below the stairs to the corridor that led to their chambers—"Locked in a room alone when he is but five years old?!"

"Now, now, dear, it is not as harsh as that." The King set his full chalice on the table before the hearth. How her moods fluctuated, with greater intensity the closer her confinement drew; diplomacy and gentleness served as his best allies.

"No son of mine will be locked up in a windowless room, in a prison!" roared his Lady, cheeks pink with rage. Marna plopped onto the heavy upholstered chair before the fireplace. "Dalock, it is horrible."

"There, now put your feet up. Rest." He bent to push a short stool under her heels.

"Do not think you are soothing me."

He smiled, handed her the other chalice. "A sip might soothe you." She grunted but allowed herself a swallow, which gave him his opportunity. "Believe me when I say it will not be all the time. Only when he wishes to be alone, when he retires for the night—"

"Who will hear him when he cries with nightmares? Poor wee lad! Do not tell me that never happened to you." She plunked the bronze cup onto the table and attempted to fold her arms over her protrusive belly. The effect would have been comic had Dalock not sympathized with her discomfort.

Marna gave up, letting her limbs hang limp at her side. "Another two months of this! Are you certain there is *no* possibility of twins?"

Dalock shook his head. "My dear, I know you will find this strange, but I enjoyed having a room to myself, even at the age of five when I left the nursery. It was not until I met you that I wanted to share my bedchamber all the time." He gave her his warmest smile.

"Did you not miss the company of other children?" Her voice softened into skepticism.

"There were times when I did, but truly, I had my fill of companionship during the day." Dalock leaned closer to her. "You will see, Marna, he will like it."

"Hmm." His wife glanced at the wine. "It tastes awful. Perhaps Cook could fry me some fennel. That sounds tasty."

"Marna, when the time comes, let us give our son the choice. What say you?" He raised his eyebrows.

"It seems the best I can hope for." Her tone was resolute, her gray eyes on the hearth.

The Queen's Chamber door swung open, and Marna's Page entered, announcing, "My Lord and Lady, Werna, Queen's Sister, and Palika, Queen's Niece just arrived. They hope to come up and see you."

"Ah, my saister and nayce." Dalock patted her knee. "Do you think they will be more companionable to me than when I stole you away from them?" He winked.

"Visiting at this late hour? They must be exhausted."

Her tone echoed her words, but the King saw his diversion, and counseled, "Why delay your reunion; they sound eager to see you. Favik, show them up."

Marna inhaled, holding an arm to Dalock. He helped her rise, feeling he had won the battle, but unsure who would win the war.

CHAPTER FORTY—ONE RICH IN THE POWERS' GIFTS

The Powers must have heard his wife's pleas, for only a month later, Dalock entered the Queen's bedchamber to find his saister Werna swaddling their crying babe. Marna lay against her pillows, her beautiful face shining with perspiration and relief.

"Your son." Werna handed the bundled newbabe to his father.

Dalock grasped the surprisingly heavy form in his hands, forgetting to breathe as he marveled at his son. Beaming at the child's tiny squinched face, stroking the little fingers, a dizzying pride swelled his breast. He knew his son supplanted his own Gift as the invincible heirless Strange King, but not a fiber of his being cared after this first glance at the wee wonder. "Marna, look, see? He has my hands."

His wife managed a weak smile.

"Ah, and see, see? He has your ears, thank The Powers!" He chuckled as Werna leaned close.

"My Lord Braither, you must know, the child is most healthy, but his mother..."

"What?" His eyes darted to Marna, whose eyes had closed, her Reader by her side resting gentle hands upon the Queen's arm.

His saister spoke quietly. "She cannot bear any more children."

"But otherwise she is well?" His voice had become a low growl.

Werna dropped her gaze. "Otherwise well, my Lord, yes."

As though The Powers had drained all the tension from his limbs, he turned his gaze back to his child. "Then all is as it should be. Thank The Powers."

His Second's voice came from behind him. "The Naming ceremony, my Lord."

"Our first adventure together, hmm?" Dalock cooed to the babe. "We shall return soon."

Jinil held the door as they departed the Queen's Chamber.

———

Marna opened her eyes a little. "Where are they going?" she whispered as Saralya patted a damp cloth on her Lady's forehead.

"To ask The Powers to protect King's Son," Saralya answered. "It must be done as soon as possible after he is born. Rest, my Lady. They will return soon."

———

"You know the words, my Lord?" Jinil asked as they walked toward the grand terrace overlooking the courtyard and distant hills, crowned with a blaze of gold at this early hour.

"Aye. And he does not need these swaddles till we are finished. The King paused to unwind the tan and scarlet coverings. The newborn wailed miserably as his father unwrapped him.

Jinil called over the din, "Healthy lungs."

The new father grinned. "There there, in a moment this will all be over," he purred. Dalock passed the cloths to his Page Trevil, who skittered along his side as they followed Jinil onto the terrace. The tapered wooden arches of the colonnade were lined with fluttering pennants bearing his colors and those of Heedlich First King. The flags seemed to tremble in anticipation, as though even the air exhibited pride for this moment. Excited murmuring burbled from the large crowd in the courtyard below: nearby villagers and well-wishers, merchants from

Queen's Market, all awaiting the Lord of Eskalind's appearance so that someday they could turn to their tablemates and say, "I was there when King's Son was named. I was."

His Second raised a stiff hand for silence as Dalock strode to the stone balusters lining the terrace edge, a tangle of King's Flowers obscuring the stone. The one hundred and twenty-fourth Lord of Eskalind gazed at the multitude of faces assembled below, his people, then at the babe fidgeting and squirming in his hands. His son, his own small son. He raised the child high to the sky, declaring, in a voice he hoped pierced the realm of The Powers, "This is my son Dalich. Gift and protect him."

The people cheered and clapped, though at the sight of the small babe held aloft, a few women clasped their hands over their mouths, eyes large with worry. Whistles shrilled, and shouts of "Hail, Dalich King's Son!" propagated through the joyful assembly.

Dalock lowered his child, cradling him with one arm, and raised the other arm, calling upon the crowd to quiet for once last roaring pronouncement. "I will see you all at the feast tonight!"

The gathering reanimated into raucous whoops, a great stomping of feet, and cascading applause. The King returned to his weary wife, finding her sleeping as contentedly as their son, who, after his presentation to his people, found nothing else worthy of interest, other than using his father's arm for a pillow.

True to his word, that evening Dalock King, carrying his swaddled son, roamed his Great Hall whilst all manner of people celebrated King's Son's birth. The Lord of Eskalind passed the newbabe into the hands of mothers and maids, who held him with pure delight, while their menfolk toasted his health. The King drank with them, while the child's nurses followed their master, knitting their fingers together, ever mindful of the wee babe's state.

So passed the first night of Dalich King's Son, cradled in the arms of his people. Perhaps this is why The Powers so richly Gifted him.

◆

Carla Fraga lives with her husband in Seattle
where she teaches and writes.

www.ingramcontent.com/pod-product-compliance
Lightning Source LLC
Chambersburg PA
CBHW070549120726
47909CB00007B/2290